PRAISE FOR K.j.a. WISHNIA

NOMINATED FOR THE EDGAR AND THE ANTHONY AWARDS

"Packed with enough mayhem and atmosphere for two novels."—*Booklist*

"Sardonic, street-smart humor. Strike back against the boredom of polite mysteries; buy this book."—*Sierra Club Book Reviews*

"Literate . . . humorous . . . finely nuanced writing that will satisfy both genre fans and a wider audience of appreciators of the contemporary novel."—*High Times*.

"Action is swift in this politically charged thriller."—*The Midwest Review of Books*.

"Everything a first mystery should be—hard-boiled, gritty, passionate, and raw. The sheer force of the protagonist's voice holds you." —*Biblio*.

"K.j.a Wishnia's work gets more complex and deeper with each book. He started strong and keeps taking chances that pay off. This is a writer I admire."—S.J. Rozan, author of *Absent Friends continued*

"Wishnia writes with a rare combination of graceful prose and hard-hitting action. His protagonist Filomena Buscarsela is perfectly realized—one of the freshest, most original voices in crime fiction today."—Rick Riordan, author of *Southtown*

"I always look forward to a K.j.a Wishnia book, because his world is bigger than most other mystery writers', not to mention a lot more interesting. He writes with as much intelligence, as much humor, and as much pure originality as anyone in the business."—Steve Hamilton, author of *Ice Run*

"Tough, fast moving, gritty and great fun to read, the Filomena novels rank right up at the top with the best cop novels being written. When you know you have other things you have to get done, but can't put down the book you are reading, you know you are hooked by a terrific writer. The Filomena novels do that to me. I've got to stay away from them for a while so I can get some writing done. Pick up one of these books. Read three pages. You won't be able to stop either."—Stuart Kaminsky

"The Filomena Buscarsela novels have the wonderful ability to be funny, caring, outraged, and informative all at once. Ken Wishnia is my favorite!"—Barbara D'Amato, author of *Death of a Thousand Cuts*

"K.j.a Wishnia is a rare author of authenticity. His hard-nosed stories guarantee strong characters, a tough hero, and an unflinching voice of reality at a time when the abyss between rich and poor is the deepest since the era of Hoover and the Great Depression. Step into Wishnia's world for an unforgettable reading experience."—Gayle Lynds, *New York Times* bestselling author of *The Coil* and *Masquerade*

"Fil Buscarsela is as smart, tart and tough as any three pop private eyes rolled into one. K.j.a Wishnia is an enormously talented writer who deserves a wider audience."—Doug Allyn

"If you are a fan of female protagonists in crime fiction, you must not miss K.j.a. Wishnia's Filomena Buscarsela series. Fil is an intelligent, independent, tough-talking, no-nonsense ex-cop who cares deeply for her city and the people who live in it. She deals with the injustices she sees by relying on a finely-tuned sense of humor that always serves a bigger purpose and never slides into cheap quips. Every book in the series is a true delight, combining fast-paced plots with outstanding characterizations and often deeply moving moments. I highly recommend this series."—Katy Munger, author of the Casey Jones series

"New York City's mean streets as they were meant to be walked, by a kick-ass, Hispanic lady cop. Gritty. Sardonic. First rate!"—Parnell Hall, author of *With This Puzzle I Thee Kill*

"The Filomena Buscarsela series is written the way urban police officers live, which is 'on the edge.' The author of these novels, K.j.a Wishnia, has a sharp ear for cop-talk, and a deft way of making it spring from the page. Enjoy—and learn from—a young Latina from Ecuador as she tries to protect and serve the citizens of New York City despite the cynicism and downright betrayal of those around her."—Jeremiah Healy, author of *Spiral* and *The Only Good Lawyer*

"Ken Wishnia's Filomena Buscarsela is one hell of a woman fighting the good fight in politicized bad-to-the-bone stories where the point is not merely to interpret the world, but to change it . . . one goddamn block at a time."—Gary Phillips, author of *Monkology continued*

"The writing is top notch. I don't think I have read any male author who writes a better female character."—Sandra Tooley, author of the Sam Casey mystery series

"Feisty female sleuth: for mystery fans, that's a well-known phrase, and the description certainly suits K.j.a Wishnia's fearless crime magnet of a heroine, Filomena Buscarsela. But it hardly makes for the whole story, since what Wishnia has done is give us a vibrant and quintessentially New York series that manages, at the same time, to be both gritty and charming—two words that rarely, if ever, appear in tandem."—Michele Slung

"Filomena Buscarsela is one of my favorite people, as real to me as anyone in my address book and a lot more fun than most. I always enjoy spending time with her energy, humor, and compassion. She is also a crazy idealist who sticks her nose in a lot of messes that are none of her business, but nobody's perfect."—Kate Derie, author of *The Deadly Directory*

"K.j.a Wishnia cuts a different path with his stories and novels, choosing subjects, settings, and characters of a sort the reader is unlikely to encounter in the mainstream of mystery and crime fiction. His fine sensibility and skillful prose will appeal to discriminating readers."—Janet Hutchings, editor of *Ellery Queen's Mystery Magazine*

"With her sharp tongue, quick mind, and stubborn will, Filomena Buscarsela is the ultimate New Yorker: a cop, a woman, an immigrant who has made the city her own."—Linda Landrigan, editor of *Alfred Hitchcock's Mystery Magazine*

23 SHADES OF BLACK

K.J.A. WISHNIA

POINTBLANK

23 SHADES OF BLACK
Copyright © 1997, 2004 by **K.j.a. Wishnia.**
Cover design copyright © 2004 by **JT Lindroos.**

PUBLICATION HISTORY:
First edition published by the Imaginary Press, 1997.
Mass Market edition published by Signet Books, 1998.

Point*Blank* Press
www.pointblankpress.com

ISBN: 1-930997-64-7

Para Mercy

ONE

"There ain't no clean way to make a hundred million bucks."

—Raymond Chandler

All this happened a few years ago, when Ronald Reagan was busy making tuna fish hash out of the national budget and trying to learn which countries belong to South America, and the second wave of Punk still ruled the East Village.

I was riding around with my partner, Bernie, a beef-brained *cabeza de chorlito* so cerebrally-challenged he couldn't pick his own nose without the aid of an instruction manual and a detailed map, when we both spot what looks like a typical Saturday night street fight. A local loser and three college-age kids are scuffling and groin-kicking in front of a glass-enclosed restaurant.

Bernie says, "I'll handle this," as he swings the car up onto the curb, hops out, and proceeds to take command of the situation by doing his Elvin Jones imitation on the head and shoulders of the loser, who looks like the principal cause of the whole mess.

I get out of the car and get my nightstick between the two peripheral participants, and move them over towards the glass walls of the restaurant, where a yuppie foursome delight in getting some free entertainment. Bernie stops conducting the acoustical test on the guy's spine long enough for me to get some answers.

It turns out to be a $30 rip-off involving a quarter-gram of what tastes like mannitol and baby laxative, and the big, curly-headed blond kid is blubbering just like a baby. I can't blame him. He's obviously not used to the way real dealers work.

It's clear that the guy Bernie's holding is a crack-head, which is unusual. The street vendors tend to be pretty sharp around here. This neighborhood is the New York Stock Exchange for controlled substances; dealing and doing are kept separate when there's that much money to be made. But the crack junkies are definitely starting to move in, making a dirty game even dirtier.

Bernie cuffs the guy while I give the three college kids a good "Don't-let-me-catch-you-around-here-again" speech, which disappoints my glassed-in audience, who want to see their tax dollars working for them.

"What's going to happen to him?" they ask.

I'm about to tell them that it would be better if they just got out of there, when Bernie says, "I'm going to kick his ass all the way to the precinct house, *that's* what's going to happen."

This seems to satisfy the kids, and they move on into the crowd, which is already dispersing. Bernie's beating has turned the guy green.

"Help me shove this snotrag in back," snarls Bernie.

"Oh no, I'm not cleaning this guy's vomit up off the back seat," I tell him.

"Well what do you want me to do?"

I notice part of the crowd has decided to stick around for more.

"You could try letting him get some air first." I can see that Bernie is wracking his brains to come up with a way of telling me off without using improper language in front of the public.

"Piss on that," he says, stuffing the Junkie's head inside the car with the heel of his hand and leaving the door open for me to deal with as he goes around to the driver's side. I'm not sure if Bernie is aware that "piss" is considered improper language in some circles.

I waste my time waiting for further instructions as Bernie parks himself behind the wheel and slams the car door. The remainder of the crowd is staring at me wondering, What is she going to do? Then the Junkie gives me something to do.

"I'm going to be out by tomorrow morning, babe!" he says, climbing halfway out of the car. "And I'm going to come looking for *you!*"

"Just get in there," I say, replacing his body on the seat and slamming the door. Bernie guns the motor as I go around the other side and climb in next to him, then he pulls off the curb and away down the street.

"Why don't you just leave me there, Bernie? You got everything under control all by yourself."

"You're damn right I do, Buscarsela. I didn't need you in there." He turns to shout through the cage. "It was just two puppies slapping each other over some baby powder."

"Watch the traffic, will ya?"

Bernie decides *not* to run over a young woman pushing a baby carriage, aiming instead for an old man with a walking stick.

"You blew it, Bernie: An old man with a cane is only forty points. A mother and baby is eighty-five points," I say. Pregnant nuns are one hundred and fifty points, but they're rare. "Okay: So it turned out to be two puppies slapping each other over some baby powder, but it *could* have been two psychos knifing each other over three thousand bucks. And one of them could have had a gun."

"I'm hungry. Let's eat," is how Bernie chooses to wrestle with that particular enigma.

"We can't call in a meal break with a prisoner in the back."

"Fuck that." That's Bernie talking. "I said I'm hungry."

I turn and get my first good look at our detainee. He's young, but already got the face of a lifer. Glazed, sunken eyes, a few requisite knife scars, and a sallow malnourished complexion that bleeds right through what in a WASP would be considered a healthy tropical tan. Without that extra melanin, he'd be as pale as chalk, pale as that powder he's trading in the world for. At least he's calm. He's been through this a few dozen times before.

"What are you trying to do, selling for yourself in this neighborhood? You want to end up as dog food?"

"Fuck you, cop," is what he says. So much for the civics lesson. *"Puta traicionera de tu propia raza."* That's supposed to burn me real bad, I guess. But I've been through this a few times before, too.

"En cambio tu eres el ejemplo para todos, ¿no cierto?"

"Fuck you," he says. So we're back to that.

Is that all the English he knows? *"¿Y porque no me lo dices en espanol?"*

The Junkie opens his mouth to speak.

"You say 'Fuck you' one more time and I'm going to feed you this," I say, shoving my nightstick through the mesh close enough for him to use it as a tongue depressor. "It's a perfect fit, too." Now he shuts up. That's the only language the lifers understand. And me a B.A. in Spanish Literature.

Bernie jerks the car to a halt in front of an all-night deli with one of those cheap, glaring neon signs that always has a couple of letters sputtering on and off and makes you feel like your eyes are going. Blink. Gddzt. Blink. Gdzzt. You could go blind trying to focus on them.

"What do you want?" Bernie asks.

The Junkie says he'll have a hotdog with everything.

"Not you, snotrag," Bernie informs him.

"Get me a whole can of salmon on rye and coffee, extra extra light." Guayaquil style.

Bernie gets out and goes into the deli. Normally, that would be my job, but tonight, staying in the car with the "snotrag" is the chickenshit detail, so I don't have to play waitress. Not this time, anyway.

Bernie does not exactly have a poker face. I can see that he's planning something by the way he is smirking at the Korean guy behind the deli counter. Hmm. Will today's gag be on me or on the prisoner? Bernie doesn't always differentiate. I see him stuffing some Devil Dogs into the pockets of his jacket when the Korean man has his back turned.

He comes back with his hands around a paper bag that is dripping wet. He has already spilled my coffee. I roll down the window of the car, letting in some of that crisp March breeze, which isn't too bad tonight. You can tell that spring is coming.

"You adding shoplifting to your growing list of petty crimes?" I kid him.

"Oh, he won't charge me for them," says Bernie, handing me my bag.

Of *course* he won't charge you for them if you stick them in your pocket when he isn't looking, I'm thinking, but my coffee cup is already tearing through the bottom of the bag, and I have to grab the bag to keep from getting soaked, but Bernie's got his hands around it in such a way that I can't get a grip on it.

"You owe me four-fifty," he says, as if unaware of what he's doing. I'm about to put my hand under the bag when it gives up the ghost (it must have had help) and an uncovered styrofoam cup of hot coffee drops into my lap, spilling about half of it down my thighs and onto the seat and elsewhere. This makes the snot-rag laugh. I'd like to dump the rest of the coffee on his head for that, but at this point in the game that would be considered excessive, and he obviously knows it. I peel myself up off the seat as best I can, but the damage is done.

"Sorry, Buscarsela," says Bernie, doing a lousy job of trying not to laugh. "You know how cheap these Koreans are with them plastic tops."

I'm struggling to keep some kind of cool here: "Bernie—wet paper bags are receptacles *not* noted for their strength."

"Huh?" he replies. You can't put anything over on Bernie.

The snotrag continues to laugh.

"Here you go—this is for you," says Bernie, passing a hotdog with everything behind me to our prisoner, who greedily starts to gulp it down. "Hey, that'll be a buck twenty-five, pal."

I'm not sure, but I think the Junkie says "Fffk yuf" through a mouthful of hotdog—with everything. Then without warning the Junkie's face goes sour and he starts spitting out half-chewed "everything" all over the back seat of the car. It seems that there are five or six live roaches crawling around between the hotdog and the sauerkraut.

"Oh, I didn't see them roaches," says Bernie. "They're extra. That'll be a buck-*fifty.*"

"(SPIT) Fuck you."

Must be his charm: He sure doesn't get by on originality.

Bernie keeps jabbing: "Hey, I thought you asked for 'a hotdog with everything.' "

"What do you carry them around in a test tube where your log's supposed to be?" I really *am* curious how he pulled that off.

Bernie is laughing. Sometimes it's hard to say. Meanwhile, the Junkie is spitting half-chewed food all over the back seat, and I'm using every napkin I've got—how nice of Bernie to provide so many—to clean up my mess, asking myself if I can get compensation for scalded thighs as a job-related injury: "Uh, yes, your Honor, that's correct, my asshole partner poured hot coffee on my lap. Well, he didn't exactly pour it. Maybe we could settle for half a million in damages?"

"While you're at it, Buscarsela, why don't you clean up the rest of that stuff?"

"Bernie—fuck you."

I am hungry, however, but somehow no longer desire to eat in the same car with the Junkie who is busy spitting on every available surface. So I step out of the car and start to unwrap my sandwich, leaning on the cold car door. The breeze is a bit nippy, but I prefer it to being in there with the Great Expectorator. I finally get half of my sandwich unwrapped, and take a bite, only to get a mouthful of cold sardines in oil, complete with bones. This is not my favorite meal.

So now it's my turn: I spit my mouthful into the gutter and storm inside the deli and shut the door behind me.

"What's the big idea charging four dollars for a sardine sandwich?"

The Korean man looks at me in that half-perplexed way of someone who is new to a culture, and still dreads every new encounter in this strange new language. I realize that he's not the regular owner.

"Fo dolla price for salmon sandwich," he says.

"Yeah, I know: The *price* says salmon, but the *mouth* says sardines. You trying to make me sick?"

The man now looks truly worried, and I can tell this is not his fault. Hmm. "Uh, could I see the can?" Nothing. I pick a can of peaches up off the shelf, and show him: "The *can.*" Now he understands, and pulls a flat, ellipsoidal can off of a pile of twenty or so identical cans and hands it over the counter towards me. "SARDINES," it reads, in big red letters. I now play a little charades, pointing out each and every noun, and trying to fill in the verbs with meaningless gestures. "Did *Officer Morgan* [point out the door] tell you [point at him] that this [the can] was *salmon?* [emphasis added]" Vigorous nodding on the part of my Korean friend. I nod back in order to show him that, See?, we *can* understand each other. I'm about to walk out when I spot the Devil Dogs on a display rack.

"How much are these?"

"Senty-fi."

I plant down a buck-fifty on the counter and walk out empty-handed, leaving the Korean man even more in the dark about the ways of these crazy Americans. And he doesn't even know the half of it. I go around to the passenger side of the car and get inside.

"Where's my four-fifty?" asks Bernie.

"Some of it's on the front seat, and the rest of it's back with the store owner. Let's move."

"Not until you get in back with the perp."

"I'm not getting in back with that guy."

He wants me to clean the crap up.

"Listen, girlie, I was pounding a beat when you were still swinging naked through the trees in the Amazon jungle. Lucky for you, too. Hell, they didn't even have TVs down there 'til *we* discovered you had some oil you could sell us."

Bernie's in-depth sociopolitical analysis of my country-of-origin's economic situation is cut short by a radio call to respond to what is reported to be a toxic leak at a food stamp center, with as many as fourteen possible victims. Now it's *my* turn to bust procedure. I pick up the mike and roger the call.

Bernie says: "We're not supposed to respond to a code with a perp in the cage. That's procedure, Buscarsela."

"Since when have you cared about following procedure?" Three more points and I'm a detective and I can dump this lousy partner. "You know how fast insecticide fumes can kill someone?"

Bernie throws on the lights and siren, and we go wailing out into traffic. The food stamp center is just a few blocks away, but it is next to the Lilliflex factory, where, among other things, they make insecticides.

We are the first to arrive at the scene, and let me tell you it's a mess. People are lying face down on the sidewalk and clouds of toxic smoke are wafting out of the building. We hop out of the car, leaving the doors open, and try to get a reading on the situation.

I ask: "Any more inside?" Nobody knows. Bernie and I look at each other.

"Should we be heroes or what?" Bernie asks me.

"I don't know, I've heard about this kind of stuff: Your lungs fill with fluid and you drown." People are standing around, more are hanging out of windows, looking down at us. I say, "Oh, shit, let's do it."

I run to the glove compartment, fish out the pair of surgical gloves that we keep there and start ripping them in half. We put them over our faces, our noses lodged in one of the fingers. We look like stagecoach bandits, except for the long rubber noses. I rip the one towel we've got in half and wrap that around the gloves. It's hard to breathe, but that's the idea.

We run inside. The fog stings our eyes like triple-strength tear gas, but we plow through it. Dead bugs are dropping from the ceiling like rain. I hadn't counted on this. We can barely breathe, and my eyes feel like they're being soft-boiled in hydrochloric acid. I try to get a fix on where some of the bodies lie, then shut my eyes tight and start feeling around where the afterimages tell me they should be. I grope around in the dark, my eyes sizzling away in their sockets, until I find one. It's a leg. I find the other leg, get the knees over my shoulders, and try to stand up. I can't. I get my knees right under the weight and try again. I can't budge this one. Much as I hate to, I drop the legs and open my eyes. No wonder. In a flash I see that the guy can't weigh less than two-hundred-and-ninety pounds. I spot a young Black woman sprawled backwards over a desktop, grab her, and run out of there, slipping and sliding on a uniform layer of dead bugs, my eyes screaming a three-alarm fire. I stumble out through the corridor and onto the street, where I can see through a veil of tears that the ambulance squad has arrived. Somebody takes the woman off my back and flings her onto a stretcher.

One of the onlookers is drinking a beer—I think. I grab it from him—or her.

"Excuse me, I need that," I explain, and begin dousing my eyes with the contents of the bottle, which are a soothing relief to my scorched cornea. I suppose tabasco sauce would probably be a relief at this point. Then the burn starts to come back, even worse.

"Allow me," says one of the squad guys, and he turns me around, forces me to my knees, and starts pouring quarts of clear fluid into my eyes, where it runs all over my face and uniform. After a few minutes, when it begins to feel like my eyes are *not* sizzling like two slices of pepperoni on a hot pizza, I breathe easier, knowing that, once again, I may yet live to see my grandchildren. If I ever get around to children.

"Feel better now?" the blurry mass above me asks.

"Much. Thanks. What is that stuff?"

"Water," he says.

I had to ask.

By the time my eyes clear, he's gone, and the people who are *prepared* for toxic fumes show up. Protective coveralls, face masks, oxygen tanks. They go in and pull out nine other victims and get busy feeding them oxygen and the same water treatment. Most of the victims are the usual shades of black and brown, but one of them sticks out like a Klansman at a Knicks game. Basically, he's white—which is not all that remarkable, I'll admit, but on this block it's a novelty, and at this food stamp center, it's practically unheard of. Other cops from the 34th are keeping back the crowd, letting only the ambulance crew through. A reporter is trying to get in to see the victims, but they keep her out. I walk over to the rescue worker who is treating the white guy.

"You need help taking these people to the emergency room?" I ask.

"Nah," he says, not looking up. "We can treat them right here, none of them is injured seriously. Just for a couple days they might get nauseous, dizzy, with persistent headaches, chest pains and throat inflammation."

"Oh is that all?"

Now he looks up at me: "Look, you wanna do this? I could be home watching *The Late Show.*"

He goes back to attending to the victim, not waiting for a response. I tilt my head sideways and get a good look at the prostrate form of the one white victim. He's pale and blond, with reasonably delicate features, but even in this condition the muscles of his face are hard, pushing up through his skin. Looks like a nice kid who fell on hard times, or maybe one of the middle-class New Jersey suburb Punk crowd who willingly embraced hard times rather than put on a white shirt and a tie and work the cash register at Wal-Mart. Yes, now I see it: He's probably a musician or a painter. He's definitely not an employee at the food stamp center. Either way, I'm not getting any answers out of this guy for a while.

I step over some of the emergency paraphernalia, glancing at each of the victims. There's a grandmother asking to see her children in a Puerto Rican-accented Spanish; I go over and talk to her. I tell her everything's all right now and I even radio in her name and her family's telephone number so someone at the station can call them and tell them she's OK. There's a young Black man who isn't moving yet; there's my three-hundred-pound friend, draining an entire tank of oxygen all by himself. It took three men to carry him out of there. Then I see the young Black woman who I brought out slung over my back. She's recovering, and is trying to push off the oxygen mask, but the rescue worker is slapping her hands away and holding the mask in place. I tap the rescue worker on the shoulder.

"How soon will she be able to talk?"

Hearing this, the Black woman tries to say something, but the rescue worker redoubles the pressure with which he is holding the mask in place. He looks at me.

"Get out of here, will ya? Can't ya see I'm busy?"

I look at the woman. Over the mask, she looks like she is trying to tell me something with her eyes, which have the wild, petrified look of an ensnared doe. But then I suppose it's normal to look that way after a brush with death. I get down on one knee and take the woman's hand in mine, I tell her we got everyone out OK. Her eyes appear to relax almost immediately. I stroke her forehead with my other hand, and she breathes deeply for the first time since I've been watching. She even closes her eyes. When she opens them, the panic is gone. She knows now that she's going to be all right. I nod and continue to stroke her forehead. I ask her is there someone she wants me to call and say she's all right. The rescue worker gives me a look.

"Don't you have something else to be doing?" he says to me.

I stare at him for longer than I'm supposed to.

"Go arrest some pimps, awright?"

That reminds me, I left the Junkie in the back seat of the car—How long ago? Five minutes? Ten minutes? A half an hour? My sense of time is shot, which looks real bad on a report. I check my watch, which reads 9:40, so it's only been about fifteen minutes, and I start looking around for Bernie and the car. I spot Bernie through the modern-ballet-like movements of the rescue workers rushing back and forth with tanks of life. He is trying to write a memo of some sort, shaking his pen like a thermometer to get the ink flowing.

I give the Black woman some more comforting. She points to my notepad with her free hand. I take it out and pass it to her. She manages to write "Kim Saunders" and a local number.

"This is your name?" I ask. She tries to nod. The medic presses the mask down harder. "I'll call 'em right now. You're going to be fine," I say, and start to get up. She won't let go of me. She squeezes my hand tightly. Then I gently remove it and get up and walk away.

I make the call as promised, from a pay phone, and keep at least one grandmother from having a heart attack tonight. The thanks I get from her make it just about worth it.

Bernie is standing near the car, and I can see that the Junkie is still in the back. The Junkie's wrists look terrible. They are bloody and torn. I think he actually tried to bite through them in order to get away while we were busy with the rescue.

"Let's get this punk down to the station before he bleeds all over the car," I say.

That's all right with Bernie. I go around to my side, and a woman stops me and says, "Excuse me, Officer"—she tilts her head to read my nameplate —"Buscarsela, Sergeant Kroger says you were the first to arrive on the scene. What do you think happened?"

She is wearing a gray trenchcoat that sets off her trim figure and reddish-brown hair a lot better than my box-shaped off-the-rack uniform does mine. I tell her, "Either General Westmoreland tried to defoliate North Harlem, or the Lilliflex factory sprung a leak."

She chuckles. "I can't print that. General Westmoreland'll sue the shit out of us *and win.*"

"Sorry, but if you really want to find out what happened, talk to Lilliflex. It's their mess."

"But what do *you* think happened?"

"C'mon, Buscarsela!" says Bernie. "Haul some ass!"

"I gotta go," I say.

"Can I call you later?" She gives me her card. It says:

Megan O'Shea

Crime Reporter

New York Newsday

"Call me Meg," she says.

"Crime reporter?"

"I was in the neighborhood."

"Okay, sure."

"See ya," and she goes off to get the story from someone else.

I climb in next to Bernie. He radios in that he is leaving the scene and why, gets the OK, and we drive off uptown. I turn my head to get one last look at the scene, but the Junkie throws himself at me, crashing into the screen. Bernie shakes his head.

"Animal," comments Bernie. This time, I agree with him.

After a bit, I confess: "Jeez, I was scared shitless back there."

Silence. Then Bernie says, "It was a bit hairy, yeah."

I can't believe I'm hearing this. "What is it with you guys?" I say. "A two-ton steel girder falls fourteen storeys and lands two inches from your nose, but, Were you scared?—No, not a bit. Well I don't mind telling you I was scared shitless back there when I couldn't lift that big guy up off the floor."

"It's different for a woman, Buscarsela. How'm I supposed to tell my wife I was scared, huh?"

"You're talking to the wrong person, Bernie. I have no sympathy whatsoever."

More silence.

"What was the food stamp center doing open at 9:30 at night, anyway?" I ask.

"Some special giveaway. A private charity was paying to keep the place open 'til 10:00, distributing surplus cheese to whoever came in."

"Get the name of the organization?"

"Negative."

"I didn't see anybody among the victims that looked like a charity worker."

"So now you're a mind reader? You want to tell me what a charity worker looks like?"

"Sure. The emergency food center volunteers tend to be bilingual Maryknoll nuns. See any nuns back there?" He doesn't say another word to me until we get to the station.

"You gonna catch this guy?" he asks.

"Sure." The usual exchange.

Once upstairs, we get the Junkie into a chair and I start to type up the report, while Bernie disappears somewhere. I believe I'm the only cop in the place who doesn't mind doing the paperwork. Some of them say it's because I'm the only one who can write. I think it's because I don't think the paperwork is any more or less bullshit than the *rest* of the job. At least I don't have to worry about the typewriter taking a shot at me.

I ask the questions, and of course the Junkie's got no address, no telephone, no next of kin, no past, no present, and no future. It's a wonder he's got a name, which he tells me is "Pepe Gonzalez." In this precinct, that's equivalent to "John Smith." Worse. Does he have any I.D.? Of course not.

When I'm finished, I call Dorset over. He is busy doing a cross-word puzzle.

"Hey Fil, what's a nine-letter word for a deadly radioactive substance, beginning with 'P'?" asks Dorset.

"Plutonium."

"Oh, yeah—ain't he that guy in *Hamlet?*"

"No, that's Strontium-90."

"You busting my balls again, Buscarsela? Jeez, I'd hate to be the first one to respond to a code from *that* place. A domestic dispute with poisoned swords?"

"Yeah, plus you'd have to write your report in iambic pentameter."

Dorset helps me dump the Junkie—excuse me, Pepe Gonzalez—in the cell, and I go to see the chief. You see, it would be really nice if somebody got it on record that tonight's toxic fume rescue was exceptional work. Or at least commendable. That and the upcoming third-year evaluation of my performance on special investigative assignment to the Rape Crisis Unit should give me enough points to make me eligible to apply for the Detective Bureau and get out of this beat garbage, which, by the way, is driving me nuts.

They were going to stick me in a Field Internal Affairs Unit, but I petitioned that knife-in-the-back job, and the Police Commissioner himself determined that I would do the Department the most good in the Rape Unit. This was seen as favoritism from the top, and ended up doing me about as much good with my peers as the FIA slot would have done. People don't exactly flip over the Department's current policy of quicker promotions for women and Blacks.

And some of the Blacks don't dig it when a *latina* leapfrogs over them. It's a mess. I don't care, I just want that shield.

"Come back later," is what I am told.

It's already a quarter to midnight, and I'm supposed to take off for the night in fifteen minutes. I go looking for my partner. He's not anywhere in sight. I knock on the men's room door.

"Yeah?"

"Bernie in there?"

"No, but there's plenty of room for you,"

I walk away from the sound of male laughter echoing off the tiles, and go down the stairs and out into the street, where I find Bernie killing our last few minutes on shift by cleaning up the back seat of the car with my half of the towel. That is, it's my half *now*. He would actually rather do that than have to contend with a typewriter and the English language.

I stand watching him for the next several minutes, until he finishes up and crawls backwards out of the car. Then he sees me. He can't think of anything cleverer to say to me than, "Yeah, so what?" so he makes up for it by adding, "Here, wash this" and tossing the blood-spit-and-hot-dog-with-everything-soaked towel at me. I dodge it. Unhappily the Lieutenant is not standing behind me to get hit in the face with it so he can bust Bernie's ass. That Lieutenant is never around when you need him.

Then a call comes over the radio to respond to a rape at 168th and Audubon Avenue.

"Uh-oh, Buscarsela's specialty," says Bernie, beating me to the driver's seat by throwing his body between the wheel and me. I run around to get in the other side to acknowledge the call Bernie sits there.

"I've acknowledged the call, Bernie, move it."

"Yeah, I can't seem to find the keys."

This is Bernie's idea of humor.

"OK, Bernie, I'm calling the precinct to tell them we haven't left the parking lot yet because you're trying to be funny."

Bernie doesn't think I mean it. He smiles at me. So I pick up the microphone and call the board: "Thirty-four-A-nine unable to respond."

"Thirty-four-A-nine," squawks the radio, "*why* aren't you responding?"

"You tell 'em, Bernie," I say, sticking the mike under Bernie's nose. He turns the key and starts the car.

"Car trouble," says Bernie. "We got it fixed now."

We pull away from the curb, make a U-turn across four lanes of traffic and head down Broadway towards 168th. I choose this moment to inform Bernie that he's going to have to explain all about the car trouble, in triplicate. He responds by driving slowly enough for me to lean out the door and pick daisies.

168th and Audubon is a bad neighborhood, as neighborhoods go. I've seen guys here rip the hoods off cars and walk off down the street holding them over their heads.

We turn the corner and pull up in front of the apartment building. People are standing around on the street trying not to look as if their very next move depends on our very next move. This house—this block—is one of those where every other person between the ages of eight and eighty deals drugs for a living. Right now I couldn't care less about that.

I dash up the stairs two at a time and into the building. I don't need to be Charlie Chan to follow the stares of the people standing out in the hallways directly to apartment 401, which is locked. I knock on the door, announce that this is the police, and that we're responding to a rape call. No answer. I knock two more times, announce this is the police twice, and were you the one who reported the rape? No answer. Oh great. The blood in my head is already pounding from sprinting up four flights, and now I get the silent treatment from an apartment where a woman has just been sexually assaulted, perhaps fatally. I pound the door with my nightstick and announce that I'm going to shoot the lock off in about ten seconds if I don't get a sign of life. There is no sound from behind the door. A breeze blowing off the Northern tundra gives me a chill. So I have to start counting: "One - two - three - four - five - six—seven——eight——"

I hear a bolt click. I jump to the side, which I should have done before I started counting. My hand is on my revolver. Another bolt clicks. A metal bar gets slid out of shot. The door opens, and a pair of severely distressed eyes peer at me over a length of eight-pound chain. The eyes belong to a very frail Latin American woman, who is clearly glad to see another Latin American woman—in uniform.

"Did you call the police?" I ask. Nothing. "Are you hurt?" She blinks. Well that's something. "Is there anyone else in there with you?"

This time I get a very soft, throaty, "No."

"May I come in?"

She is about to unlatch the chain when Bernie bounds up the stairs and shouts at me:

"Jesus, Buscarsela, you'd think you were chasing Son of Sam!"

The door slams shut in my face. Thanks, Bernie.

"You know it's after midnight," Bernie reminds me.

"So go home."

"What's the deal here?"

"I got it covered."

He looks at me, then at the door. "Women," he says.

I bring my voice down to a whisper. "You know, Bernie, I don't know what's wrong with you—if it weren't for women, you wouldn't be here."

"Who needs being here?"

"So get out of here. Tell 'em where I am, that it's under control, and go home."

It's not. There *could* be six crack dealers with Uzis in there. But I'm not getting the door open with Bernie there.

"Suits me," he says. He pushes his way through the conglomeration of the curious and he's gone, his steps clomping down the stairs and fading away.

And I'm back to an unresponsive door. But I don't remember having heard the bolts. I try the knob, and it opens. I let the door fall open to where the chain goes tight. I turn to the wide-eyed neighbors and ask if anyone knows what this woman's name is.

"Doris," I am told by a tall thin dude who's probably waiting for me to be out of sight so he can get back to business.

I put my face up to the opening.

"Doris," I say, "my name is Filomena. I'm a police officer with the 34th Precinct. I'm here to help. Just come closer to the door so we can talk. I'm alone."

I quickly look around to make sure that I'm telling Doris the truth. The few remaining bystanders try to step further into the background, even though most of them are already leaning against the walls with nowhere else to go. I tell everyone to beat it. They do. Must be something in my voice. When I turn back, Doris is facing me about six inches away. If this woman were dangerous, she could have had my eyes out. Something tells me she's not dangerous.

We start talking, in Spanish. After a few minutes she lets me in. I step inside and she slams the door behind me and throws both bolts. I take a quick look around. The place is sparse but clean. What I can see speaks of a working woman who is trying to keep her integrity above water in a very deep ocean of scum and misery. A sanctuary has been violated.

She asks me if I want some coffee. I don't, but I figure that going through the motions would be good for her, so I say sure. I follow her into the kitchen and watch her filling the kettle with water, putting it on the fire, getting down the can of El Pico, getting out the sugar. Unfortunately a family of roaches has moved in with the sugar.

"¡Caramba!" she shouts, swatting at the scattering roaches. Under the circumstances, anger is actually a good emotion for her to be showing. Anyway, it's a big step away from paralyzing fear.

"*¡Tantas cucarachas!*"

"You call these roaches?" I say in Spanish. "The roaches in Guayaquil could *eat* the New York roaches for breakfast!"

She laughs at my joke, thank God: This is the best sign there is that she's not going to turn into one of those poor people who are so afraid of dying that they stop living.

"*¿Tu eres del Ecuador?*" she asks.

"*Sí. ¿Y tu?*"

"*Soy de Colombia.* So we're neighbors."

"Hey, neighbors!" I say, not really knowing what to say, because what I want is to know some details while the trail is still warm, but, seeing Doris enjoy a moment of talking about pleasanter things, I hesitate. So we talk. It turns out she's from Cali, which helps explain why this tiny woman is so tough inside instead of being in complete shock. Maybe this has happened to her before. Cali makes Guayaquil look like Playland Park. Or so I hear.

Eventually she brings up the subject herself: She woke up with a knife at her throat and was raped. Did she see him? No, it was too dark, but she felt his face and is pretty sure she would be able to identify him by that alone. Did she mark him in any way? She might have scratched his face a little. With which hand? Her right. Maybe. OK, possible scratches on his left cheek. He was very big. How big? The length of the bed. I go check it. It's at least six-and-a-half feet. Hair? Curly. Did he talk?

"He just told me not to move."

"What were his exact words?"

"*No te muevas.*"

"Caribbean accent?"

"*Sí.*"

"Puerto Rican or Dominican?"

"I—It was only three words."

"It's OK. Try."

"If I had to, I'd say Dominican."

Hmm. Well, we're getting somewhere. I make note of all this. Did he take anything? I don't think so. Did he say or do anything else? No, he got up and left. Have you showered yet? No. Good. How long did you lie there before calling the police? I don't know, maybe twenty minutes. Maybe as much as an hour. And then you got up and locked the door?

She looks at me, her dark eyebrows drawing together, leaving a few worry wrinkles in their wake.

I rephrase it: "Did you lock the door before or after you telephoned the police?"

Two-second pause during which I can feel both our pulses rising.

"I—I didn't lock the door. The chain—yes, but not the door."

I stare at her. "Are you sure?"

"*Sí.*"

Oh shit. What's going through my mind now is *He's still here.* I slide the chair out and I'm on my feet. I have to check my near-instinctive move to the gun.

"Stay right here. Don't move."

When I'm out of the kitchen I unsnap the holster and palm the Police Department's .38-caliber revolver. Now I have to check the whole apartment. It's a very small place; there's only the bathroom and the closet, unless he's in the freezer. It takes all of about thirty seconds to assure myself that he's not in either of these places. The windows are closed and locked tight. The bed is just a mattress on the floor, so there can't be anyone under it. I check anyway. Satisfied that he's not in the apartment, I go back to the kitchen.

"Who else has a key?" Another blank stare. I know I should be more patient, but right now the adrenaline has me hopping. "What I mean is, do you have a boyfriend, or any male friend who might have access to a key?"

"No."

Then it's either the super or the landlord; whoever it is must be an unbelievable schmuck, because he went and locked the door behind him.

"Wait here," I tell Doris. "And don't open the door for anybody. And whatever you do, *don't wash*. Got it?" No response. "Got it?"

She nods, and I let myself out. She locks the door behind me. People are back out there. I see some dime bags disappear into pockets as I step out into the hallway. (All right, I couldn't swear that they were dime bags in a court of law, but what the hell else could they be?) I step up to the tall thin one and ask him where I can find the super.

"First door on the right in the basement, mon—I'll go." He starts down the stairs.

"Get your ass back on this landing," I tell him, and I swoop down the stairs past him. "I'd rather talk to him myself."

"Was jus tryin to be a gentleman, *guapa,*" he calls after me.

Right.

I go down to the basement and turn right, past the laundry room. At the end of a narrow, mildewy hall is a faded red door with a sign that says "Superintendent" that looks like it has been there since the day they dug the foundation. There is a party going on inside. I can hear it and I can smell it. Rapid-fire Dominican Spanish is being shouted over loud, thumping *merengue*.

There's a bell button which I push a few times before anything happens. The music quadruples in volume as the door swings in and there stands one bad-looking Dominican with forearms that are bigger than my legs, and a face that looks like his sweetheart caresses it three times a day with a tire iron. He has curly hair. There are also three parallel rows of fresh scratches running across the left side of his face. A single red lightbulb that glows in the corridor behind him adds a nice touch, too.

I don't wait for introductions this time. I throw my weight against the door, pushing him back about an eighth of an inch, and I'm part way in the apartment with my nightstick wedged between us—although this one looks like he could take it away from me and eat it if he wanted to. He doesn't have to fight me, he just stands there. I pull my gun, aim it just above his groin and tell him to turn around, that he's under arrest. He turns around and lets me put the cuffs on him. They almost don't make it all the way around his wrists.

At least he doesn't resist.

Now the rest of the party shows up, wondering where the host has been. Three guys that are built more to scale appear in the dull red glow. Their eyes shine at me as they come closer.

"Is there a phone here?" I ask.

The three red-tinted zombies stop. One of them says, "Yeah." I give him the number of the precinct and tell him that if he's real nice and calls them up and asks them to send a car over, I might be nice back and not make the three of them spend the night hanging by their aortae in a jail cell. None of them know what an aorta is, but they get the general idea. The one I'm telling this to leaves, and I hear him picking up the phone, dialing, and delivering my message.

I turn the big guy around to get another look at his face. He bares his teeth at me.

"Whadayou want from me, bitch?" he says.

I tell him I want him to know how it feels to wake up with a knife at his throat.

* * *

An hour later I'm back in the station house booking the super on suspicion and waiting for Doris to show up and identify him for me. But I'm not moving fast enough to satisfy the super, who wants to get back out on the street and rape some more women, I suppose.

"Hurry it up, will ya?" he says to me. "You're getting paid for this time, I'm not."

I look at my watch. It's just past 1:30 A.M. I inform him that not only am I getting paid for this and he's not, but I'm getting overtime, and How about that?

I get the high sign from Carrera—who, by the way, is one of the few sympathetic male cops in the place—which means that Doris is here and is being taken to the observation room. I nod to Carrera, and turn back to finish booking the subterranean.

"You're just doing this to me because I'm a man, right?" he says. I ignore that and keep typing. "You know I'm goin' to be out by three o'clock tomorrow afternoon."

I look up at him, directly into his slimy eyes.

"Tomorrow's Sunday," I tell him. "You can't have a bail hearing until nine a.m. Monday morning."

"Then I'll be out by noon on Monday at the latest, bitch."

He's probably right, but how does he know this? Unless he's been here before. No wonder he didn't resist. Personally, I think he should get two to three hundred years, but that's just my opinion.

I call up Gladys downtown and tell her I need some info fast. I know she can't deliver any hard copy right now, but I ask her as a favor just to check this guy out for me and get back to me as soon as she finds anything. She says, Why not?—She doesn't have anything better to do than honor about five hundred other similar requests, but she'll see what she can do. I tell her that's all I can ask for, and she hangs up.

Then I get some help and haul the worm into the Sweatroom. As the arresting officer, I get to go and be with the victim.

Doris has cleaned herself up, but not too much I hope. She is pale and nervous, shivering blue-lipped with cold and aftershock. I don't even want to think about how I'd be reacting in her place; but then not thinking about it isn't much of a solution.

During the time that I've been booking the worm, his lawyer has shown up. Well, I guess it's his lawyer. I sure didn't invite him. He's wearing a splotchy pinstripe suit that looks like it was pulled from The Costume Collection at the last minute when the actor failed to show and they had to fit the bellboy for the part.

Over in the Sweatroom, the worm deliberately comes right up to the one-way mirror, which makes Doris take a step back, and starts to comb his hair arrogantly. When he is finished, he takes out a magic marker and manages to write "FUCK YOU" backwards on the mirror—that is, backwards for *him,* it comes out just fine for us—before Carrera grabs him and shoves him back into the room. It's late and we're all tired. I get right to the point:

"Is that the guy?"

"I can't tell from here," says Doris. "It was too dark."

The worm's lawyer is beaming.

"But I ran my hands over his face, many times. It was very rough and had a lot of scars. He also had a smell that I don't think I will ever forget. If I could touch his face—"

"—NO!" injects the lawyer.

"—I might be able to identi—"

"—Not a chance, baby."

I have a brief shouting match with the worm's lawyer. It seems he has come prepared with some legal fucking precedent whereby a legally blind rape victim was barred from identifying a suspect by touching the faces of men in a police line-up.

"What about the scratches?" I say. "We can compare skin samples."

"I washed my hands," confesses Doris.

"She washed her hands," parrots the lawyer unnecessarily.

"Fingerprints," I say.

"Get with it, Officer Buscarsela. My client has been up to that apartment a dozen times during the last six months as part of the normal course of his duties as building superintendent."

It occurs to me to bring up the pot smoking, but I don't want to—I beg your pardon—cloud the issue, and I don't even want this sleaze to *think* about plea bargaining.

"Well, there's always the semen," I say, mentioning the forbidden subject.

Now the lawyer looks cornered, but Doris says, "No," and he perks right up. I look at Doris.

"I'm sorry," she says. "But I can't. Not that—"

I ask to have a few minutes alone with the victim. The lawyer says that I can have five, as if he runs the place.

And I talk to Doris. It's very difficult. She knows what kind of torment they're going to put her through. She knows it and I know it. And my good friend the lawyer has made it a point of telling her that even if we book his client on evidence, he'll be out on $250 bail by Monday afternoon, as promised, because—Hey, he didn't take anything, or hurt her, really. I say yes, that's true, but she has to think of the next woman this creep decides to rape. She's on the edge now. But I can't push her. She has to jump. Then there's a knock on the door that makes Doris jump with fright. It's Carrera. I tell him to come in. He leans his head in and says:

"Phone for you, Fil." Oh please oh please oh please . . .

I excuse myself and leave the room, heading for the desk. It's Gladys. She asks me if I'm ready. I say shoot. She goes on to say that this will be the fourth time this worm will have been booked on charges of rape, but that none of the victims have ever pressed charges.

"Thanks, Gladys. I owe you one."

"You owe me about five, honey." And she's right.

I go back and give Doris the full report. It's hard for her. She is fighting back the tears when she says, "All right. I'll do it."

I hug her, and she starts shuddering as the pent-up tears of the past four hours' pain finally surface. I have to swallow a few times myself.

The chief is no longer in, of course, so my bid for a Career Program Transfer will have to wait until Monday. Doesn't everything?

I stay and wait with Doris until the medics arrive, stay with her through the whole nasty business, confirm a Monday morning deadline for the lab results, and take Doris home so she can finally take that shower. She makes me enter the apartment first and check it out before she'll go in. I ask her, Doesn't she have any friends or relatives she can stay with, at least for tonight? She says not yet, she's only been in the country for two months. Jesus.

It's just past four in the morning by the time I get back to my apartment, which is empty because this Saturday night shift was a last-minute surprise. No French boyfriend tonight.

I hope tomorrow's better.

TWO

"Pluck out his eyes."

—Goneril

It isn't.

Megan O'Shea of *New York Newsday* quoted me as saying "It's their mess," meaning the Lilliflex Corporation, and I get the shit dropped on me for it. The Lieutenant spends about twenty minutes screaming at me that even a baby-faced recruit knows enough not to comment to the press on an open case. I say I didn't realize it was a "case," so he shows me the Lilliflex press releases denouncing the regrettable incident as sabotage. So it's not their fault.

"Sabotage? By who?" I plead. "The roaches? They got together and chewed a hole in a 16-inch pipe? 'Cause if the roaches are getting organized, I'm out of here."

The point is that it's now under investigation, so any public comments are to be made by Departmental press release only, so they concoct some crap about how I really said "It's a mess" but was misquoted by an irresponsible member of the press, and the decent human being that surfaces in me every Groundhog Day makes me fish out Ms. O'Shea's card to call her up and warn her. She can't be reached all afternoon, she's out covering a lover's revenge murder in

Queens, one of those wonderful cases where the girlfriend dumps the boyfriend for being such a violent S.O.B., so he comes back a couple of days later and shoots her. A half-hour before the Departmental release goes public I finally get her.

"Megan O'Shea? This is Officer Buscarsela of the 34th."

"Off—oh sure. What's up? Got a good quote for me?"

I tell her No, sorry, and spill the whole deal, warning her that we're about to issue a statement claiming *she* misquoted me. She's pretty nice about it, says as long as she can get me down as "an anonymous Police Department source" who confirms the authenticity of the first reported version her boss will buy it. I say, Sounds like an OK boss, and ask, "What's all this about sabotage?"

"They say one of their monitors was snipped and someone cut a hole in a scrubber duct right next to an air vent that fronts the food center."

"They let you in to see that?"

"Well, not me, but it's in the pr—"

"—in the press release," I say, finishing her sentence. "Can you get in there?"

"Why should I? Page Three murders are my specialty."

"Then tell your boss that your 'anonymous Police Department source' says this may have been an attempted murder."

"Is that official?"

"It's not impossible. *Don't* quote it."

"You're making this up, aren't you?"

Pause. "Can we meet somewhere and talk?"

"No. We're two men short and I gotta help put 'er to bed tonight."

"I just think *something's* screwy when a cop gets her head chewed off for chatting with the press at an accident scene. They usually like folks to know we showed up in time."

Pause. Or is that the sound of hush money?

"OK . . . Listen: I've got a list of the victims' names. Eleven of them. You've got their addresses."

"Somewhere," I answer.

"What say you interview the victims and I have a look inside the Lilliflex factory?"

"I'd say you're getting the sweet end of the deal."

"You want me to take a few of the names?"

"Yes."

"OK, OK. Why don't you take A to M and I'll take N to Z? Call me with the stats, Officer Buscarsela."

"Filomena. Call me Fil."

"OK. And I'm Meg."

"Right. Meg?"

"Yeah?"

"Get me some photos."

* * *

Three days later we meet in an East Side coffee shop to split what we've got, which is nothing times two. Megan shows me some 8 x 10's that certainly look like an air-quality monitor whose cables have been cut and a big metal pipe with acetylene burns around a three-inch hole.

"How the hell did the saboteur survive this?" I ask.

"They say a breathing mask was missing from the main office."

"Who is this guy? James Bond? I sure could have used one of those masks. My lungs are still stinging."

"Now what have you got?"

Nothing. All of the victims were locals, unemployed, underemployed, or just plain hungry, waiting to get some government-surplus cheese, who didn't know what hit them and don't remember a thing.

"Even the white guy?"

"White guy?" says Megan.

"Yeah: The *white* guy." Nothing. "Let me see your list." She shows it to me. It doesn't tell me anything. Dead End. I toss it back on the table. I say: "Maybe it *was* sabotage . . . "

* * *

I've got no personal stake in the Lilliflex business, so I let the cops who are getting paid for it chase down the sabotage angle. They come up with enough evidence to admit the possibility of sabotage by the proverbial "disgruntled employee," but that's as far as they get. They scour every employee that's worked there in the past ten years without turning up a serious suspect. Which leaves the white guy. I mean, if he had just turned in the same story as the other ten victims it would've slipped right by. But a little legwork with Megan's half of the list confirms that he gave someone else's name and address, and when Megan knocked on the guy's door, he was just so thrilled about getting his name in the paper that he said yes to everything.

Great.

We relay this info to the detectives in charge of the investigation. They don't get any further with it than we did. It's tough to get an eyewitness account from people who were being blinded by carcinogenic chemical fumes at the time. I tell them I'd know him if I ever saw him again and that little remark buys me seventeen hours of cross-referencing a half-ton of mugshots with the Lilliflex employee records. Whoopee. But if he's a suspect, what the hell was he doing inside the place he was trying to poison? That doesn't make too much sense, but then, neither does his disappearance. Maybe he wanted to create a leak to discredit the company or make their stock plunge or something, and then he saw that the food center was open late that night and ran in there to try to get everybody out—but then, that points to a pretty humanitarian saboteur, and you'd think one of the witnesses might have mentioned something about a guy running in and trying to get everyone out.

I decide to talk to all the witnesses again and see if maybe I can jog something from their memories that Ms. O'Shea couldn't. After all, I was there. Maybe some detail will click. But all I get is the same old nothing. When I get to Kim Saunders, her mom answers, remembers to thank me again and tells me Kim's at the doctor. A lung specialist. It doesn't sound good. I promise to call back.

And I ask myself, What kind of saboteur would risk his life to save some unintended victims at a food stamp center?

* * *

A few days later I'm walking to work. Spring is now close enough so that every once in a while we get a day where an occasional breeze from the south carries with it a warm hint of the summer to come, and the Korean grocery on the corner has started putting fruit on display out on the sidewalk. Forget that jazz about spring starting on March 21st. I don't know who came up with that. Some neolithic meteorologist. This far up in the Northern Hemisphere it doesn't really get warm and stay warm until about the second week in May.

But it's nice enough to walk, if you walk fast and get the circulation going.

I'm even a few minutes early as I report for the eight a.m. shift and am told that the Lieutenant wants to see me. Must be a slow morning if he has time for me. I look around. There are two university students in the holding cell discussing Pliny, of all things. They have presumably been busted for possession of a quarter-gram of cocaine or some similar infraction, and a night in jail is supposed to throw a scare into them, which it probably did when they were first picked up and brought in, but now the scare has worn off completely; they know by now that they'll be out on probation in a few hours, and here they are calmly discussing whether or not there is a certain inevitability in nature when a tree falls or some such nonsense, and gathering data on Departmental procedure that will serve to fascinate and impress future girlfriends for years to come—all free of charge, courtesy of the N.Y.P.D. Other than that, the place is practically asleep. The stillness of a battlefield before the next barrage.

I knock on the glass door and the Lieutenant gestures for me to come in as if he were trying to capture a mosquito and crush it with his fist.

He is on the phone, so I sit down and wait. When he hangs up, he starts going through the papers on his desk and in his drawer, saying my name over and over as he looks. This is all an act to make me realize how many other things he has to do besides review my request for promotion. He's done this to me about ten times before, and I know he's got my application within easy grasp the whole time, but I wait it out.

He makes a big show of "finding" it under some case files, and looks at it as if he's trying to refresh his memory as to what this trivial matter is about. He has time to read the thing three times in its entirety before he says, "Bad news, Officer Buscarsela. Your application was rejected because it's half a point short."

"But the review board gave me an evaluation Well Above Standards."

"It's not that. They nixed the Exceptional Merit."

"Down to Meritorious Police Duty?"

"Down to nothing."

"What?"

Up to now he has been holding the report up in the air between us, half-hiding behind it. Now he fans it away from himself so that I can see it—although he doesn't let go of it. I scan the denial.

" 'Uncorroborated Testimony'?" I say, incredulous.

He slaps the report down on top of the other papers on his desk.

"No witnesses, Fil."

"No witnesses? What about my partner?"

"He says he ran in first, and that he can't say where you were, it was so confusing in there."

"That—" I stop myself. "How about the paramedic who treated me?"

"He claims he only saw you after they got everybody out."

"Kim Saunders."

"Who?"

"The woman I carried out—"

"Yeah. Unfortunately, she was unconscious at the time."

"Look, Lieutenant, she might have been unconscious, but one of the medics took her from me the *second* I got her out of there."

"Can you identify which one?"

"I already told you my eyes were totally blinded with irritants. I wrote that in the report. What's the matter, my sworn statement isn't enough?"

"In a case like this, I'm afraid the answer is 'No.' "

I sink back in the chair. I don't believe what I'm hearing. I don't want a frigging brass plaque and the Key to the City, but what's the point of risking your neck to pull people out of a deadly circumstance when this is what happens? Then the full irony of the situation hits me, as I remember the one other participant in that night's events who might be able to corroborate my statement.

"The Junkie," I say, hardly believing myself that I am saying it.

"The who?"

"We had a perp in the back of the patrol car the whole time. He must have seen what went down—he was watching our every move."

The Lieutenant starts to stack some papers. "Well, what's his name?"

Oh great. Pepe Gonzalez number 3002. I tell the Lieutenant the name and the S.O.B. starts *laughing*.

"Sorry, Fil. It's just that you got all the rotten luck."

"I know," I say, getting up and leaving him laughing.

Always leave him laughing.

Now what do I do? I can't remember having seen the Junkie around lately, but even if I managed to find him, why would he want to do anything to help me? I could promise him something, but what? Maybe I'll get lucky and catch him robbing a liquor store, but I doubt he has the brains or the motivation for that. If only he would fulfill his threat to "come looking for" me. The least they could do is get me away from this asshole partner of mine. Here he comes now.

"Get it in gear, Buscarsela, let's go," he says, heading for the stairs without really looking at me.

"One phone call," I yell after him. I try to call Kim again. She's not in. Anyway, they don't give you promotions for holding someone's hand.

I walk out past the university students and start down the stairs, where I meet Carrera, who is coming off shift.

"I'm finished with this," says Carrera, holding out a slightly used copy of today's *El Diario*. "You wanna see it?"

"Thanks," I say, taking it from him.

Once inside the car I use the paper to build a wall around myself and hide Bernie from my sight for a little while. On the front page is the major U.S. news. I see that three days after telling reporters at a press conference that the U.S.S. *Nimitz,* which is only the largest frigging warship in the fleet, was nowhere near the Gulf of Sidra, Reagan & Co. have shot down two Libyan planes—in the Gulf of Sidra—with jets launched from the *Nimitz*. Reagan himself is staring into the camera as if he's telling the reporters, "Oh, *that Nimitz!* Oh, sure, *that Nimitz* is in the Gulf of Sidra, yeah . . . "

I lower the paper just to make sure Bernie hasn't set up an elaborate practical joke whereby he sneaks out of the car to watch it drive off the University Heights Bridge into the Harlem River with me inside it, or some such hilarious project. No, we're still on Edgecombe Avenue, overlooking the rift between Manhattan and the

Bronx that was once occupied by a glacier, where now spindly high-rises seventy storeys high and about twenty-five feet wide are sprouting up, and being rented to people under the delusion that they are standing on "waterfront" property.

Bernie makes some stupid comment about Spanish language newspapers that I am pretty successful at blocking out, shuffling the pages loudly while I turn to the *Nuestros Paises* section, where I see it's time to elect Miss Banana again in Panama. Some people have all the fun. It seems that the infamous death-camp doctor Josef Mengele was sighted in Paraguay. The Simon Wiesenthal Center, in conjunction with the Israeli government, is offering a total of $3.4 million dollars reward for information leading to his arrest. What on earth am I doing here in this car when I could be down on my native continent racking up $3.4 million?

I turn to my own country, and see that the big item in the news today is that a voicebox for the Ecuadorian armed forces has reiterated their promise to allow the upcoming presidential elections to take place. How nice of them. Now if we can just get the C.I.A. to make the same promise.

I was a student at the University of Guayaquil during the last two military dictatorships. General Lara was thoughtful enough to nationalize the oil industry, which brought in a nice pile, but as the man says, the money turned into color TVs and Mercedes-Benzes instead of schools and hospitals. I saw kids fry themselves trying to rob electricity from the power company by running uninsulated wires to their shacks from the high-tension lines that criss-cross the sky above the poor neighborhoods on their way to the foreign-owned factories. Legend has it that Guayaquil was founded by a blind man, on a swamp, which would explain a lot.

So I came here. And when I got tired of having bosses yell, "Hey, college girl! Type this!" I became a citizen, and joined the force.

And suddenly I became the interpreter for people who never realized that my Andean *mestizo* Spanish was not always enough to relate to people who grew up on East 116th Street speaking Nuyorican.

Worse, before I had even one week on the job, I found out what a sardonic Fortune had cooked up for me: Being a cop suddenly cut me off from most of the *latino* community—but I wasn't accepted into the "Brotherhood," either. So I was, am, left an observer, stuck in an endlessly revolving door between the two cultures, able to catch glimpses of both, often acting as a link between the two, but never able to step out and unequivocally join one or the other. For some reason the Dominicans always thought I was Cuban, the Cubans always thought I was Colombian, and the Colombians thought I was Puerto Rican. Buscarsela is not a common name.

My reverie is interrupted by a 10-18 call at the construction site where Columbia Presbyterian Medical Center is sending up its new office towers.

"That's us," says Bernie, steering past Trinity Cemetery and turning uptown. Bernie flips on the lights and the Jimi-Hendrix-Live-At-Woodstock bootleg that we use for a siren, and we wail through ten blocks of lights and stop in front of the hospital construction site, not more than fifty seconds after having gotten the call.

We rush into the cavernous, unfinished lobby of the new building, where a supervisor meets us and leads us inside the rickety open cage that serves as the temporary elevator. Now, I got used to precipitous five-hundred-foot drops to certain death on the legendary roads between Guayaquil and the small-town-to-end-all-small-towns where I was born, Solano, which lies ten thousand feet above sea level and still has no paved road leading up to it; but frankly, this semi-floorless hanging cage is the kind of vision that usually gets a starring role in one of my nightmares. I age a few years for every level we climb. They really can't be called floors yet. They are just concrete levels, open to the cold April air, several hundred feet above the unyielding blacktop of Fort Washington Avenue.

We finally stop at the twenty-third "floor," and step out onto a rough concrete shelf without so much as a strip of day-glo orange plastic between us and Nowhere. Cold needles tingle my toes. Dust is everywhere, and the chalky smell of freshly cut sheetrock clogs my nostrils. There is another, chemical, smell that I can't quite identify.

The supervisor leads us to one of the rooms where the wiring is being installed. Everything's that drab gray of unpainted wallboard and poured concrete, so it's a real shock to see so much blood. There's a big splatter from an exit wound, and what's left of the construction worker's body is lying in a bright red puddle surrounded by chunks of blood-soaked plaster and cement. Half-baked wiring hangs down lifelessly from the ceiling.

What a lonely death.

The place is so bare. The acetylene torch nearby looks like it was wheeled in from a slaughterhouse. There are other people standing around in the bright, wind-swept area, all fellow construction workers. The supervisor brings one of them forward, a long-haired kid who looks like he's seventeen, and frightened. The supervisor plants the kid in front of us with all the grace of a trash compactor and says with equal delicacy:

"Spill it."

The kid looks at us cops as if he's looking at forty years of hard labor at Ossining, which, incidentally, you would be able to see from this height, looking up river, except that it's too cloudy and overcast.

"It was an accident, I swear it," is how the kid begins.

"No shit," says the supervisor. This guy would make a terrific social worker.

"Go on," I say.

"I was working in the other room, putting studs into the sheetrock with this—"

The kid practically takes off my nose with one of those .22-caliber nail-into-cement guns they use when nobody feels like drilling. I know he's nervous, and for good reason, but I can't help swatting the thing away from my face with an angry gesture.

"S-sorry," says the kid.

"What's your name?" asks Bernie.

"His name's Tommy Osborne," says the supervisor. "And he's fired."

"That's the least of his problems," offers Bernie.

"Just a minute," I step into this. "Tommy, how old are you?"

Tommy blurts out "Nineteen" so fast you'd think someone had just performed the Heimlich maneuver on him.

"Uh-huh Could I see your driver's license?"

Tommy looks worried, but I'm watching the supervisor. A couple of his neck muscles involuntarily tighten as I'm asking this and Tommy reaches for his wallet.

The driver's license that I'm given looks like it was printed up in Times Square in one of those places where you can get a three-dollar bill with your picture on it. I ask again:

"Tommy, how old are you?

Tommy gets this look on his face that I once saw in a painting of General Cornwallis surrendering his sword at Yorktown. He says he is sixteen. Now it's time to make the supervisor sweat.

"And you let this kid load the shells for a .22?"

The supervisor hides behind one of the older lies in the history of Western civilization: "Hey, he *said* he was nineteen. Plus he had references."

"And he's a full-fledged, dues-paying member of the union, right? Let me see your union card, kid.—Don't have one? Well well . . . ! So now we have a fatality on the job due to unauthorized operation of equipment. We might even be able to halt construction over this, which would probably cost the contractors—for this place—about $150,000 a day, to say nothing of a possible jail sentence for you, my friend, for criminal negligence. Firing this kid is the best thing you could ever do for him."

The supervisor lets the dust settle, literally, before he says, "Jesus, you're serious."

"You're damn right I'm serious! What did you think, you were gonna be able to pin this all on the kid—?"

I'm fixing to throw this guy off the ledge, but Bernie crams himself between us.

"Look, let's just leave judgment in this matter to the experts. I'll go call it in. Buscarsela, you wanna watch the body?"

"Love to," I say, moving away from the supervisor. Guarding the body means I get to be rid of Bernie for the rest of the day, if I'm lucky.

"I'll be back," says Bernie, walking out.

"No hurry," I call after him. Then I turn to the others. "All right: As far as I'm concerned, this is a crime scene. The rest of you clear out of here."

The supervisor does a worthy imitation of Napoleon on his way *back* from Moscow, slinking out the door with the weight of a possible $150,000-a-day violation for his bosses weighing on his shoulders. The other workers trail out after him.

"Not you," I say to a guy in dark coveralls whose shirtpatch says his name is Morty. "I've got to search the body and I need a witness."

Morty stays. I bend down to have a closer look. It's pretty bad. The guy must have been working on the wiring when he was hit, and fell clutching it, because in addition to a very jagged 350 m.p.h. exit wound in the back of his head, he is scored with several deep, curved electrical burns. I knock the deadly tendrils away from the body with my nightstick, get my hands under his left shoulder, and lift him up to get a look at his face. The hideous entrance wound isn't enough to keep me from recognizing the solitary blond-haired white survivor of a toxic leak that still hasn't been fully explained.

The next second my radio is in my hand, and I'm calling Bernie, who answers, his voice crackling over the played-out speaker, "Yeah?"

"I know this guy. I've seen him before," I say, my voice sounding strangely tight.

And what does Bernie have to say to that? "So fucking what?"

* * *

I do my job and call in the detectives on the Lilliflex case. I also order some hot coffee. It's getting pretty chilly up here. I'll say one thing for New York City, my coffee arrives before the detectives do, and the Chinese delivery boy smiles when I tip him like he brings coffee to the edge of the freezing abyss of death all the time, but he usually doesn't get a tip for it. I'm about halfway through my rapidly cooling cup of coffee when the detectives arrive and they *take over,* acting as if I'm not there. At least I get a kick out of being ignored by someone besides Bernie.

Hours later I'm into my fourth cup of extra extra light coffee (I told them to warm the milk up. They did. Thank God for small miracles) when the detectives finally pack up and call it a day. All kinds of questions have been rolling around in my head, but I keep them to myself. Questions like Why is there an acetylene torch in the middle of this windswept mausoleum? Who loaded the .22 shells? Was there more powder than there should have been? Then I think, shit, let *them* do the investigating. One of them, Detective Meehan, is actually nice enough to tell me I can call him for the results, since I did him the favor of finding the body. He tips his hat to me and keeps looking at me as the cage slides out of view.

No one in forensics is available to come sign a death certificate, so I have to accompany the body to the morgue myself. I'm sure Bernie tried his hardest to find an available doctor. On the way down to the morgue, I keep thinking about Tommy, who, in spite of the fact that he ended up believing me that it really wasn't his fault directly, is still going to have to live the rest of his life knowing that his incompetence, albeit shared with someone who *should* have known better, killed a man. What can I say to that?

Hours later, when I've finally got the body processed, and have learned that he was, in life, Wilson McCullough, who lived at 135 Avenue B, Manhattan, I notice that I still can't get the chemical sting from the construction site out of my nose. This brings back memories of when I used to work on those goodwill housing projects back in Ecuador—a land still unburdened by worker protection laws: I would wake up the next day with the taste of yesterday's lacquer thinner in my mouth.—And I was only present at the Columbia Presbyterian site for a couple of hours.

The site was pretty damn well ventilated, too.

I take McCullough's effects, sealed in a plastic bag, to have them registered. One very curious item is a blood-spattered $20 bill that was lying under the body. But it's really just a naturally shocking graphic, it probably doesn't mean a thing. A brand-new bill.

The next day they finally honor my request to "at least get me away from this asshole partner," and I get to spend the rest of the week on the shit details—like the shift I spend guarding the entrance to the South African Embassy on *the* day that P.W. Botha arrives to address the United Nations, and about 100,000 people show up to tell him what they think of him. They call out every cop who's got a pair of shoes to cover this one. But I don't mind. I'm free of Bernie.

I get back to the precinct in time to put out a description of "Pepe Gonzalez." You can imagine how much good *that* does. But it gets me thinking about fake names. If there was one fake name on Meg's list, it's possible there are others. I call her up and suggest we go over the list for the fifteenth time, but she says Why? they all check out.

I tell her, "Maybe I can get something out of Kim Saunders. She seemed to want to tell me something."

Meg says, "That old fool? She had trouble remembering her name."

"Old—??" Sure enough, Meg talked to Kim's mother. They have the same name. Don't ride Megan too hard about her mistakes. I make mine often enough. A few quick calls and I find out Kim's in Jackson Hospital ICU with shredded, soggy lungs. She's been there for a week. And they won't let her talk to anyone. Shit. As soon as I get off shift I go down to see her. Jackson Hospital is the poor folks' hospital so it's not as hard as you think to get past the restrictions and walk through the rarefied air of the oxygen-tent hallway, my regulation heels echoing callously off the sterile tile walls. Kim looks horrible. The stuff she breathed in has gotten to her. She's dying. They've got her in a mask, under a tent, with so many tubes I can't tell which are going in and which are going out of her blotchy, purplish chest.

I can only ask Yes/No questions.

I describe Wilson. Does she remember him? Yes. Had she ever seen him before? Yes. At the food center? Yes. Did he ever talk to you? Yes. I figure I better ask a "No" question just to make sure this system is working. Did he work there? No. Good. When he spoke to you, did he ever say anything against the Lilliflex Corporation? Yes. That night? No. Because he had only just gotten there? No. Was he there for more than five minutes? Yes. More than ten minutes? Ye—No. Around ten minutes? Yes. Okay, here it comes: That night, did he tell you or anyone else to leave the building, that maybe it wasn't safe to be there? No.

Because, of course, it was a cold night in March, and all the windows and vents should have been sealed tight. But those old buildings aren't too seaworthy, so when the fumes started to hit it caught *everyone* by surprise. Or maybe not . . . Still, it's beginning to look like Wilson could have been the saboteur.

The doctors tell me it's time to go. I tell Kim, "We're going to find out who did this, okay?" But it's not okay. Poor Kim is beyond caring. I say my goodbyes and get myself out of there.

I'm about to call Jean-Luc but I change my mind and call Meg instead. I give her the scoop on Wilson, who was not an employee of Lilliflex (I only checked the damn records twenty or thirty times), and tell her she should dig for a connection between the two. "Thanks, Fil," she says. "You're getting to be a pal." Then I call Jean-Luc. No answer. Damn. I could use some serious loving. And since I'm having so much fun tonight, I decide to go down to the morgue to find out what the autopsy is. Since I brought in the body, they let me in. I am not expecting it when the coroner's lab assistant says, "He was killed instantly by the projectile. It certainly seems to have been an accident, but all the same, somebody could have gotten tired of waiting."

"What do you mean?"

"McCullough had enough tetraethyl lead in his system to open his own gas station."

"What on earth is tetraethyl lead?"

"Tetraethyl lead comes from cheap gasoline. Boil off ninety-nine percent of the gas and you've got it. Just being near the concentrated liquid or the vapors is enough to croak somebody if they're around it long enough."

I think of the persistent sting in my nostrils after my brief visit to the site. "Wouldn't day to day exposure on the job build up—"

"—Not in these quantities, honey. Getting a dose like this under normal workplace conditions is about two hundred times better than chance. I have little doubt that his death was an accident. But sooner or later it probably would have been murder."

I call the precinct and tell them I need to get in touch with a Tommy Osborne immediately. Dorset answers, and tells me, "Osborne was found OD'd in his parents' house in Flushing. They're calling it suicide. —By the way, Fil, you know Spanish. What's a nine-letter word beginning with L that means 'maze' . . . ?"

"Laberinto."

* * *

Now the wheels are turning. Is this an accidental death and a suicide, or two murders? Ether way, the two people who might have been able to tell me aren't talking.

And this is getting messier than I thought.

It's time to see the Lieutenant again. I go up the back stairs from the parking lot, and pass by the men's locker room, where I am privileged to see the precinct's three newest members, a couple of kids who chose the police academy after the local street gang turned them down, actually *playing* with their guns—ejecting bullets from their chambers up into the air and trying to catch them.

I'm waiting to see the Lieutenant, pondering why I keep subjecting myself to all the obstacles that the people who are supposed to be on my side keep throwing up at me. Why am I even in this country in the first place? is the subtext of many of their not-so-innocuous remarks. Don't ask me, friend, I don't even know myself sometimes. What are the advantages of being here?—Besides the relative luxuries of an imperial society: Things like dishwashers, electricity, drinkable water, predictable government . . .

"Okay, Buscarsela, you can come in now, but I've only got five minutes," barks the Lieutenant.

The first part of our conversation plays like one of the routines Abbott and Costello rejected before they came up with "Who's on First?":

"I want to be assigned to the McCullough murder."

"You can't get a murder case unless you're in Homicide."

"So process my application and put me in Homicide."

"We can't process your application until you score another half point—"

"You mean, like if I crack the McCullough murder, that'll give me enough points to apply for Detective and crack the McCullough murder," I say.

"Look, Fil, until your Junkie witness turns up, or you get a positive from one of the victims, that's the situation. Or you gonna go over my head and take this one to the Commissioner too?"

So that's what this is about. And I thought we were all working together fighting crime, or some such nonsense. Silly me.

"All right, Buscarsela, if that's the way you want it, but you're gonna do body detail all week."

"Why don't you just stick me with the night shift at the Brooklyn Navy Yard?" Unless the dark side of the moon is available.

"If I have to," says the Lieutenant.

"And I came to you for help," I say, getting up to leave.

"That's your problem."

* * *

It's raining outside, but I decide to wait and catch the bus. Somehow I just don't feel like going underground.

Sitting inside one of those brand spanking new buses where the plastic always smells like someone threw up on it, I look out the windows that some fool designer, who must live in Los Angeles or a similar place where it never rains, decided to tint gray. Rain is pouring down the windows in rivulets that infiltrate the allegedly impermeable window seals and form puddles in the perpetually-depressed plastic seats. This did not happen with the old bench-style seats, but progress marches slowly on. Something is wrong when the company that successfully landed Viking 1 and 2 on Mars can't build a bus that will survive two months of crosstown traffic. Somebody's making money somewhere, I'm thinking, as I stare out into the undulating images that the sheets of rain on the windows are making of the bleak stretch of Broadway that you never see in the movies: Mile after mile of utterly characterless buildings that are just the wrong age for the Manhattan cycle of real estate value: Most of them were built in the 1920s, so they're not old enough to merit refurbishing in the eyes of the speculators, or new enough to be in good condition. They just reach sixty, seventy years of age and quietly fall apart, and nobody's doing anything about it. And I live in one of them.

People try desperately to generate some life in this inhospitable environment, but on block after block of slate gray quasi-tenements the only color comes from the stores whose garish yellow-and-red plastic signs look just like those fuzzy day-glo tufts of mold that infest the otherwise featureless neutral background of a failed high-school biology experiment.

My mind is wandering, but it keeps coming back to the same thing: It's the *method* of offing Wilson McCullough that makes me feel that there is something behind it. Slow poisoning is not the typical method of your average loan-shark enforcement agency, jealous husband, or barroom bigmouth. Even Bernie would be able to dope out that the death the same day of McCullough's nearest co-worker points to a certain amount of organization, with a lot to protect.

The bus drives through the George Washington Bridge under-pass, and in the sudden darkness my reflection appears on the window in front of me. With a sudden shock of recognition I ask myself a disturbing question, Is that the only reason I'm so deter-mined to get at the heart of the matter?—My own personal interest in the fact that I think it's a big case, and would ultimately lead to Departmental recognition? A wave of guilt seizes me. Am I really so anxious to see justice done, or am I just after The Big One that'll get me that promotion? I turn my face from the bleak streets and look around at the faces on the bus. Middle-aged Black women in long woolen raincoats are heading back downtown, protecting their shopping from enemy attack. Somebody is trying to convert 181st Street into a kind of shopping mall. Sister, all the polish in the world wouldn't make these streets shine. To think this used to be an Indian trail that led from the tip of Manhattan island all the way up to what is now Albany.

Now there's a string of gin joints so thick lining the way that if you stopped in each one to have a drink you'd be dead before you got ten blocks. Now there's a thought.

I never had much of a taste for the hard stuff until I came here. And if you've ever tried the hard stuff of the Ecuadorian highlands, you know why. Half the men in town would get falling down drunk on homemade brew every weekend, while the women stayed home nursing the babies and scrubbing the floors. They all said I should have been a priest, the way I castigated them. I probably would have been a priest if the local Church weren't still caught in the fourth century. I always figured being a cop was the next best thing: Helping others, saving lives, plus a pension. Needless to say, the Academy was no seminary, except for the similarity that there, too, the first rule of survival was to become "one of the boys," which meant rule bending with the boys, cruising with the boys, and going out drinking with the boys.

So after a few hard-earned lessons in how to be sick like one of the boys, I learned how to hold my liquor like one of the boys, how to know my limit night after night after night just like the boys. And I went along with it because it made my job easier. Even if it meant turning my pink young bronchia black with burnt offerings, and my healthy liver semi-cirrhotic with toasts to every god in the pantheon. Funny: I never compelled them to share the experience of my abdominal cramps. And when I learned not to care if there was a fly wing floating in my drink before I gulped it down, or where the glass had been before that, or care about the wet T-shirt show that was getting my "buddies" so in touch with their primal selves, or about the ethnic slurs they'd all let slip after too many rounds, then I made the grade: One Of The Boys. Congratulations!—You've sunk down to our level.

And I realize rather abruptly that I must have been staring right at a tough *latino* kid with a radio that's larger than my bed.

"What are YOU looking at?" he says, loud enough for everyone on the bus to hear, with a tone that conveys more malice than I would have thought could be conveyed with five printable words. I have committed the unpardonable sin of invading the dude's space; that bubble of protection that each of us dons in order to get by in the city. For some of us it is physical, as in, You can sit next to me, just don't touch me; for others, like this product of a sick society, it's You so much as *look* at me, man, I cut your face. Bad.

So much for my purgatory of self-doubt. I divert my eyes, that requisite millisecond response for all riders of the subways and buses, but which is still not fast enough for the kid with the radio. He sits staring at me and saying stuff like, "Ain't it your stop yet, bitch?" every three blocks for the rest of the trip.

That settles it. Whether or not I stand to gain from investigating this business on my own is pretty damn uncertain in the end. What matters is that if I can try to do some good for somebody . . . But who? I don't know if these guys had families, or anyone who will benefit from my efforts. Oh, forget it. You can drive yourself crazy thinking this way all the time.

It's getting dark as I get off at my stop, my mind made up to head down to the East Village tomorrow after shift and start sniffing around. I figure that my Inwood Heights beat is far enough from Avenue B so that no one down there will know me.

I go up to my apartment and call up Jean-Luc's number. No answer. I open the bottle of whiskey and pour myself a shot, then I call Meg. No answer. I try calling Meg after each shot and give up after three. There's a very strong urge in me to get drunk. Or stoned. I resist it, but it isn't easy. The left half of my brain is simply not coming up with a reason not to that's good enough to convince my right half. Because right now there just isn't one. But I feel so bitter and disoriented, my mind is already feeling altered, so I clamp down on it and try to escape for a short while in the comparatively safe and legal drug of television.

And it's time for the seven o'clock news. A reporter is standing in the rain interviewing one of about thirty Queens parents who are protesting the sex-education course in their local high school. She is giving the religious right's party line that abstention should be taught, even emphasized, as a major part of the course. Oh, not this again. The purpose of education is to make sure that people stay ignorant, is that it? During the ads I call up Kim's mom to find out how she's doing. I find out Kim died around 3:30 this afternoon, in great pain (despite the morphine), gasping for air. She had been coughing up bloody pieces of lung since late last night. I can't take it. I shut off the TV and reach for the bag.

THREE

Reporter: Mr. Gandhi, what do you think of Western
    Civilization?
Gandhi: I think it would be a good idea.

"Guess what, Buscarsela?"

"What?" I say, looking up in time to catch the sheaf of papers Sergeant Belasco is tossing at me.

"You got four-to-midnight rape duty all week."

"Great."

Belasco isn't such a bad guy, in spite of being a Sergeant. At least he just wants the job done, and treats you with equal indifference regardless of your age or sex. I have to respect him for that. He sits down next to me and opens a manila folder.

"It's the usual decoy stint: You'll be wired for sound, and cruise the likely areas, all the time staying within hailing distance of a prowl car that will be assigned to the job. Got it?"

"Got it, Sergeant."

He flips a page and we're looking at a map of the precinct.

"Now where's the best place to get raped?" he asks, in all seriousness.

Maybe I'm tired at the end of my shift, but for some reason I find the Sergeant's way of putting this and the fact that he is oblivious to what he said wrong ridiculously absurd. I suppress a giggle, and the Sergeant looks at me as if I just admitted that I've never heard of the Dodgers. The *real* Dodgers. I try to get ahold of myself, but the forced effort only makes it worse, so I let it all come, laughing unreservedly until it works itself out.

"I'm sorry, Sergeant, it's just that you sure have a way with words sometimes."

"Well, I won a poetry award in eighth grade one time, but I haven't, uh, written much since then. I wrote one for my wife on our fifteenth anniversary." I told you he was an all right guy. He turns back to the map. "I figure Highbridge Park."

I am looking at the map.

"Okay. How about one park per night?" I suggest.

"Ah, who the hell hangs out in the fucking Cloisters after dark?"

"All the more reason. I mean, that area around Washington High is pretty rude."

"You wanna talk rude, take a walk in the Subway Yards. But it's not a place where you'd expect to see a woman walking alone at night. We better stick to the park."

"Roger."

The Sergeant is one of those veteran cops who are becoming all too rare: He may not be up on the latest developments in criminal psychology, but he can spot a purse snatch five blocks away in a snowstorm.

"Starting tomorrow at 4:30," he says, getting up. "And try to wear, you know, like a miniskirt or something."

"Right." See what I mean? The Sergeant is a dependable, stolid, workhorse, but he obviously hasn't heard, or has never believed, the rape statistics showing that what a woman is wearing is not a relevant factor. There are more rapes in August because there are simply more crimes committed in August. It's hot and people are up late, hanging out on the streets long after midnight. But there's no point at all arguing this sort of thing with a guy like Belasco. Besides, I'm willing to put up with it from him. After all, he made Sergeant when the subway still cost a dime. It's the young brats straight out of the Academy who've also got these ideas dug in to their brains that get me. *They* don't have the excuse that I allow the Sarge. *They* should know better.

However, it is now the first week of May, and just barely staying warm enough at night to wear clothes where you can distinguish a woman from, say, a tree trunk with a winter coat on. So in a way Belasco is right. And it'll be a change from a week on body duty . . .

The coroner down at the morgue is a creepy, withered old man who I would just as soon *not* run into in a dark alley, but I got to know the swing shift attendant well enough to beg some information beyond the call of duty. I'm calling him up now for another session. "I just got on duty, Fila," says the voice at the other end of the line. "What's on your mind?"

"Luis Alberto—"

"*Oye*, baby, don't call me that. Call me Beto."

"No, I was shot at three times once by a guy named Beto."

I hear him laughing.

"Lucho?" I ask him.

"Too many Luchos in the world already. I got about seventy-five cousins named Lucho—"

"Me too. So what'll it be?"

"Well, my girlfriends call me 'Gordo' because I—"

"Okay, Gordo, listen: Have you guys isolated the pharmaceutical compound that the Osborne kid checked himself out with?"

"Sure, some kind of prescription antirheumatic. In pill form, of course. His mother probably kept them around for arthritis."

"They were that powerful?"

"You can OD on aspirin if you take enough of them, girl."

"Any idea what make?"

"Give me a break: We would have to do a microscopic structural analysis and maybe a few dozen other tests to pull up that kind of detail."

"But it's theoretically possible?"

"Sure. Why?"

I lower my voice a little, but not enough to make people take notice and think I'm doing it deliberately "Just a hunch. I'd like to try to trace where the kid's dope came from."

"Think he had help?"

I answer by not answering.

"Can you give it a shot?" I ask him.

"Only by special investigative request."

"—Which has to come from a detective."

"Right."

I sigh loud enough for El Gordo to hear it.

"*Escucha*," he says, "what I might be able to do is tack it on to another request. We get multiple assignments all the time."

"Could you?"

"I can try, baby."

There's a little too much spin on that "baby" for my liking—it has that "nobody rides for free" quality to it—but for the moment I have to let it go.

"Great. Let me know as soon as you find out anything."

"I'll give you the word *personally*," he says, in case I missed it the first time. Just now I'm not exactly in a position to raise hell over it.

"Just call first, all right?" I tell him.

"You got it." He hangs up.

I get up to leave, but the phone rings. I answer it, and get a tingle from my tummy on down when I hear Jean-Luc's resonant, mannish voice.

" 'Ello, Filomena. Are you free this Friday?"

I have to sit down before the guys across the room pick up on the vibes that I must be sending out.

"I'm working 'til midnight, but we can get together after."

"That would be perfect, *ma chère,* Per'aps we could go and 'ear some jazz."

And maybe make some jazz, too.

"Terrific. Listen, can I call you in a little while?—From somewhere else I mean? The guys are looking at me."

"Nonsense, Filomena. You are not an animal in heat—" That's what *you* think, loverboy, "—humans cannot detect the presence of pheromones."

"The presence of what?"

"Pheromones. They are airborne sexual signals that creatures such as bees and other insects emit, and can be detected by the opposite sex several miles away."

"Sounds like what I've got all right."

"The root word is *feral,* which is to say, *beast.*"

"—And not for nothing, either."

Jean-Luc laughs, "Oh, Filomena, you are such a wild creature."

"You bet your ass I am."

"Okay. I shall be waiting for your call." Click. My excitable emotions are like those old TV sets where the residual static would keep the tube glowing for long after you turned it off. Not like today's solid-states. When my sap rises, it's not that easy to get it down again.

In the women's locker room I change into my street clothes and throw on a splash of Punk-like camouflage. Then it's down into the subway for the long, thrashing trip down to the East Village.

It's still light out by the time I walk through Tompkins Square Park and up the steps of 135 Avenue B. There's no buzzer, but then the door swings open with a light push, revealing some chewed-up wood that testifies that the building hasn't had a secure lock since Truman fired MacArthur for trying to start a World War III with China.

I walk up the stairs, passing sheepishly under exposed wires that hang down naked from holes in the ceiling that once were lighting fixtures, I presume, and have to hold my breath between the third and fourth floors due to the unbearable odor of fermenting tomcat piss. The door to McCullough's fifth floor apartment is open, and I can see a man inside going through the broken drawers of a railroad flat dresser.

The floors in this decrepit building creak loud enough to be heard across the street, so as I step up to the open door, the man turns around. He is not much taller than I am, but he is a lot more muscular. He is wearing a rumpled trenchcoat, and is old enough so that some of the muscle is starting to turn to flab, suggesting that he was an athlete back in college, but that was maybe fifteen years ago, and he hasn't kept it up.

"What the fuck do you want?" is his introductory comment,

"Ease off, Detective," I say. "Where's the uniform who's supposed to be guarding the door?"

"Did that jackshit walk off for another cup of—ah, forget it. I repeat: What do you want?"

"I heard they were investigating his death as a possible murder. I thought I might be able to help."

"How come?"

"We went out a few times," I say, which has a grain of truth to it, in a sick sort of way.

"You mean you were fucking?"

"That's none of your business."

"Uh-huh. Where have you been for the past week if you're such a close friend?"

"I have a bad schedule. I have to work all kinds of crazy hours."

"Join the club," he says, whipping out a small notepad. "What did you say your name was?"

I tell him. He stares at me a moment, then hands me the pad and pen for me to write it myself.

He turns. We hear the sharp, flat slap of regulation leather rising up the stairs and he goes to the door to chew out the beat cop for quitting his post.

I start flipping quickly through the pad with my thumb, which gives me enough of a glimpse at his notes to get an idea of where this man has been in his investigation. I learn that McCullough was a painter, was arranging for an exposition in one of those 11th Street and Death Row galleries, and hung out with a lot of fellow artists and rock musicians at A7, Low Life and the East Village Community Center basement performance space, where this man has been and has talked with everyone he can. He has also talked to the owner of the SlapDash Gallery about McCullough. All this in about ten seconds, but the brain can register key words flashing by at 1/12th of a second under ideal conditions. He comes back in.

"There a clean sheet in this?" I ask.

He takes the notepad, flips to a blank page and I write my name.

"What's yours?" I ask him.

He looks at me, takes the pad away and looks at my name. "Detective Snyder, Miss Buscarsela. Now, what was your relation to the deceased?"

"Like I said, we went out a few times."

"And how do you think you can be of any help to me?"

"I thought maybe if I could take a look around I could see if anything doesn't look right."

"You're only about the forty-seventh 'friend' to show up today with the same offer. Every freak on the block's looking to cash in on this: 'Oh, there's the stereo I lent him'—'That's my TV, didn't he tell you?' Yeah, right."

I push both my sleeves up past the elbows and display the smooth undersides of my arms to him.

"Satisfied?" I ask him.

"It don't mean shit to me, babe . . . Okay, I'll give you two minutes to take a look around, but you so much as touch anything and I'll break your friggin' arm for you."

"I won't even breathe on anything."

I start looking around, but the place has a lot of rooms, each one a bigger mess than the last. Two of the rooms have artists' oil paints spattered all over the walls and floor and there are empty cans of turpentine, laquer thinner and some other bad chemicals piled in the corners together with a mess of blackened, oily rags. The place is a powder keg, and it seems like being an artist is about as dangerous as being a fire-eater with hiccups.

"So what can you tell me about Wilson?"

Wilson?—That's right, I'm supposed to be his friend. Hmm.

"Well, he was acting kind of weird lately, like his mind was being affected by too many drugs or something."

"Yeah? That's what everyone's been saying about him. Any idea where George might be?"

I saw this name flash by three times in as many notepad pages, so it's not a bluff, but I also have no idea who on earth it might be. Better play it safe.

"No," I tell Detective Snyder.

"Everyone's been saying that, too. Nobody knows where the goddamn roomie's gone. But he sure is gone. As in didn't even take his stuff, which would point to a bit of haste on his part, wouldn't you say?"

"I didn't really spend any time with George."

"So what the fuck are you coming here looking for?"

"Wilson's diary," I say. It's a belt to extreme left field, but I'm hoping it will appease this bulldog for a while.

"A diary, huh? Nobody mentioned that—but I guess it figures only his girlfriend would know about it."

"I already told you I was not his girlfriend."

"Yeah, yeah. Where'd he keep it?"

"Over by the bed."

"What bed?"

"I mean where he slept."

Detective Snyder saves me the trouble of showing him where Wilson slept, going into the next room himself and rummaging around in piles of dirty clothes. On a hunch, I locate the bathroom and open the medicine chest. It's completely empty. That's worth noting. I shut the mirror, and Detective Snyder is standing right there, smiling at me.

"Over by the bed, huh? Bullshit, girl. Let's see what you're *really* after."

He pushes past me and opens the medicine chest.

"Ha! Looks like George beat you to it. Okay, babe, out of here." He grabs my arm and starts to give me the bum's rush out the bathroom door.

"Hold it, Detective Snyder," I say. "Open your eyes, will you? That medicine chest isn't just empty. It's been cleaned out, which would make it the only clean surface in the whole place, or haven't you noticed?"

There is a brief pause, then I can see that I have connected with something inside him, as the acceptance of my observation begins to visibly diffuse across his face. He starts with indignation that this Punk girl has put him on to something that he didn't spot, but that passes and transforms into more of a 'What the hell, maybe I can get this Punk girl to do some of my legwork for me, if she's that sharp.' He loosens his grip and lets me have my arm back.

"Sorry," he says. A cop who says he's sorry!—A Detective yet! I almost hit the floor. The guy might be for real. "I get so used to dealing with people who can't spell 'cat,' I forget there's some people out there who still got active brain cells."

"I hear that," I say.

"So what else can you tell me about the bathroom, Miss Buscarsela?"

The bathtub is filthy. The toilet is suffering from a severe personality crisis. The floor looks and smells like they fished it up from the wreckage of the *Titanic* after seventy years underwater. And the garbage under the sink is overflowing. I get down on my knees and start going through it. Detective Snyder hunches down next to me and watches.

"It would follow that people who are not all that particular about leaving eight months' worth of dirty laundry lying around wouldn't think of emptying the garbage, even after having scoured the medicine cabinet," I say, pulling out snot-soaked toilet paper, bloody maxi-pads that Detective Snyder obviously thinks are mine, dirty band-aids, and all kinds of empty capsule packets, the leftover husks of too much partying, until I come up with something interesting: An empty bottle of black hair dye, along with a towel that is soaked with the stuff, in which are embedded a few partially-dyed, undeniably red hairs. I turn to Detective Snyder. He is practically speechless. But no New York City Detective ever sees anything that keeps him or her speechless for too long. It takes Detective Snyder all of a second-and-a-half to recover.

"By all accounts George was a flaming redhead," he says.

"Now all you've got to do is comb all the joints for a freckle-faced white boy with jet black hair."

Detective Snyder takes the towel from me, examines the hairs. Then he looks at me long and strong, before saying, "You really want to help?"

"Any way I can."

He puts his hands on his knees and stands up.

"Let's go talk on the couch. This place is making me sick."

* * *

An hour later I'm sitting under a tree on a bench in Tompkins Square Park, Detective Snyder's words still in my ears: "You pegged me as a cop before you walked in. That's my problem exactly. Everybody's seen me, they all know I'm conducting a murder investigation, and the net result is they clam right up. Nobody wants to talk to a cop, least of all these Punks. How'd you like to do some eye and ear work for me?"

I got in through the back door, but I'm in.

It's too early for the action to be starting in the East Village, so I head west until I find a working pay phone that is not being used as the central office of the local drug dealers. I find one at First Avenue and 10th, and step under the little half-shell that is supposed to protect only the phone from the elements, but not the customer. Why on earth did they ever get rid of the venerable phonebooth? I don't really want every leather-and-metal-studded passerby to pick up on the fact that I am on speaking terms with the four-to- midnight attendant at the city morgue. After three rings I get El Gordo on the line.

"Fila, baby, wha's happening?"

"Get anything yet?"

"Relax, doll, I got it covered, but it's gonna take a week or two. The Stewart case has got us all sewed up tight."

"Hmm. Listen, I got the name of a pharmaceutical here, I was wondering if you could tell me what it's about."

"I'll try."

I reach inside my leather jacket and take out one of the empty six-capsule packets that I pocketed when Detective Snyder was examining the partially dyed red hairs. I read the brand name into the phone. El Gordo tells me to wait, and I use this time to turn around and make sure no one is backing a garbage truck over me. So far, I'm okay. Two young Black men in black and beige vinyl jackets are waiting to use the phone, sharing a joint between them. They offer me a hit.

"No thanks," I say, without much conviction. After all, why not? What difference does it make? I'm off duty. But we are not dealing with logic here. Somewhere inside my head there is a relay that won't let the action through to the mainline, diverting it to a side track. I have learned not to argue logic with the relays: Just listen. I turn back into the alcove as El Gordo returns.

"It's a legitimate prescription medicine for migraine headaches," he says. "Help you any?"

"Maybe, maybe not. Could be interesting," I say. He insists on chatting a bit more, and I put up with it though I am always amazed at people who are supposed to have these incredibly important high-pressure jobs, and yet they always seem to have time to spend twenty minutes yakking on the company phone. The phone company computers finally break in to tell us that I have to put another nickel in if I want to keep talking. I lie to El Gordo, saying that I don't have any more change, hang up, and relinquish the phone to the two Black men.

Night has fallen, but it's warm. The traffic down First Avenue is heavy, and row after row of dancing ellipsoidal headlights glare at me as I cross 10th to go get something to eat.

Twenty minutes later I've got some barbecued chicken congealing in my stomach that ought to be enough to have the place closed down by the Board of Health and have the owner run out of town on a rail, if only they still did that sort of thing. Maybe we should bring it back. I decide to head for A7, which is reputed to have a bar, so maybe I can order myself something caustic enough to eat a hole through the meal that is imploding down to the density of a small cannonball in my stomach to allow it to start what is promising to be a long and memorable journey through my digestive system. Maybe I should stop eating meat altogether.

I have to walk slowly, and by the time I get to A7, which is a hole-in-the-wall Punk rock club on Avenue A and 7th Street, it is 9:30, and the creatures are just starting to come out for the night.

There's a bouncer out front who is big enough to bully a couple of pale, undernourished Punks, but who wouldn't last a minute in one of the tougher places in town. He stops me with a hand that is all knuckle and tells me,

"Three dollars."

I look at him. It evidently took him all week to learn how to say this, and the effort has almost been too much for him. He reminds me of one of those intelligent chimpanzees that some very patient linguistics researcher has taught how to form sentences, even original sentences, out of colored plastic symbols, but the basic question still remains, Does he have *language* capabilities?

"There's a band tonight," he adds.

"Who?"

"The Shitz."

I give Mongo the three dollars and he lets me crawl under his arm and in through the door.

At first I am plunged into blackness, then my eyes gradually get used to the dimness, and I realize that there are two yellowish 15-watt lightbulbs glowing dully over a 4 x 8 platform sixteen inches off the ground that must be the stage. I walk towards that, and suddenly the wall on my right disappears and the room opens up into a bar and two tables that I can only make out by the light of the twin pinball machines on the far wall, which are by far the brightest sources of light in the club.

The terms "opens up" and "far wall" may be misleading, however. The "far wall" is about twelve feet away from me, and, with the pinball machines taking up about one-quarter of that side of the room, the whole club wouldn't be big enough to hold a Saint Bernard *and* its fleas at the same time.

The general impression is that of an underground bomb shelter during an air raid. For all I know, a decorator spent weeks striving to get just this effect.

I feel my way over to the bar, where a single red-and-white neon "BUD" sign provides the only respite from total obscurity. There's a shape catching a bit of neon light around its edges that must be the bartender.

"What's your monthly electric bill?" I ask. "Eighty-nine cents?"

"You want something to drink?" says a voice that comes from

the general vicinity of the shape with all the friendliness of a mother alligator defending its young from poachers.

"Give me a straight-up shot of Wild Turkey," I say. It's like talking to a shadow. I hear some clothes rustling, a bottle cap being screwed off, the angry clink of a bottleneck against the rim of a glass, and the faint liquid sound of the contents of the one being transferred to the other; then a shot glass is slammed down on the bar in front of me.

I run my fingers around the rim of the glass to make sure it isn't cracked, then put it to my lips and take a sip. What enters my mouth is corrosive enough to make me shudder even before I swallow.

"What is this?" I ask, my voice still quavering a little from the unexpected encounter with uncut dragonwater.

"Whiskey, like you ordered," says a voice that could be coming from inside a closet somewhere.

"The hell it is. Lucky for you I'm in urgent need of a digestive," I say, and swallow the rest, exclusively for its medicinal properties.—Yuggh!

"How much?" I ask when I've recovered.

"Four dollars," says the voice, with perfect clarity this time.

"I mean the price for *one*," I reply.

"Four dollars," says the shadow. I could be talking to a tape recording for all I know.

"How much is a beer," I ask. "Two-fifty?"

"Two-seventy-five," comes the response. This means it's not a tape recording after all. A computerized robot, maybe. They never could program a sense of humor into those things.

I step away from the bar, the Liquid Plumber I've just swallowed going to work on the goo clogging my drains, thinking that I can get a half-pint of the best for four dollars in any liquor store, and here I get a short shot of Stain Remover in a dirty glass, and a bad attitude thrown in for free. I guess that's not so bad after all: There are places that charge extra for the bad attitude.

By 10:30 the place is crowded, although twenty people constitute a "crowd" in this rat hole, and I can hear snatches of every conversation in there.

"Yeah, like nobody asks John Kennedy Junior to type fifty words per minute," intones an emaciated young woman who is standing under the standard jet black spike hairstyle, this one with a few shocks of peacock blue.

"Whenever the first line of a limerick ends with 'Nantucket,' you know you're in trouble," says one literary critic to another. Belly laughs follow.

A buyer and a seller share the following exchange:

"I don't spend a buck a jay on Morning Thunder tea, man."

"OK, OK, tell you what: I'll give you a break on a quarter of Jamaican, OK?"

A single man and woman who are evidently not together the next:

"Where do you live?"

"Why?"

My attention is momentarily caught by, "Freud says the penis is a phallic symbol," as I fight my way to the bar, struggling as hard as any electron bouncing around in a cloud chamber, to order one of those gold-plated beers. I get my order in between two guys who are having a discussion that you don't hear every day. One of them is the only white non-Punk around. He actually has naturally curly hair and a full black beard. Maybe he's a Punk on the inside.

"Sure, I always piss out the air-shaft," he is telling the other one, "just to bug my asshole super. He lives in the basement room four floors down at the bottom of the air-shaft, and the best time is late at night when it's dark: I start pissing, and it arcs out, then there's this great delay for several seconds before I can hear it starting to hit bottom, then after I've stopped, the sound of it hitting bottom keeps on going for the same amount of seconds. It's a trip—"

I am getting kind of absorbed in this when a deranged face plants itself in my way. The face has a long scar on one side, a head shaved clean except for a bandana wrapped around the forehead, and breath that the Department of Defense should really think about deploying instead of nerve gas. Do you know how strange someone looks who has more hair coming out of his nostrils than growing on his head? Give this guy an eye patch and a parrot and he could pass for Captain Morgan's cabin boy.

"You're new here," says the matey.

I try to step back, but bodies are pressing against me and there is nowhere to go.

"I know everyone who comes in here and I haven't seen you," he says, slowly choosing his words the way someone who is genuinely brain-damaged might do.

"I used to have orange hair," I tell him, reaching across for the beer that I no longer have the thirst for, "but I changed it."

An unseen hand is riveting my beer to the bar. I slap three dollars down on the bar, and the hand releases my beer and performs a very smooth disappearing act with the three dollars. And I don't see my quarter anywhere as change.

"You can change your hair, but you can't change your mind," says the salty dog breath, far too close to me.

I tip up the bottle and drink four quick swallows of beer in a row and hand the Space Invader the rest. He drinks some and hands it back, but I signal that the rest is for him. He empties the bottle in one draught and puts it on the bar, where I still don't see any sign of my quarter.

"George changed his hair a—"

"We had this real candy-ass, hot-shot Second Lieutenant," continues my drinking companion, "straight out of the academy. Wanted to win the war in two weeks and cross all the way to Peking, right? We had to patch his ass together for him."

"I can imagine. George just changed his hair a few days ago—to jet black. Of course you don't have to worry about changing *your* hair color—"

"Hey-Yo! Don't you *never* touch a skinhead's bandana!"

"Oh. OK. Why not?"

That stumps him.

"—Uh—I don't know. Just *never* touch a skinhead's bandana."

"OK, sure. Like I was saying, George just dyed his hair black. It looks pretty good on him, don't you think?"

The Long John Silver impersonator screws up his eyes, and I'm waiting for him to say, "Ayar, Jimmy boy," and when he says "George?" the intonation isn't all that far off. "I don't know anyone named George," he goes on.

"You know, Wilson's roommate."

Now he twists his face to achieve a look that he must have practiced for hours in front of a mirror to perfect. The training shows.

"Look, you can drop the act, friend, 'cause I'm not buying it," I tell him. "I'm sure it's great for bumming quarters on St. Mark's Place—the poor, deranged Vietnam vet bit—but frankly, it's getting on my nerves."

He looks at me like a man who has just awakened to find himself standing naked in front of a live audience, then a second later the look is gone, back behind the crazed vet mask, but with something darker added in this time.

"I don't know anyone named George," he repeats, stepping backwards into the crowd, and leaving me wondering if I haven't been a trifle indiscreet, violating some local taboo, as I watch his unmistakable skin head bob along through the tightly-packed bodies near the stage.

I turn to the bar and see that there is still no evidence of a quarter turning up with my name on it, nor is there likely to be. I signal to the bartender by holding up the empty beer bottle. After a few moments he comes along the bar to take it from me. This time I'm the one who won't let go. Now that I've got him where he can hear me, I say, "I prefer it when charities ask me for a donation, rather than just taking it."

I let go of the bottle, which hovers in mid-air for a moment before disappearing under the bar without a rejoinder. Not an audible one, anyway.

Suddenly some lights go on that I never imagined the place had, and the members of a band separate from the crowd and get up on the stage.

I'm half expecting a bottle to come swishing past the side of my head, so I put some distance between myself and the invisible bartender and watch as the band plug in their guitars and check the mikes by beating them against the floor of the stage. Amplified test chords leap out of nowhere as the sound technician, who must be in the broom closet (or under the stage), turns the volume up full.

The drummer is a heavy-set guy with *very* pale skin, black sunglasses as thick as manhole covers (I expect it's too bright for him in here), and a black T-shirt that says "FUCK YA IF YA CANT TAKE A JOKE," in white block letters. He is throwing his sticks at his drum set to see if any of them are broken.

Then a pimply-faced teenager with an incurable Long Island accent and a few hairs that could only be spiked out that far with the aid of airplane glue stops checking the mikes with his tongue and announces,

"We're The Shitz."

That is the evening's only concession to formality. What follows is a series of excursions into determining whether or not demolishing a human being's will to survive with sound waves is feasible.

The first song goes something like:

FUCK YOU
FUCK ME
FUCK THE WORLD
FUCK EVERYBODY

—and some of the others are even less upbeat. Yet, through it all, there is a certain sensation that creeps up on me, against my will, beyond any single unintelligible syllable or jackhammer guitar chord, of a pervasive nihilism that can't be expressed concretely—after all, how can you use conventional narrative techniques to describe the indescribable *angst* that is life on the other side of this impossible experiment called New York? And there is an identifiable act of *release* in the slam dancing.

I begin to be truly amazed that these whining Punks are actually close to *It,* maybe closer than any revered philosopher whose works are required reading in private colleges, to spelling out that dreadful, underlying, primordial SEND-ME-BACK-TO-THE-WOMB-IT'S-COLD-OUT-HERE! banshee wail that we all have deep inside of us somewhere. Speaking the unspeakable. It's quite a job, and very few people are up to it. I wonder if the kid even realizes it himself . . .

But all this is the brief luxury of reflection. What first caught my eye and continues to hold my attention throughout the entire set, is the bass player, half-hidden though he is behind a 5-foot high Peavey speaker. What's so interesting about the bass player? Maybe it's the red eyebrows and jet-black hair.

After the set I push through the crowd and grab ahold of the bass player.

"Where you been, George?"

"My name's Natz. Got that? Natz."

"Okay. You forgot to do your eyebrows, Natz."

* * *

Friday night of an otherwise uneventful week. I'm supposed to be disguised as a lonely and vulnerable woman, which is pretty damn easy, and I'm wandering around Fort Tryon Park, watching the afterglow of what was a marvelous sunset fade into a lurid violet. I'm also wearing a radio transmitter that's being received, I trust, by a squad car holed up two blocks away on Cabrini Boulevard, where two lucky cops get to sit and drink hot coffee and read the newspaper while I'm out here being live bait for an animal trap. I stand leaning on the railing that overlooks the wide expanse of the Hudson, which is flowing very high and mighty today down to the Atlantic, fortified as it is with the runoff of half-a-dozen spring rains. The violet sky is beginning that imperceptible edging towards indigo and the ultimate black of night, and the lights on the George Washington Bridge are starting to stand out in a glittering, mile-long jeweled arc. Traffic in both directions is still clogging the two levels of the bridge, even at this hour. There is so much activity out there, but at this distance it's all a bit unreal. It's hard to believe that every other set of orange pinpricks of light drifting across the suspended blackness of the bridge is a massive, eighteen-wheel, tractor-trailer hell-bent on delivering twenty tons of pig iron to a foundry on the mainland by 11:30 P.M.

My conversation with George/Natz revealed almost nothing that I didn't already know. He swore and swore again that he got away from the apartment because he knew someone was after Wilson for some reason, but that he doesn't know what the reason was, and he doesn't ever want to know what it was. That sounded like bullshit, and I told him so. So he said Wilson knew someone was out to get him, but never talked about it openly. I told him *that* was obviously bullshit, too. Then he said Wilson would just talk into his pocket tape recorder and drown himself in his painting. So he had a tape-recorded diary? Yes. You better not be shitting me. I'm not. Honest.

I'm going to have to go see some of those paintings.

So I didn't learn much, but I got to turn George over to Detective Snyder and earn myself a few unofficial but useful points with him. He ought to be able to shake a little more information out of the guy. And I got to take Detective Snyder back to the apartment where we found five 60-minute cassettes with all kinds of ramblings about women—none of them mentioned by name, so my presence in

Wilson's life is still an established fact in Detective Snyder's mind—about how much he hates doing construction work for a living when he should be painting, about how even working with artists' materials is unhealthy, and very little else. No "Nicasio Sangurima of 551 Jerome Avenue in the Bronx is after me because I know his laundromat is really a front for an international organ-smuggling operation." Shucks. There were, however, indications during the last recorded month of something consistently going very strange in Wilson's view of the world:

"March 5th. Everything tastes like chemicals. I have eggs for breakfast and they taste of paint thinner. It's in the President's coffee. Industries are fouling every inch of this globe, and the government isn't doing anything to stop it because the industries own the government. Environmental Protection Agency—Ha! That's a laugh. What do they care, they all have their estates in the country, far from it all. I have to make my living breathing in slow death every day. The bastards. What's the difference between a corporation that knowingly poisons people for profit and a Mafia hitman who just does it more quickly and violently? I know they're going to win, but maybe I can at least take some of the bastards with me when I go . . . "

Food for thought. Snyder says he's going to spend the whole weekend grilling George and listening to those tapes over and over, and that if I want to get in touch with him here's his number. Day or night, if I come up with anything, I'm to get in touch with him.

Darkness is slipping over the city. But it's a relative darkness. It never really gets completely dark in New York because even in the middle of the park the lights of the city reflecting off the day's pollution light up the sky with an unnatural rosy-pink-and-yellow glow.

I walk along the rampart and go down the steps beneath the arch that supports the lookout point, to Margaret Corbin Drive. There's a plaque commemorating Ms. Corbin's having taken up her fallen husband's rifle and unflinchingly firing on the advancing British troops in what was unfortunately a siege that the patriots lost. Right on, Margaret. Nice try, anyway.

Otherwise, I didn't get to do much investigating this week. First of all, I had diarrhea all the next day after my barbecued chicken, plus I've been working every evening until midnight. At that time of night it's easily an hour-and-a-half to the East Village from the precinct, and still another hour back to my apartment. But since many Punk shows don't even begin until 2:00 A.M., I always arrive right on schedule. Besides, I think it would be best if I were just seen hanging around for a while, let people get used to seeing me, rather than have them notice that I always seem to be buttonholing key people involved in Wilson's life. But tomorrow I'm going down to the SlapDash Gallery to have a look at some of Wilson's paintings.

I'm walking along past the imposing medieval tower of the Cloisters, a structure as out of place in New York City as an oil derrick in the Ecuadorian rainforest. The Rockefellers had it brought over from Europe stone-by-stone during the Depression. Can you picture the Spanish peasants' faces when this rich American family offered to buy the monastery that had been benevolently overshadowing their town for six or seven centuries, and then proceeded to tear it down and remove it? It must have blown their minds, to say the least. Their first, unforgettable encounter with "After-All-It's-My-Wall" Nelson. I wonder what they filled the hole in their past with. There's probably a shoe factory in its place now.

I'm also thinking—It's Friday! Three more hours and I get to knock off the lady cop stuff and hop the A train down to meet Jean-Luc in time to catch Art—Ka!-Ka!—Blakey's last set at Sweet Basil's, Oh ¡jés! And then, after that . . . ?

I circle around the far side of the Cloisters, turning back towards 193rd Street and the squad car, dreaming of the night's coming delights, when a calloused hand grabs my face from behind and throws me backwards over his leg to the ground. Fortunately I land on the grass and live to tell about it. But an unshaven white man of about thirty-five is now sitting astride my abdomen, a stranglehold on my neck with one hand, undoing my buttons with the other. This is definitely going to put sex out of the question for later in the evening. I'm lying there, reasonably calm, because the left-handed stranglehold is just to keep me from struggling. It's not cutting off the blood to my brain—yet—although I can feel the pulse in my neck against the pressure of his sinewy fingers. Or is it his pulse? Now I can't tell.

The Cloisters is nothing but an upside down, seven-hundred-year-old shadow towering over my head. I wonder what the thirteenth-century monks would have thought of this scene taking place on their front lawn.

If they can hear what's happening to me, the patrol car should be pulling up in under two minutes, so I spend my time etching this man's features in my mind just in case he gets away and we need to put out a description. He's got a three-day growth of black sandpaper on his chin, a hawk nose, and arteries that bulge out about a half-inch along his temples. His thin, angular face shines with a greasy pallor. I figure he's an assistant electrician or something, and he's probably married and has three kids, which suggests that he's not likely to kill me. But I don't feel like being raped tonight.

"That's right, honey," he says. "Just keep still and you won't get hurt."

I can feel some pressure around my eyes, but I force myself to stay calm. My backup will be here any second.

But the seconds are flowing by, and the guy is yanking my bra up around my neck so he can clutch my breasts. I'm not sure exactly when, but within very few of those seconds it hits me that I don't hear a car coming, and, in my assurance that they would be here within an instant, I have made the serious mistake of letting this guy get complete control of the situation. Now he's hiking my skirt up around my waist, feeling around for what's mine, and they're still not coming. How did I let myself get pinned down like this?

I blink away from the bony face above me and look towards the road beyond the bushes. There isn't a car in sight, and now my panties are being ripped in half. He reaches up with his right hand and starts to undo his belt. And I'm trapped. Alone, and unarmed. The edge of my vision starts to turn blue. Zip. Oh my God.

"Wow, you really turn me on," I say, but it's someone else's voice, someone who is trying to sound calm. There is a slight pause in his just-about-unrecallable momentum, so I go on. "But not here. Not like this." He swallows. "Let's go back to your place."

"No, we can't go there," he says. But at least I've got his attention.

"Then let's go back to my place."

He asks me where it is. I tell him.

"Too far," he says, and prepares to thrust. I grab him by the business end.

"We can take a taxi," I say. "It'll be ten minutes."

I'm stimulating him in a way he didn't imagine, and it takes hold.

"Okay," he says, and backs off me, zipping up his pants.

I pull my skirt down, but he's not a very patient guy, and he hauls me to my feet in one rough motion.

"Come on," he says, shoving me along in front of him. This guy really loves women. "And don't try to get away."

I'm going to have to soak my hands in formaldehyde for a few days.

He grabs my arm and is bringing me over to the stone steps that lead down through the park to Broadway when a pair of headlights curve around the bend together, and suddenly the beacons flare up and start flashing. He tries to get away, but I've got his arm. His other arm flails through the air and slaps me, hard. He keeps smashing his fist against the side of my face and head, but I'm temporarily blind to the pain and I stick to him like a remora fish on a shark, until the car pulls up and two patrolmen jump out and grab him. Now my face is starting to sting. I can feel the blood rushing to the skin. My normally soft skin.

"Where the fuck were you guys?!" I demand to know.

"Hey, your radio went out."

That's it. "Your radio went out." Did it? I wonder.

Now I have to return to the precinct to file a report and it can't wait until Monday. They don't even give me time to shower. So I'm still wearing the same torn, grass-stained clothes I was nearly raped in when I have to call up Jean-Luc to tell him that I'm afraid I have to cancel, and at the last minute, too. He tries to be understanding, but, in the end, how can he be?

"Well, of course I am disappointed, but it's okay. It's your job. You 'ave enough to worry about weethout my making a fuss."

"You're one in a million, Jean-Luc," I tell him before he hangs up on me.

I am even more disappointed than Jean-Luc is. I could use some warm caresses right now. Instead I've got to book this fuckhead.

Even catching the guy is of little consolation. I turn to him and start to roll a sheet into the typewriter.

"You just ruined my Friday night," I tell him.

"Yeah? Well what about mine?" he says. "You sure ruined mine, too. So we're even."

Not quite.

—"Name?"

FOUR

"You're either on the bus or off the bus."

—Ken Kesey

My trip to the art gallery has to wait. This isn't my day to begin with. First, I wake up and my face and head are still sore and my cheekbones black and blue from the pounding the rapist gave me last night trying to get away. Then the Laundry Room Fates walk off with most of my underwear. Then my toast-r-oven turns my daily bread into a smoky chunk of carbon. Then I get to the station house only to find that two of my more abusive colleagues have caught themselves a Nazi Punk—for whom I have no concern whatsoever, but the problem is I recognize him from A7, and I don't particularly want him to recognize me. I grab the precinct copy of today's *New York Times* and climb inside it.

Two inches from my face, buried in the last paragraph on page thirty-seven, it says the C.I.A. is paying mercenary pilots in cocaine and other drugs to fly weapons to the *contras* in Honduras.

And I wonder how many throats will be slit before they're through. How many women will be raped, how many wombs will be ripped open before the place is safe for democracy. But it's a crime to ask such questions, to show such sensitivity. How am I supposed to bring a baby into this world? My nurturing insides, my active and aromatic cyclically flowing womb yearns for me to fulfill its course—the seeding, breeding and feeding of a new life. Boy, do I not have room in my life right now for that. Not yet, anyway. Jean-Luc doesn't even want a *cat*.

And, of course, you can't drink if you're pregnant.

So what, you say? Just another shitty day in paradise, and what do I plan to do about it?

I put down the newspaper and see that they have removed the Nazi Punk into interrogation for a bit of fun, so I fold up the paper and head to the women's locker room to change. As I'm passing by the men's locker room, I hear a small group comparing notes on how to handle women.

"—And she says, 'Is that a real gun? I bet it's *big* and *powerful*—' Ha! Ha! Ha!"

I shake my head, and start down the back stairs to the claustro-phobic ex-storage room that now serves as the women's locker room. I meet Sergeant Belasco coming up the stairs,

"Don't bother to change, Officer Buscarsela, the Lieutenant wants to see you," he says.

I turn around and head back up the stairs, the Sergeant following me. As I draw near the top step, masculine laughter barrels out of the men's locker room and a voice floats out my way. It's the voice of one of my backups from last night, and this is what I hear:

"—By now the guy's got his zipper open and out comes his dong, so she says, 'Wow, you really turn me on! But not here. Not like this. Let's go back to your place.' " This followed by another peal of laughter.

My eyes widen in disbelief and I storm into the forbidden defenses of the boys' room and confront four male cops in various stages of undress.

"So the radio *was* working, you bastards!! I mean I've heard a lot of pretty offensive macho shit come from in here, *but deliberately holding back to see if I got raped or not—!!*"

I can feel a wave of hysteria welling up inside of me, rising to the very brink.

Sergeant Belasco takes hold of me from behind and damn near picks me up and carries me out of there.

He sets me down outside the Lieutenant's office and lets go of me. I turn to face him. I can feel the tears of rage just waiting for a fragile surface tension to let them overflow. He looks down at me to see if more restraint is going to be necessary. It's not.

"Thanks," I tell Sergeant Belasco, lying: "I probably would have just made a fool of myself in there." I'm shaking.

"That's more like it," he answers back. "Now sit here and wait for the Lieutenant.—They're just boys," he says, and he walks away.

Just boys. Just boys who are entrusted to use their judgment in domestic disputes and battered-wife cases. Just boys who quit their posts to go screw scared, single women in the projects who figure the occasional uniform will make living there safer and I'm not supposed to say a word about it. Just boys who occasionally beat a suspect to death.

I feel like going outside, walking into the first travel agency I can find, and asking them to take me the hell away from here.

How can I continue to work in the same place with these people? They're probably selling bootleg tape recordings of last night's comedy out behind the vans in the parking lot.

Dorset looks up from his crossword puzzle and sees me patiently waiting for the Lieutenant's blessing.

"Hey Fil, how do they say 'barbecue' in Argentina?" he wants to know.

"What am I, a fucking dictionary?" is the answer he gets from a very bitter woman.

The Lieutenant opens the door to his office and invites me in. I go inside and flop down in a wooden chair that wasn't built for flopping down in.

"Guess what, Buscarsela?"

"You're transferring me to the dark side of the moon."

"Almost," he says, flourishing a report under my nose. "The screening panel reviewing your request has recommended you for a temporary position assisting the DEA."

"I specifically requested to be assigned to rape, homicide, or robbery, in that order of preference."

"What's the matter with you, Buscarsela?" I think he was expecting me to do some back flips through a hoop for him or something. "This is an international case. The Feds need some local assistance. The panel recommended you. So what's the problem?"

"The problem is, why should I risk getting shot to bust somebody for a few pounds of coke when the C.I.A. is bypassing federal laws to back the *contras* with arms paid for in drugs?"

"What are you babbling about?"

"Did you see this morning's paper?"

"What the hell has that got to do with it?"

"Just the fact that buried at the bottom of page thirty-seven it says—"

"Buscarsela, I called you in here to give you the good news you've been pestering me about for months, and you start in with this bullshit—"

"—In Ecuador they always televise the destruction of tons and tons of confiscated drugs. They don't do that here. What are they doing with all those drugs?—Paying off a bunch of murderers."

"Officer Buscarsela, we are talking about cocaine. Tons of it. Not some commie fairy tale—Now are you gonna shut up?—Cause I think you've already said more than enough."

He's right, of course. In the heat of the moment, I have allowed myself to speak freely. I guess that finding out that my partners were giving four-to-one on whether I'd get raped or not kind of pisses me off, though. Gee, Lieutenant, I'm sorry. Did I hurt your feelings by suggesting that you all were full of shit?—You probably put down five bucks on the rapist yourself, you creep. But I can't help it. Maybe you'd be more understanding if you knew what I've been through, how I feel about things like nearly being raped, and how my brother was killed during an uprising that the C.I.A. later admitted sponsoring. Tell me, how would you feel if it had been your brother who they killed? That's why I have so little patience for these utterly confusing, intentionally elliptical The-CIA-is-out-to-get-me-because-I-know-something-that-they-don't-want-me-to-know books and movies. Why not just tell the truth? That would be the scariest horror story of all.

"Well?" says a voice above me somewhere.

Have I been digressing again?

"Sorry," I hear myself saying, again. Sorry for hurting your knee with my stomach when you kicked me onto the floor. "I guess I'm still a bit shaken from what happened last night."

"Let me tell you something, Fil. You're up for this position *because* of what the panel considers your admirable performance last night."

But *you* don't consider it admirable, do you, Lieutenant. After all, you lost five bucks.

"But seeing you carry on like this . . ." Now he is eyeing me with unmasked suspicion. "There isn't some other reason for your not wanting to assist the Drug Enforcement Administration, is there?"

"Just give me the assignment, will you, Lieutenant?"

The Lieutenant looks at me like the wicked stepmother who can't figure out what to do with that pesky Cinderella, who keeps insisting on doing the right thing all the time, damn her. He jerks the folder at my eye and holds it there at arm's length.

"Get your butt out of my sight and report to room 1402 of the midtown Hartley. Now."

By the way the Lieutenant is looking at me, I would say he lost more like fifty bucks on me last night. Tough break.

I take the folder, and get my "butt" out of the Lieutenant's sight as ordered.

I take two minutes to check in with Detective Meehan. They've compared the shells that were in Tommy Osborne's .22 to others found at the site and have determined that they were loaded with nearly double the powder needed, but the company is sticking to its story that Osborne loaded them himself. And what about the torch? They claim it was just being stored there for a while. "On the twenty-third floor of an empty structure?" I ask. He says, "How much do you know about building construction?" Fair enough. Do they know if Wilson ever worked a torch for this company? Detective Meehan tells me to take it easy, it's pretty slow going through the company records. I tell him while they're at it, see if they can find out if Wilson spent a lot of time working in sealed, unventilated rooms before moving to the topless tower, and what use a construction company would have for concentrated doses of tetraethyl lead. He says they're working on that, too, but something in his voice tells me I just gave him the idea.

On my way down the street to my new assignment I stop in at Ortiz's grocery store to get something to steady my nerves. I settle for tomato juice. At the counter, Ortiz asks me in Spanish how it's going with me. I tell him it's been better. He says hasn't it always? While we're talking two kids come in and ask Ortiz if he has any lighter fluid.

"No," he tells them, and they leave.

I notice he's got enough lighter fluid stacked behind the counter to burn down a warehouse.

"Good going, *hombre*," I tell him on my way out of his store to catch a bus.

The bus turns out to be a trip in itself. First of all, the driver has "RING OR RIDE" scrawled in crayon on the back of a cigarette carton that is displayed above his head, taped over the broken "Stop Request" sign. Next, we are treated to an uninterrupted patter that the *Tonight Show's* writers should hear about:

"Good Morning, Ladies and Gentlemen, Welcome aboard Metropolitan Transit Authority Bus Number 3045 to Houston Street, making all local stops. We will be traveling at a top speed of thirty-five miles per hour. The weather is clear, so we should have no problem arriving on schedule," says the driver. Then he starts in with the jokes. "Let's leave this old lady, whaddaya say?" And he guns the motor as if to drive past the stop without picking her up. "Aw, what the heck," he says, and swerves into the bus stop, where the old woman climbs aboard the bus, unaware that the giggles are being derived from her unwitting performance. I have to hand it to this driver. Even I'm smiling. I didn't think it was possible. Not today, anyway. Whatever this man's salary is, it's not what he should be getting, not by a long shot, for being able to make the toughest audience on earth crack a smile when it doesn't want to.

By the time I get off at Columbus Circle—the driver advising me that "The safest part of your trip is now over"—and walk down and over to the Hartley, I'm a rational human being again, which is no small transformation, let me tell you. Double that driver's salary immediately.

The lobby of the Hartley is a cavernous, glittering monstrosity with enough room inside to moor a dirigible. I get myself announced, shoot up fourteen flights in a glass elevator that brings back shades of Wilson McCullough's destitute and disfiguring death, and get shooed in to room 1402 by a box-shaped Fed who looks so much like a Fed it's a wonder they've got him doing undercover work when he should be out working in the garment district—as a clothes form.

"Officer Buscarsela?" he says to me in a low voice. I nod. He slides the door closed behind me.

There are two other Feds in the room. The one looking out the window is a thirtyish Black man dressed as a street kid; the one sitting on the couch is a white man of about the same age, dressed as a businessman, minus the jacket, which is draped over the back of the couch. He is the first one to look at me.

"Hey, the girl from Wuthering Heights is here," he yells to his partner.

"Washington Heights," says the man who let me in, blankly.

The Black man turns and nods at me, then goes back to staring out the window. The young one says, "We heard about your little escapade on the heath last night. We understand you defended your honor admirably."

Great. So my genitalia are being held up as an example of law enforcement at its finest, and being pictured in all their intimate and glorious detail in the minds of every young stud in the entire Northeast. I expect another round of bets is being placed concerning who will succeed where the rapist didn't.

"We need people like you on the team," he says, coming towards me to shake hands, and putting his arm around my shoulders with excessive familiarity. "You hip to the scam?" he asks.

"I just spent an hour on the bus reviewing the briefing my Lieutenant gave me."

He goes on as if he hasn't heard me. "We're talking fourteen agents on two continents working for eighteen months to trace the source of over $140 million worth of cocaine, my friend."

"She says she read the briefing, Matthews," says the first Fed.

"Yeah, yeah," says Matthews.

"And what's your name?" I ask the first Fed. I always like to know the name of the one who seems to be the horse among mules.

"You can call me Ryan."

"How do you do, Ryan." We shake hands.

"That's Eddie," says Ryan, pointing his thumb towards the man at the window, who does not acknowledge the introduction.

"So where do I start?" I ask. "I speak a mean street-Spanish, and I know most of the holes in the neighborhood pretty well."

"Well, we're kind of hungry," says Matthews. "But we're

expecting a phone call, and room service in this place is outrageous, so how'd you like to go over to the deli on 43rd and Eighth and pick us up something to eat?"

* * *

While I'm out I call Detective Snyder's office. It takes a while to get him, then he comes on the line and says, "Your friend is scared shitless, all right, but he doesn't seem to know why."

"And you believe him?"

"Yeah, far enough, anyway. He coughed up a missing tape. I'd like you to come by and give it a listen. Maybe you can help us identify some of the voices on it."

"Sure, maybe. Did you say voices? It's not one of his diary tapes?"

"No. It's a live performance of extracts from his diary."

"Oh?" I mean, "*Ohh*."

"Yeah, George said it was recorded at an open-mike benefit for the 13th Street squatters at the Pyramid Club a couple months back. He says he wasn't there. Were you?"

"—Uh, yeah, I think I went to one of those."

"Great. So when can you come in?"

"Is George going to be there?"

"Nah. We let him go home. Being stupid isn't the crime that it oughta be. But I warned him: No more disappearing acts. They really piss me off."

"Right. Can we meet somewhere neutral?"

It takes him a second.

"Don't like the smell of precinct houses, huh? All right, tell you what, I've got some paperwork to catch up on. I can do it while I'm waiting for you. I'll be in an unmarked van facing south at East 15th between Stuyvesant Town and the Con Ed plant. That neutral enough for you?"

"Sure."

"Don't worry, none of your friends will see you talking to a cop."

"Thanks. I'll be there around six."

Then I call Meg and she says she checked the connection and that Wilson did have friends at the Lilliflex factory. I give her Detective Meehan's number but Meg says she's filing the story first.

"So you think he did it?" I ask her.

"I'm not saying he did it, but he had friends."

He also, apparently, had enemies.

* * *

By 5:15 the deal is set, and the federal agents are preparing to go out and make the exchange. What have I been doing all day? Well, when I wasn't going for breakfast, lunch, and coffee I was counting out $240,000 in hundred-dollar bills, and marking down each and every serial number in a three-hole loose-leaf binder.

When it's time to go connect, Matthews turns to me and says, "You can go now. But report back here the same time tomorrow."

"If you don't mind I'll check with my precinct first."

"Suit yourself."

They are waiting for me. I grab my jacket and step outside, while Matthews's eyes give my body a thorough going-over.

"What are you checking to make sure I'm not lifting any of the silverware?" I ask him.

The Feds laugh. I should be proud: Making the Feds laugh is probably my biggest accomplishment so far today. We walk down the hall to the elevator together, ride down to the lobby together, go out to the street together, and there separate. "Eddie" still hasn't said one word to me.

I get on the subway and take a ride to the East Village. Detective Snyder is right where he said he would be, in an unmarked van. I climb in next to him, looking south across East 14th Street straight down Avenue C. From here, it looks like downtown Beirut, We exchange hellos, then he plays the tape for me. There are noises in the background of people chatting and glasses clinking while a woman who sounds like she is being stretched to death on a steam turbine howls in a high-pitched shriek that makes it very hard to make out individual words. Fortunately, I've heard the words before, so I'm able to piece most of it together. She stays pretty close to the script:

"Everything tastes like CHEMICALS!

"I have eggs for breakfast and they taste like PAINT THINNER!

"It's in the PRESIDENT'S COFFEE!"

When it's over, there's a noisy response, applause and shouts, some table banging, then a hundred people start talking at once. You'd go nuts trying to isolate one voice in there. It's like listening to "Revolution #9" backwards through an Echoplex on two stereos that are out of synch. Then a guy with a nasal Southern California valley accent steps up to the mike and says, "Okay, okay, I don't want a freakin' riot in the middle of the freakin' party, man."

Snyder says, "Boy is he far from his natural habitat," as someone near the mike let's out a big, brawling laugh. I shush Snyder so I can hear the rest:

"Wasn't she great? Okay, we got Rat At Rat R and the False Prophets coming up next so don't go away—"

The tape ends there.

"That's it?" I ask unnecessarily.

"That's it. Want to hear it again?"

"No, but I guess I'd better."

"That a girl," he says. He rewinds it and plays it again. This time I try to block out the performer and listen to everything else. It isn't easy. "Who's the woman?" he asks me when it's over.

"I wasn't listening to her, I was listening to the other voices."

"Sheesh!" Detective Snyder throws up his hands in frustration. "I was playing it for you so you could identify the woman!"

"Didn't George tell you who she was?"

"George wasn't there, remember?"

"Oh. Right."

"Do I have to play the whole damn thing again?"

"No—it sounds like it could be Hazel, the lead singer for Health Hen, or maybe Gloria from The Slutz. Or Jackie from Soviet Sex. I'll ask around."

"Got any *last* names for me?"

"No. A lot of them use stage names, anyway."

"Tell me about it. I've already spoken to Natz, Slash, Bobby Blender—"

"Let me listen to that last part again."

"You mean the displaced Beach Boy? You know who he is?"

"—No, I mean the other stuff."

Detective Snyder sighs. Then, after a pause, "Okay." He rewinds the tape about a minute and plays it. We listen.

"Again," I say. He plays it again. "Just the last ten seconds."

We listen to it one more time. "You picking out a voice?" he asks.

"No."

"Then what the hell are we listening to?"

"The laugh."

"You kidding me? You think you can tell me whose laugh that is?"

"No, I can't. That's the problem. But it sounds like a laugh I've heard before."

* * *

The SlapDash Gallery lies deep in the heart of the Alphabet Jungle, which is to say 11th Street between Avenues B and C. To get there, it is recommended that you walk along 10th Street until you get to B, then turn up one block, rather than walk down 11th Street all the way. 11th Street is one of those blocks where the only steady occupations are recycled automotive parts and retail pharmaceutical distribution. Some of the operators on this block actually haul industrial winches out onto the street in broad daylight to remove car engines in one shot.

Even taking the "safer" route, it is necessary to negotiate a course past tenements that are burnt-out but not vacant, bricked-up "abandoned" buildings with human-sized holes in the brickwork that lead in to dank, foul-smelling, self-made dungeons, and the shallow eyes of many a lost soul of human jetsam. You might have to negotiate for a whole lot more.

The SlapDash Gallery is an outpost beyond the edge of the tamed frontier, a cabin above the timber-line: It has eight-foot-high plate glass picture windows instead of sheets of 3/4-inch plywood boarded over empty windowframes; bright, surgically meticulous pinspot lighting instead of scorched wires that haven't fed electricity to a socket since the Summer of Love; and instead of the decaying, ghostly shadow of a junkie on the corner who asks me if I want to see him turn a quarter into a million dollars as his way of begging for some spare change, the well-lighted, antiseptic gallery is peopled with that select race of the few, the ambassador class from the art crowd, each one wearing his or her credentials on their sleeves. Clothes make the man, and some of these people are so representative of this dictum that if you took away their clothing, there would be very little left.

Finding this crowd on 11th Street near Avenue C is a bit like coming across a bunch of bronze-skinned Club Med members playing water polo in a hole cut in the ice off Baffin Island, in January.

Heads sprout up from clear plastic cups filled with cheap white wine to look at me expectantly as I enter the gallery: Who is that? Sheila from "The Name?" Bob from "Inksplotch?" Timothy from "Subtrends?" No, it's just some Spanish girl from the neighborhood. Tsk, tsk. Ought to be a law. Perhaps they don't realize how useful I would be as a guide. "Frankly, darling, the sun will be setting soon, so we shall be needing one of the natives to guide us back to civilization. Go see if she speaks English. Baksheesh? Much-y money, yes? You take-y us to great big boat on great big river for much-y money?" But the natives have never seen the piece of paper with the White Man's picture on it, doubt its value, and figure it's safer just to kill the white hairless ones and eat them right there.

There's so much ego grease on the floor from everybody buttering each other up that I nearly slip and fall flat on my face as I skid between the forgers of new modes of American—like, expression, man—to a woman who is sitting at a desk in front of a huge painting of the inside of a stovepipe.

She looks like she works here. By that I mean that she looks like an artist who, even though she spends three-quarters of her income on clothes, can't possibly hope to dress like the patrons. She is wearing a simple, seasonal light dress that some psycho designer was let loose on with a kitchen knife, and her auburn hair is tied back in a bun that is pegged in place by a paintbrush positioned in such a way as to give the illusion of it piercing through her head. You have to be so much more creative when you don't have the money. In a way, it's an interesting effect. Eye-catching.

"Don't commit any crimes looking like that," I tell her.

"I beg your pardon?" she answers. I don't think she heard me. So much the better.

"Where can I find the owner?"

"She's very busy right now with some buyers. What was this about?"

"I'm interested in seeing the paintings of Wilson McCullough."

"You're looking at one," she says, not so much with scorn—she's still too humble among the powers for that—but rather with an awareness that I can't possibly be here for artistic reasons if I don't recognize a McCullough when I see one.

I look up at the painting above the woman's head. It's big, about six feet by nine feet, and it *still* looks like the inside of a stovepipe.

There are a lot of arcs and fragments of circles, all in shades of gray and black, curving perpetually inward, ending in total blackness at the center.

"Marvelous, isn't it?" she says, as though talking to an Aborigine who she is trying to get to trade her 100,000 hectares of uranium-rich desert mountain in exchange for a handful of colorful plastic beads.

"Is this representative of his work?" I ask.

"This is one of his finest."

"I'd like to see some more."

"Take a walk around," she says, gesturing at the gallery walls. "They're on display."

"I'd like to see some of the ones that are not on display."

"Well, we have quite a selection in the back, but they're for interested buyers only."

"I'm an interested buyer. Show me."

She smiles because she knows I'm making this up, but she's bored enough with watching the cream of the crop titter at each other's oh-so-very-witty comments that she welcomes the opportunity to slum with a native for a while. As she's leading me through a narrow corridor to the back room, I ask her, "How much does one of these cost?"

"The one you were looking at is $12,000, and it's a steal at that."

Gulp.

We turn a corner and we're in the back room. She waves her arm along the length of one wall, where several dozen paintings are stored, upright and visible, for the duration of the exhibition. Nothing like dying to boost your sales.

I approach the first battery of paintings, and kneel down to get a better look. It's another gray and black painting, though this one looks more like a minnow's eye-view of terminally polluted water. I reach out and take the edge of the painting, looking up at my companion.

"Go ahead. I'm here," she says. To make sure I don't damage any, I suppose.

I gently tip the outer painting forward, and have a look at the next one. It looks like the life being drained from the sea by an oil spill. Followed by the poison seeping out of a contaminated underground reservoir. And another. And another. All different shapes and spatial relationships, but all the same, grim, gray-on-black death-by-slow-poisoning point of view.

"The cumulative effect has quite an impact on one's sensibilities," I say to my fellow traveler into Wilson's personal torment. She looks at me the way someone might look at a two-year-old who has just spotted a few inconsistencies in Einstein's General Theory of Relativity. She apparently didn't believe I had it in me.

"They're very powerful," she says, with new-found interest. "Particularly his last ones."

"Where are those?"

"Over here."

We go over a few rows to the last set of neatly stacked canvases. I look through them. This last series is the grimmest of all. No more half-suggested landscapes of despair. The last paintings are full-tilt, headlong dives into the absolute depths of bleakness. There aren't even the grays that were in the earlier paintings. Just black on black on black.

"I'll never think about black the same way again," I confide.

"Black," she says. "Wilson once told me that he could distinguish twenty-three separate shades of black, each one equivalent to a specific level of human despair."

"That's quite a theory. So you spoke to him?"

"Lots of times. But it got difficult towards the end. I think he was having a breakdown. What a shame that he was forced to prostitute himself to that shoddy building contractor just to pay his bills. And they killed him with their ignorance."

"Well, that's nothing new," I say. "Kafka and Melville were clerks all their lives. Cervantes and Mozart died broke. Even the Wright Brothers had to fix bicycles to support their strange habit of trying to make aeronautic history. Nobody pays you for being different."

"What a waste."

I nod in agreement. Wilson is dead, and his paintings are selling for $12,000 and up. "So who's getting the money?"

"Wilson donated some paintings to the Environmental Action Foundation for their annual fundraiser, but I hear they liked them so much they hung them up in their offices instead. He always said he wanted more of his money to go to them, but he never put it in writing."

I repeat my question: "So who's getting the money?"

She directs me back to the corridor and discreetly points to a tall woman in her mid-fifties with a flattop blond crew cut, a fashion model's body and a strong German accent. Erika Schnelling. Owner of the SlapDash Gallery.

"How'd she get them all?" I ask.

"Wilson rented studio space from her. When no one came by to claim the paintings, they became Ms. Schnelling's legal property."

I look around the gallery again and return to the back room, taking inventory. At these prices, Ms. Schnelling just got about a million dollars richer. I wouldn't kill for that kind of money, but lots of people would.

"You mean somebody who never gave the artist a break while he was alive inherits a fortune as soon as he's dead? That doesn't seem fair to me."

"Ms. Schnelling was *very* supportive of Wilson. She rented him studio space at ten percent below market value. She even let him pay her in paintings when he ran out of money. So, many of these were hers before—" She leaves that part unsaid. "Ms. Schnelling had been planning to mount a major installation of his, but he got killed before he could finish it."

I notice that she keeps saying "killed," not "died."

"What do you mean, 'installation'?"

"It was going to be a twenty-foot-high walk-in mixed media construction—part sculpture, part video, part sewer, part nightmare. He even had some empty barrels of industrial waste fitted with day-glo green neon tubes, so it really looked like they were glowing, while a pre-recorded voiceover recited horrifying statistics of toxic spills from the EPA's own Superfund reports over the amplified sounds of dripping water."

Gee. George didn't mention anything about all that. I'm going to have to tell Detective Snyder to revoke his kitchen privileges.

"Sounds like an awfully big studio."

"Oh, it's a shared space. Most young artists don't have the money for a loft that big."

"How many people share the space?"

"Oh, dozens."

"Is it open now?"

"Probably."

"What's the address?"

She looks at me.

"I've got a lot of friends who are artists," I tell her. "They're always looking for affordable studio space." She gives me the address. I thank her, and take another look around. I kneel down to examine the signature on a floor-to-ceiling painting of black human misery seeking blacker relief in the deepest blackness of death. Kind of like the last thing a starving coal miner would see after being buried for a week, half a mile under a mountain, just before he dies of suffocation; or what it feels like to stand on a dead asteroid and watch the stars burn out. That kind of black.

It's the weak, watery signature of a dying old man.

"This is a late one, isn't it?"

"Yes," she says.

"His signature was much bolder in the earlier ones."

"Yes," she agrees. I've impressed her.

"Are these all his paintings?"

"Most of them. Except for a handful that he gave to his friends, and his classmates—"

Classmates! Did I just wake up or what? "He was taking art classes?"

"At the New School."

"Which classes?" I say out of reflex. She isn't going to know that, you fool.

"I don't know."

Told you. No matter. I can find out from the school records. But not until Monday. Hmm.

"Do you have any idea where I might be able to find some of those classmates—the ones he was close enough to to make them gifts of his paintings?"

"You'll find Amy Anxiety giving a performance tonight at Low Life," she says. That's just what I need. Then she adds, "Listen, what's your story? What are you after?"

"The truth, honey," I say, getting to my feet. "And believe me, it's as precarious a calling as avant-garde painting."

"You think there's more to Wilson's death than they made out in the papers?"

I don't really want to open my heart up in this matter to anyone I don't know *very* well.

"You sell anything else, besides paintings?" I say, walking back out to the brightly-lit gallery.

"Of course," she says. "We have some very unusual antiques."

And she points to an item that sears its image into my brain: A ewer, which is to say a ceremonial drinking cup, made out of an entire human skull. The cranium is sliced horizontally clean through, allowing you to remove the top and fill a silver bowl lining the bottom half with the libation of your choice. A typed label informs me that it's from eighteenth-century Tibet. Remind me not to visit eighteenth-century Tibet.

* * *

The studio door was unlocked. I went in and spoke to a twenty-something Nuyorican who was hard at work turning portraits of herself and other women into art. Each figure was isolated in a corner of her own separate canvas, painted entirely with shades of amber and yellow, making it hard to see where they began and ended—the only thing you were sure of were their faces. Nice style. After Wilson's paintings, the sight of all that white space in her canvases was doubly powerful. We spoke mostly in Loisaida Spanglish, first about her work, then about Wilson's unfinished installation, which she told me was dismantled and removed from the studio just a few days after his death. The spot where Wilson's last project once stood is now broom clean. I told her that seemed a bit premature, considering the current rate for one of his 4' x 6' canvases using shades of one color. It was unfinished and studio space is expensive, was the explanation. Where was it taken? She didn't know. But I kept talking with her until I jogged her memory. There *was* one piece of his installation left. She had once borrowed an empty "toxic waste" barrel to use as a pedestal for a still life. It was under a drop cloth. A 30-gallon drum with a bonded enamel "Biohazard" trefoil permanently affixed to it, and then hand-marked, "Extremely Toxic: Ship to Zone 3." It still had the bill of lading taped to it in a plastic envelope. Wilson must have stolen it right off the loading dock. Underneath the shipping label was the inverted-triangle logo of the Lillifiex Corporation. A division of Morse, Inc.

* * *

There's a crowd outside Low Life waiting for the doors to open. I sidle up and mix in. Two white Punks are smoking some buffalo grass in front of me.

"Yo, red light," warns someone in front of them, and the flame disappears as a police car cruises by. But the smoke still lingers. We used to have the same problem back home in Ecuador, but we would say, *Tapa la olla:* "Put a lid on it." The only difference is that up here you spend a punitive night in the slammer; down there you disappear from the face of the earth.

The doors finally open and the crowd piles in in an orderly enough way. I walk inside and am mildly amused to hear the disc jockey playing the pseudo-oriental opening gong and chords of the New York Dolls' "Bad Detective." Did someone pick this especially for me? Is there a deeper meaning here? Is God trying to tell me something? David Johansen is telling me, "Bop she bop she bop rabadaba ding dong, Bop she bop she bop—oogie boogie boo." I interpret this as meaning that I should go to the bar and order myself a drink. The bar is one of these long, neon affairs with colored water being pumped through clear plastic tubes embedded in its surface, for that psychotic effect.

"We got a special on frozen margaritas tonight," says the bartender, who looks like a fashion plate from *The New Dictator Magazine.* He's wearing a white jacket with glittering epaulets and a pencil-thin Hitler moustache.

I tell him I'll try one.

A blond bombshell, dressed entirely in what look like loose-fitting, cream-colored silk pyjamas, is chain smoking cigarettes while cleaning them up at the pool table, against what appear to be predominately gay male opponents. I wonder what her angle is.

The two post-Punks next to me are engaged in an engrossing subject: Personal grooming and appearance:

"It's easy for straight people to look weird," says one. "It's the weird people who look straight you've got to watch out for."

There may be more truth in that statement than she realizes. I'm evaluating this when I get a very sharp jab to the lower back and a voice says, "—Don't be *frightened,* Ha! Ha! Ha!" That's the laugh.

I can see in the mirror that it's my friend, the crazed vet impersonator.

"How are ya?" he asks.

"Except for my kidney, I'm fine. You know that kind of punch is
even illegal in boxing?" I say. He laughs. What a card.

The bartender delivers something that is semi-solid and bright
pink. I look at it.

"What's this?" I ask.

"A strawberry margarita."

"Sorry, I never drink anything fluorescent. It's basic self-preser-
vation—a habit I got into ever since I swallowed radium one time
thinking it was a banana daiquiri."

"House rules. You asked for it, you bought it."

He walks away, leaving me with my day-glo snow cone. I try a
sip.—Eh? Well, if I've got to pay for it I might as well finish it.

"You here to see the show?" says the vet.

"Yeah. I haven't seen her since the squatters benefit when she did
that bit from Wilson's diary. She really ripped into it: 'Everything
tastes like CHEMICALS!' She *rules.*"

I figure it's a 3-to-1 shot that he'll say something like, "That
wasn't Amy Anxiety, that was Kim from Sonic Youth."

He doesn't. He takes a step back from me and tries to imitate a
smile. Not even close.

I look at him. He has changed his appearance. At A7 he was
wearing torn blue jeans, a hardcore T-shirt, and a headband.
Tonight it's leather. But leather everything: Leather pants, leather
jacket, leather tie, leather hat, with belts and straps of
metal-studded leather criss-crossing his body every which way.

"You put on any more leather and people are going to think
you're an escape artist," I tell him. He laughs. I should go on TV
with this guy as my straight man. Then a voice from out of nowhere
announces Amy Anxiety. I'll get back to him later.

I turn to look at the stage. A woman who looks to be twenty-two years old under the half-pound of clown white she's got on comes out on stage in a flat-black skin-tight dress and black spike hair. At least I think it's flat black. Her skin is so white the lights bouncing off her temporarily burn out my retinas. When I can see color and form again, I notice that the vet has slunk off, but is eyeing me from the other side of the room. I see all this in the mirror that's behind the bar.

Something that sounds like a train wreck diverts my attention back to the stage. It's only Amy, who has been joined on stage by a specimen of man who has definitely just escaped from the asylum within the last twenty-four hours. He's wearing a reflective chrome spacesuit and sunglasses that probably allow him to see the electro-magnetic spectrum of our planet. He is presently eating an electric guitar. Maybe I should telephone the asylum.

Amy is screeching along with this accompaniment. She continues to screech for about ten minutes, then starts delivering a rap. It's her voice on the tape all right:

"You know there are three ages to this society. You know what the three ages of this society are?"

"No, tell us!" yells someone in the audience.

"Primeval, Mid-eval, and *Most*evil!"

This gets applause. (Why are my hands so clammy when it's so hot in here?) Then she launches into a speech concerning her thesis that the hero of the Mostevil Age is the antihero. In truth, the first part of her performance—the screeching—was kind of interesting. This part of the performance—well, let's face it: Some of this sort of stuff can get pretty pretentious. Who says that the antihero is a new idea? Read *Oedipus* lately?

The Germans behind me love it though.

It takes me her whole performance to finish the strawberry margarita. Then I get Amy interested in me by offering to buy her one. (Why do I feel so nervous? My heart is palpitating.) After I compliment her performance, I say, "I'm looking for a missing person."

"So try all the John and Jane Does in the city hospitals."

"Is that where you found him?" I say, indicating the escaped inmate who is now bumming drinks from the Earthlings.

"Which missing person?"

"Wilson McCullough's closest friend."

"Try George."

"George bowed to the four quarters of the universe and disappeared over the hill. Try again."

"Leon."

"Leon who?"

"Leon something. I don't remember. But definitely Leon. They saw a lot of each other."

"What about you?"

"Me? Listen, I did a reading of one of his poems, and he gave me a painting. Nothing more. He was like that."

"His paintings are worth a lot of money now." It just comes out of my mouth. Normally, I would have kept that tidbit to myself. She makes a sour face, and I can see that I'm going to get nowhere plugging *that* angle.

"Sorry. I didn't mean that. I don't know why I said it." Nor why I said *that,* either. Why am I speaking all my thoughts out loud? Let's change the topic: "Where can I find Leon?"

"You're not gonna believe this, but he dropped out of school to become an apprentice stonemason on the Cathedral of Saint John the Divine."

"Why shouldn't I believe it?"

This interview is not going right. I'm not connecting with her, not my usual subtle self.

Amy gets up to join her fans, and I pay for the drinks with a hand that is getting strangely cold and quivery. I wait for the change, and when I count out the tip, my hands won't stop tingling as if I've just hit my elbow on something. Patti Smith is singing "Into your starry eyes, baby . . . " over the sound system. I look around at the other patrons. They are wiggling and grappling with each other with that sudden, emblematic, exaggerated camaraderie that a certain amount of alcohol is known to produce on live humans. A woman comes up to me. Her breasts look like they're made of silicon, jutting up as strongly and unrealistically as a pair of plexiglass paperweights. She offers me some grunt weed they've been smoking out here in the open, and I reflexively accept some of it: Now I know something's wrong. I look at myself in the mirror, and a face with shiny black eyes grimaces back at me from somewhere away underwater. Now's when the realization seizes me—*I've been dosed.*

As soon as my mind makes this discovery, the walls cave in around my defensive controls, like the first crack in the dyke that floods the valley. I know one thing. I'd better get out of here. Now. No more investigating tonight. If somebody were to pull a gun on me, I'd probably laugh. My knees are like jelly under me, as I undulate over towards the door, past the bouncer who looks at me like he's the gatekeeper of hell who just got fired because of an attitude problem.

The balls on the pool table collide with a sound like the sky breaking apart. I blink my eyes, and in the normally suppressed flash of darkness the whorls of Wilson's imagery engulf me.

Somehow I get myself out of there, and my first impression of the outside world is that all of a sudden it's raining: Everything looks so shiny and reflective in a liquidy way. I wobble out onto the flexible sidewalk, pitching and rolling from side to side like a ship weathering rough, choppy seas, and my experience gradually changes. It's not raining at all. I look up and see that it's a clear, starlit night. But then I look down and see that it's a clear, starlit sidewalk as well. Those little incandescent dots will get you every time. The bus driver's words, "The safest part of your trip is now over" are echoing through my head. Oh, my head . . . Thank God for automatic pilot. Something inside me is leading me inexorably towards the subway.—Come on back, girls! I'm shouting inwardly—at least

I hope I'm not shouting outwardly—are those people looking at me??—I'm shouting to my neurons, which all seem to have closed up shop and gone out to party somewhere, without telling me where to meet them. It makes me wonder how anything stays together. How flimsy the pretense of "society" is. How is it that we all agree to show up and participate? What if one day we didn't?—We just stopped showing up? Maybe I should have called the asylum—to come get *me*. De-e-e-ep breath . . .—Whew! . . . I'm getting near the hole in the ground that is the subway. I'm sure it is. It always looks something like that . . . Well . . . Here goes . . . Down the steps, hold on to that guardrail. My footsteps are echoing against my eardrums . . . The oddly concave walls of the subway tunnel swallow me up with an uncharacteristically luminescent peristaltic motion . . . Thick ribs of undulating light guide me down the throat and into the stomach of the system. Careful now . . . Don't want to have an acident. . . I mean a—No, I don't . . . A—An acident . . . This is an acident all right . . . I've made it. I've gotten my token out without dropping it into the next world, and gone through the turnstile without leaving an arm or a leg behind . . . I reach the platform without breaking anything valuable . . . This is going to be some ride . . .

At first rivers of silence wash against me. The clock in here says 5:15. But the clocks are never working down here in the subway. Or is it 5:15? Did it reaaa-a-lly take me seven hours to walk five b-blocks? I try to look at my own watch but my eyes can't focus on anything that close. I'm waiting for that train to come and take me away, and a paradox occurs to me: If we split a wishbone, and my wish is that you should get your wish, and you win, do you get your wish??—Because you got your wish, but I *didn't* get mine, which was that you should get yours . . . so. . . . Which is it?

A kid walks by wearing a T-shirt that says, "BEAM ME UP, SCOTTY." Oh, how true! How appropriate! "Aye, Captain," I say with a Scottish accent, and I start laughing. I fall against a pylon, laughing, laughing, laughing . . . The pylon is holding me up. My one semi-solid link with reality. Thank God for the pylon. It feels good to laugh. Relieves the tension. And nobody's turning around to look at me or reporting me to the police . . . That's what I like about New York. You get to go completely insane whenever and wherever you want, and nobody gives a damn. They don't give a damn about anything, not even a little girl who is losing her mind please mommy take me home I'm scared is that an earthquake or what no it can't be an earthquake at this hour it's getting louder it must be the subway thank God get me out of here here it comes RRRRRRRRRRRRR-RRRRRRRRRRRRRRRRRRRRO-O-O-O-A-A-A-A-A-RRRRRRR RH!!!!!!! — Sque-e-e-e-e-e-e-e-e-ak! Shngirk! Hmmm mmmbmbm-bmbmbmbmbmbmbmbmbmbmbm. . . . .

I get on the subway train. The whole car is peaking my brains out God how much of that stuff did they feed me? I sit down. It feels good to be attached to something. I can feel the seat pushing up against me with the same force that I am pushing down against it. If it weren't, it would collapse!—Hey! I remember my high school physics!! I'm so proud of myself. Let's see, what else can I remember?—Spin states, spin states . . . —Nuclei with an . . . *odd* number of nucleons have . . . spin. Alignment . . . *with* the field ... is the *low* energy position . . . resistance requires *higher* energy . . . The amount of . . . *energy* . . . you can . . . absorb . . . depends on . . . field . . . strength. Field strength is affected by . . . local . . . density . . . of . . . —Local density of opposing electrons! But electrons also have a spin, and therefore orientations in the field! —Wow! The cosmos is a gay, fractal dance! With God gluing it together in the rhythm section and Coltrane blowing the interstellar sax. And in the swirling silence I hear the sounds of Jimi Hendrix destroying a stack of Marshall amps.

Shngirk! Clank! Dr-r-r-r----Oh thank you God for getting me on the train that's heading in the right direction. *Oh, Dios, ten piedad en mí. Por mi culpa, por mi culpa, por mi gran culpa.* I'm beginning to think that I actually might make it home. I even have the presence of mind for a little near-rational thought: If they've dosed me with mescaline, I'll be out of commission for at least three to six hours; if it's LSD, which is the most likely, I can look forward to more like eight to twelve hours of psychomimesis. My only fear is that whoever did this—going to have to look into who did this later—*much* later—gave me STP or some such designer drug that lasts for three days, because while you're being overwhelmed by waves of undulating everything, it's hard not to worry that you'll never find your way back again. It's like being stuck on an elevator that keeps rising higher and higher, and the floor buttons reach up out of sight into the infinite, black reaches of space. And if all that isn't enough, the serial numbers of all those bills I counted today keep flashing before my eyes. I can't believe that this sort of information has been stored and retrieved by my hyperactive brain. How much more precious inner space is being taken up with vast quantities of useless information, I wonder?

It's the graveyard stint on the subway. A friendly-looking transit cop enters the car and plants himself in the molten linoleum that is slowly bubbling up over my shoes like lava. He is generating standing wave patterns in the goo. He says something like, "Where now now now now rygngths at this at this late hour?"

I smile at him. That is, I think I smile at him. My heart is trying to pound its way out of my chest, and, failing that, is now trying the alternate route up my throat. Now, dear, that's ridiculous, the heart is just another muscle, yet it is understandable how for millennia it has had the reputation it does for it can be felt beating and beats more strongly under certain circumstances and you DO feel something in the middle of your chest when emotionally charged so there must be some physiological reason for it but what and if the brain is just an unfiltered collection of electrochemical impulses how many neurons does it take to make a soul . . . ?

And I swim home that way . . .

I get up thinking, Where does your lap go when you stand up? and make it upstairs to my apartment where I spend the rest of the night in Sidneyland playing with the television by turning it to one of those channels with nothing but "snow" and fidgeting with the contrast and brightness knobs to form swirling, full-color, four-dimensional fractal geometries—and all with a $69 black-and-white TV (you should really try it sometime), and taking a pickaxe to the ego shell with which people normally surround their sensibilities, and a few other explorations that the words to describe haven't been revealed as of yet. There's a phrase that Patti Smith used earlier in space and time when I used to go to clubs to see performance art, about advancing through this "spectrum of age." And she's right, I can't get it out of my head. You're born like a ray of light shooting through space: Pure and delightful energy in motion. Then sometime around age twelve, depending, you strike that first wall of the prism (ouch!) and you start refracting, diffracting, expanding, growing. That was all right. Why? Because everywhere you turn there's all this talk about adolescence, and how tough it is. Why don't they ever talk about all the *other* crises of age? I was totally unprepared when at seventeen I struck an unexpected second wall of the prism. And again at twenty-two. And I continue to strike them. Slamming into invisible barriers, and always coming out wiser, but black and blue with bruises. And on and on like this until morning, when the sun shows up to announce that a new day has risen over one very burnt chick. But at least the walls have stopped breathing.

* * *

I don't even have time to dry out before I have to go to work. So I drink about a half gallon of orange juice to aid in the detoxification of my abused system and the repairing of damaged synapses, and ride the once-electric train that has now faded to a grey, filmy reminder of last night's light show, up to the precinct. On the train it hits me: I was supposed to call up Jean-Luc last night! I hope he'll understand. . . .

I report to work on time, and except for the beautiful, brightly colored first fruits of summer in front of the Korean grocery, everything seems just a little too solid, a little too drab. I've still got enough residual GDZZZZT! infesting my brain to produce that abnormal attention to detail, but the detail is now frozen, drab, the attention to the dirty rather than the marvelous.

The first thing I do is call Jean-Luc. No answer. At eight a.m. on a Sunday? I can't help feeling that for lack of news from me he went out to find something better. . . .

I look up from the dead phone to see the Lieutenant standing over me, looking flat and haloed like a medieval Russian icon. A few hours ago he would have looked like a living Andy Warhol seriagraph. Icons I can deal with. But there's a pale, dark-haired woman alongside him who looks like the disciplinarian from a women's prison.

"I asked Sergeant Bantry to come uptown and help me with your case," says the Lieutenant, sounding like the Archangel asking Eve where that apple went to. He gestures for me to get up and follow him. We form a silent conga line and snake our way through the desks, no one saying a word, until we get to the top of the steps. Then the Lieutenant stops and Sergeant Bantry takes over, turning to me and saying, "Come on," the way someone talks who is used to dealing with people guilty of crimes against the state.

She leads me down the stairs away from the Lieutenant and towards the women's locker room, and a somber premonition begins to take root in my frazzled cranium. Uh-oh . . . .

We get to the locker room, and sure enough, Sergeant Bantry asks me to take down my pants and deposit a urine sample in the company bottle, if I don't mind. Oh, shit . . . There's nothing else to do but go along with it. These surprise drug tests are a new item on the agenda; still another way of policing the police who already have enough to worry about. I finish performing my function under the unflinching eyes of Sergeant Bantry, and hand over the specimen bottle. Here you go, God, here's that apple core you were asking about . . .

My urine has come out of me extra-dark orange. Probably because of all that vitamin C. Would that be enough to neutralize the acid?—No, of course not, orange juice is citric acid, you fool. Alcohol is a base. I should have gotten drunk instead. I should have stayed home.

I strangle the brief, self-defensive urge to bash in Sergeant Bantry's skull as she turns away from me to walk back up the stairs, and instead opt for just following her like an obedient little fallen sinner. You've got to watch those post-acid depression urges. In some ways LSD is most dangerous *after* you come down from it.

Sergeant Bantry displays Exhibit A to the Lieutenant. They are both behaving as if they have just found the fingerprint on the revolver that's going to send the suspect to the gallows. Maybe they have.

The Lieutenant informs me that I am *not* to report to the DEA undercover today, but I am to stay here on desk duty (which sounds strangely like a euphemism for "under constant surveillance") until the urinalysis is complete. He has already spoken with agent Matthews, and they won't be needing me today anyway. Imagine that. But I should report to the Hartley tomorrow morning at seven a.m.

I spend the next several hours sitting at other people's desks, playing musical chairs every time someone with seniority wants to use the one I'm at—and when your ass is on the thin blue line, my friend, *everybody* has seniority. I return the salutations to the few people who take the trouble to acknowledge that I'm there waiting for the axe to fall, but I can't concentrate on anything. I suppose that this is what some provincial challenger feels like in the hours before he's supposed to step into the ring with Larry Holmes. You have a drink of water, but no amount of water can stop the dry tightening in your throat. You mechanically do the backlog of typing and filing on your desk and afterwards wonder if you did it right. You read a headline or two but you can't concentrate on them, nor do you care. How horrible it is to be so concentrated on yourself. A headline says that twenty-four Haitians have drowned trying to float to the Land of Liberty on a rubber raft. But I can't feel for them, I'm just waiting for my own private disaster to strike. And that's not like me. You say hello to people but you don't see them the way you're used to seeing them. Sure, they might feel for you, but they're all going to be spectators when you're in there getting the living crap beaten out of you by a 6'4", 220-pound heavyweight with a reach sixteen inches longer than yours.

Finally around 3:00 the hour strikes. Okay, Buscarsela, come on in here. I don't even get my last meal.

The Lieutenant closes the door that's just soundproof enough so that every word can be heard by those outside if the Lieutenant talks above a certain volume. Which he does.

"Do you know what this is?" he asks me, tickling my nose with the corner of a report folder. I sure am getting a lot of report folders shoved at me lately.

"Result of the urinalysis?" I answer needlessly. I'm also trying to keep my voice down. Just because my co-workers can hear everything the Lieutenant is saying doesn't mean they have to hear my answers.

"Uh-huh. Do you know what it says?"

I nod. "Enough LSD to kill a horse. Lieutenant—"

"Not just LSD, Buscarsela. We got, 'Sufficient traces of THC and other residues to suggest chronic use of marijuana,' not to mention some alcohol that I suppose you just threw in for kicks."

"Lieutenant—I was out trying to dig up a lead on the McCullough killing. Somebody knew it and their way of warning me to lay off was

117

to slip me a Mickey that you wouldn't believe." I'd like to see *you* survive five hundred accidental mikes of freshly made LSD, Lieutenant. "I'm prepared to sign an affidavit to that effect."

"Since you're not officially connected with that case in any way, Officer Buscarsela, I fail to see why I should even consider what you're telling me as relevant to the issue at hand, which is, in case you haven't figured it out, illegal drug use."

"Call up Detective Snyder from downtown. There's his number. He'll back me up on my assertion that I am acting on his behalf, investigating the scenes that he would otherwise be unable to infiltrate."

The Lieutenant tosses Snyder's card on his desk. I think he was aiming for the wastepaper basket and missed.

"All right, Officer. Even if I bought your cockamamy story about involuntary ingestion of LSD—" You make it sound so easy and straightforward, Lieutenant. How would you like to confront the limits of your consciousness alone in bed at four a.m.? "—There's this 'Chronic use of marijuana.' What have you got to say about that?"

"Why should I say anything? That report says it all. Lock me up already and get it over with."

"This report does not 'say it all,' Officer." Now he lowers his voice, for the first time since he called me in here, below the threshold of transmission of the interoffice message system. *Now* we're in private. "This kind of drug use tells me one of my officers is having emotional problems."

All right, Lieutenant! A grain of humanity in the traditional stone wall. I'm impressed.

"My job is to run the ship here, and if one of my crew is sick—or having problems—it affects the whole precinct. Now in view of your years on the force, and the Department's recognition of your outstanding performance in a number of instances, I'm willing to work this out, on the condition that you clean up your act, Miss

Buscarsela. I don't have to tell you that this is not really going to help your bid for a promotion. This happens again and you're out of here. Is that clear?"

"Can I go now?"

"I asked you if that was clear."

"It's clear. Can I go now?"

"Yeah. Beat it."

I'm beginning to understand what Wilson may have meant about there being twenty-three shades of black, each one akin to a specific level of human depression. I think I've just sunk down to about Level Five. Or maybe Eight.

* * *

I'm signing out for the day, relieved that the axe hanging over me is not going to drop on me—today—but its shadow is still there making me nervous, when I get a phone call. It's El Gordo.

"You ready for this, *flaca?* I got you your death medicine: It's a product called 'Mentherax,' and it's manufactured by Flexum Industries, which also manufactures the migraine medicine you asked about the other day. But get this: Flexum Industries is a subsidiary of the parent company that also owns and operates that insecticide factory that blew up in your face two months ago."

"You've been working overtime, Gordo."

"—And I get off in fifteen minutes. How about getting together for a drink?"

"Sure."

I could use about ten. It's been one of those days.

FIVE

"And why is my life a page plucked from a holy book
And the very first line torn away?"

—Kadya Molodowsky

I wake up badly hungover, which, by the way, is even *worse* than being burnt from an acid trip. The defining condition of LSD burn is depression. But you generally aren't left feeling sick enough to want to die.

I guess I drank myself half-silly last night. I can remember pouring myself into the subway, where the combination of the long ride underground and the spastic lurchings of the car slowly transformed a head high and dizzy into that dull, get-me-home-so-I-can-pass-out-before-I-throw-up condition that always makes you swear "never again."

I also remember having to push El Gordo away from me ten or twenty times during the extremely serious operation of getting trashed. No thanks. All I ever needed was that one abysmal one-nighter not to ever repeat that again: "No, don't bother to turn on the light. I'll find my coat in the dark.—Glp!" I have never gotten drunk enough to black out. But last night I think I came close.

I promise myself I'll go easy next time (—*next* time!!) as I limp towards the subway, mold growing on my brain and a prairie fire slowly eating its way through my colon. Even watching the train come in is too painful for my eyes, which over-saccaded themselves while rolling loose from my head sometime last night.

I drank between five and six glasses of water this morning to rehydrate my scorched and brittle tissues, and now I have to pee like you wouldn't believe, and it's only 120 blocks via underground rail to the Hartley, and a toilet, which is a sobering experience in itself.

El Gordo couldn't tell me much beyond what he had said over the phone, but that was enough. I resolve to check out the possible connection between Wilson and Morse, Inc. as soon as possible, which is to say when I'm feeling better. Morse, Inc. is the parent company of those two stepchildren, Flexum Pharmaceutical, and Ven-All Insecticide Corporation (a division of Lilliflex), and God knows how many other legitimate and illegitimate heirs.

But first I've got to show up at the Hartley and perform my Gal Friday act, and then if there's time, I must go and look for Leon X.

And I'd better stay away from the Punk scene for a while.

By the time I get to the Hartley, my bladder is ready to burst, and I have the greatest urge to just relieve myself in one of the gigantic potted palms in the lobby. But I make it up to room 1402, rush past Ryan to the bathroom just in time. The pressure against my insides has made me nauseous, and I have to wash my face with warm water until some of the color comes back. Then when I'm ready to face my partners in crime-busting, I step out of the bathroom and into the main room. For a very expensive suite in a midtown hotel, the place is pretty ordinary.

Matthews is looking at me with a dim smirk. I *trust* the Lieutenant kept the results of my drug test confidential . . .

"You didn't say 'May I?', Buscarsela," says Matthews. "Now you lose a turn."

"Grow up, Matthews," says Ryan. I like Ryan. He's all right for a Fed. "Jeez, you look like death on toast," he says to me.

"Does it show?" I ask.

"On you? Like a newspaper, babe—and you're about the same color, too. Now if you were a man you might could get away with it. More body weight to absorb it and all that. But I admire you for trying."

"Thanks."

Matthews pipes in: "What say we two get together sometime and find out what your limit is?"

"I think she's already reached her limit of you, kid," says Ryan.

"You should open a fortune teller's shop," I tell Ryan.

"I did once. We were investigating fraud in the prognostication business. Lot of nice retired couples getting conned out of their life savings."

"Come on, Ryan," butts in Matthews, "how can retired couples prognosticate? That's strictly for young, red-blooded—"

"It means 'predict the future,' pea-brain, not what you're thinking," says Ryan. "Listen, Officer Buscarsela, I know we had you just kind of hanging around the other day—"

"—I'll say," I comment parenthetically.

"—But we were setting up a good, solid scam. We want you to keep an eye on a construction site for us."

"Much as I hate to say this, you can't send a woman to a construction site, unless you dress me up as an I-beam."

"You've sure got the disposition for it today, Officer. Rust and all," says Ryan. "I have to agree with him."

"Here's what we want from you," says Matthews.

"Let me guess," I say. "You want me to bring you the broom of the Wicked Witch of the West."

"The deal is this," says Ryan. "We got a corrupt building contractor on our hands."

"Don't let that get out," I say. "It's liable to cause a panic."

"What have I got? *Two* jokers now I gotta deal with?" complains Ryan.

"Sorry. Monday morning," I say.

"That's all I need."

"Look, it's been a tough weekend for me, too," I say. "Let's just forget about it."

"Tough?" says Ryan. "Listen, babe, we went out Saturday to make the buy. After the cop we follow the damn car halfway to fucking Canarsie, where it parks in front of a single-family house and doesn't move for the rest of the night. Nobody went near the stuff for eighteen hours, eighteen hours that we spent sitting in our cars watching the stupid fucking car. The stuff's still in the trunk. They must have known they were followed. Now what have you got that would compare to that?"

I could think of a thing or two, but I keep silent.

"Uh-huh," Ryan goes on. "Like I was saying, the deal is this: We got you a job in a deli up Eighth across from where they're throwing together the Columbus-Air Condos. Heard of it?"

"I've seen the hole."

"Well it's not a hole anymore. They got five floors already. They got something else, too. They got a guy who's supposed to be an assistant plumber. But there's no plumbing yet. So what does this guy do all day?"

"I don't know, tell me."

"He waits for a runner to bring him four to five ounces of coke at a shot, which he then cuts up into grams and distributes to street dealers."

"That sounds like a really stupid way of moving a half-ton of coke," I mention.

"Sure, it's dangerous as hell. But it brings in a lot more money that way, too. Grams can go for up to $120 each. In bulk, you're lucky to get $60."

"I do work in the Police Department, Agent Ryan."

"Then act like it. We're talking about a greedy son-of-a-bitch, Officer B. Someone who's probably figured the cost per gram per courier to six decimal places on the company computers, and decided it's worth it—provided there's enough insulation between the street and the source. And there is all right. It took us six months to trace a street squeal to this man—"

Here he takes out a 3 x 5 color mug shot that looks so much like my would-be rapist that I have to look at it again to make sure it isn't him; but it could be his older, meaner brother. They've both got the same three-day growth of sandpaper.

"This shot's a couple of years old, but it'll be good enough to go by," says Ryan.

"Has he shaved since this was taken?" I ask.

"He looks about the same," says Ryan. "We had him under surveillance, but I think he knew we were out there."

"Sounds like you have some holes in your security."

"Look: Anyone who'd squeal to us isn't exactly going to behave like your great-grandma at the Sunday picnic."

"They tell me my great-grandma used to poach mountain lions out of the cornfield. 'Course the neighborhood has changed since then."

"Yeah, I bet," says Matthews.

"Shut up, you," says Ryan. "Here's the address," he says, handing me a slip of paper. "It took us a long time to land this thing right. No one in the joint is hip to your being a cop. I expect you to remember that."

"Well, if you don't complicate it by asking me to chew gum at the same time I think I can remember it."

"Then get going."

"You got our number?" asks Matthews.

I nod. Ryan opens the door for me and shows me the way out. Eddie hasn't moved from the windows the whole time. I bet you forgot he was there at all.

On my way out, I tell Ryan, "I bet you don't get bored listening to Eddie's conversation."

Ryan shuts the door in my face.

I go down into the street and walk up Eighth Avenue until I get to the address on the piece of paper. It's just like they told me: a respectably-sized deli, directly across the street from the site of the new set of luxury highrises.

I take a good look at the construction site from outside the deli. Behind a wall of splintery boards is a deep pit one street block wide and half an avenue block long, which I can see through the steel mesh that covers the sporadic holes in the fence. I'm really not going to be able to see much dealing, unless they come out onto the sidewalk under the platform that's supposed to catch falling debris to do it. Maybe this whole business is a dead end for me. If it were for real, they'd have to have agents planted in a dozen locations to keep this site covered, and there'd still be a hundred places to hide. On the other hand, if they just want to see who goes in and out, I suppose it makes sense. But I wouldn't know. I'm just the meter-maid here. They intentionally keep me from knowing about anything but my own little piece of the pie. So be it.

I can't get over how shitty the construction looks. There's hardly a superstructure to speak of—although it's true that major earthquakes are less common in New York than in the Andes—and the whole thing when finished is going to be made of the same kind of "sheetrock" that Tommy Osborne shot a nail straight through into Wilson's face. We used to call that stuff "plasterboard." "Compressed dust" would be more like it. Built to last, it's not. Built to cash in on the second-longest-running land ripoff in history, maybe.

I shrug and go inside.

The Feds have told my Chinese boss that I am a recently released offender who they're trying to help get back on the track to an honest way of life. There's actually some truth to that. His name is Wang, and he gives me some very serious once-overs before letting me put on one of those ridiculous white paper hats and start slicing the bologna. The other two workers for the middle-aged Chinaman are both *latinos,* too, Rafico, and Mateo, and they spend about 88 out of my first 90 minutes there making highly explicit references to my anatomy, the fine points and the gross points. The leftover two minutes they spend talking about the *other* women passing by on the street. All of which is in Puerto Rican Spanglish, but my boss is with it enough to know every word they're saying, and is suitably impressed by my coolness under fire to actually let me alone with the cash register for thirty seconds when he goes to the bathroom.

But he comes right back and the first thing he does is open the register, pretending that he's looking for a lump of gold he might have left there, or something. Now he's satisfied that I'm honest—or at least more honest than my co-workers—and he shows me how to work the cash register. So I spend the whole morning making sandwiches for the construction workers across the street, for the 42nd Street winos who have managed to panhandle the necessary five quarters for a grilled cheese sandwich that is probably their only protein all week (I toss on an extra slice of American), and for scurrying condo-tower executives, who, by the way, make far ruder comments about what they think my sexual tastes are than the construction workers do. There's a lesson in there somewhere, but I'm too busy keeping one eye out across the street for the assistant plumber, and the other one on the meat slicer to make sure that I don't serve anyone a liverwurst on whole wheat with mustard and thinly sliced thumb of Filomena, to think about what it might be.

When I finally get to sit down and have lunch, I have to turn down an offer to spend my twenty minutes in a hotel that one of the boys knows two blocks away near Tenth Avenue.

"That's two *avenue* blocks, bimbo, it'd take twenty minutes just to walk there and back," I tell him.

"Then let's go in the freezer, baby."

How romantic.

"Make me heave," I tell him, and sit down to eat a BLT, which is without a doubt the freshest thing around. I made it myself. I'm sitting on a plastic milk crate, my head below the level of the counter, but I can still see clear across the street through the hams and salamis on the glass shelf, which is the critical thing.

Gee, boss, Sonny Corleone hasn't driven up in his limo yet, stepped out in full view and handed a construction worker a paper bag leaking cocaine so far today. I swear I kept my eyes open, too.

But what does happen is a young urban professional—what they used to call a "go-getter" back in the twenties, and in some ways the term is more appropriate—comes in, suit and tie, briefcase and all, and orders the fried chicken, which is weird to begin with, today being one of the first real scorchers of the season, and chicken being one of the messier items on sale here. My sexually deprived co-worker says, "A whole, a half, or a quarter?"

The go-getter-*cum*-yuppie says, "Uh, just a half." This guy's going to eat a half chicken with that light green three-piece on? This I gotta see.

So my interest is piqued just in time for me to observe that the young businessman has handed Mateo enough money to buy three 20-pound turkeys; then my co-worker gets into some excessively elaborate wrapping of the half chicken, and hands it back to the young buyer, along with change that is about $65.00 short, if that package contains only half a chicken.

The young man looks more than satisfied with the deal, however, and steps lively out of the store. Only $5.00 goes into the cash register.

"That's a neat trick. Where'd you get it from?" I ask, looking up from my low angle on the milk crate. Mateo turns around and leans back against the register, real cool.

"Get what from?" he says. Now where have I heard that before?

"That coke switch. That's sweet. Tell me you thought that up yourself."

He's looking at me like "Should I knife her now or later?" when I can see the other thought enter and displace the first: "That's right, this bitch just got out of jail." Those are his thoughts, not mine.

"Why? You want a piece of it?"

"Hell no, bro. I just did time for working my share of the family business. I just think it's too high-class a scam for a mutt like you to have come up with it."

He laughs. These macho men always laugh when a woman insults their intelligence. They think it's sexy.

"You must of got real lonely in there, baby, with no one to hold you," he says, changing the subject.

"Who says?"

A shadow falls over him. Nothing shuts up a macho man quite like the suggestion that you just might not be interested in what he's got, *ever*. Tell them you've got a boyfriend, and they'll laugh and tell you how he can't be half as good as they are. But you drop "dyke" on them and they turn just plain limp. What a waste of womanhood.—As if you care. But it doesn't faze this one.

"One night with me, babe, you'll change your mind."

"—About whether or not I should kill myself? No thanks."

"You don't know what you're missing."

"I missed out on Prince Charles, too, but I survived. You still haven't told me about your deal. I just want to know what's going on so I don't screw up your oper—you know, your system."

He thinks about this a bit and starts nodding slowly, pursing his lips. "Fair enough," he says, finally. "Come here."

I get up and walk over to him. There's nothing to show me. He just doesn't want the egg salad to hear.

"We only got barbecued chicken, see? Someone comes in and asks the old man for fried, he say, 'No fried, barbecued.' Someone comes in and ask me, I ask 'em a whole, a half, or a quarter, then I slip in what they want from here."

He shows me the upper pocket of his butcher's apron, which has about a half-dozen postage-stamp-sized folded packets in it. I whistle.

"You wanna go in the back and do some?"

"My parole officer is giving me twice-weekly drug tests. She spots coke in there and I'm back inside before the pee cools off, you hear?"

"I hear, I hear."

"Where do you get it from?"

"Whoa whoa whoa, babe, you gettin' mighty chummy."

"Okay, forget it." I start to turn. Fortunately, he wants to impress me.

"Right across the street, man. It's easy. If anything ever goes wrong, I'd see it from here long before it got to me. Is that a deal or what?"

It took three Feds six months to find the construction company connection, and I just got it in three-and-a-half hours. Either I'm lucky, or they were talking to the wrong people in the wrong tone of voice.

"It's a sweet deal, all right," I tell him.

"Any time you want a piece of it—"

I waggle my finger at him.

"All right, I get it," he says. This boy is quick. It only took him half a day to get it.

Now that it's about noontime and I've had something to eat, I feel that my poor little stomach has recovered enough for me to test out its reaction to my first cup of extremely light coffee. I draw off about a third of a cup in one of those paper "I ♥ NY" containers and open a fresh quart of milk. I'm sitting back down to enjoy the inner warmth of the magical liquid's rejuvenating powers on my dissipating hangover. Most folks I know wake up the morning after with a head that threatens to split open, and a pale green complexion, but they're both gone in an hour or two. I just feel like a starched collar all day long. I drink in some more coffee. Yes, professor, the subject is beginning to respond to the stimulus. We will soon be able to continue with the experiment.

My boss comes back from whatever errand he disappeared to in the first place (after all, he doesn't have to answer to me), and tries to look casual as he scrutinizes the cash register for signs of tampering. Finding none, he turns to me.

"How's it going?" he asks me.

I'm in the middle of sipping coffee, and my new pal answers for me.

"She's doing fine, chief. Slices meat like a pro. She's got good, fast hands."

"Not as fast as yours," I say, putting a stop to the uncalled-for commentary.

The chief comes over by me.

"That's good," he says. "You eat lunch?" I nod. "What'd you have?"

I tell him a BLT and coffee. He says that's fine, that whenever I want to have lunch, I'm covered for $3.00 worth of whatever I want. Anything over that I get charged for. I tell him that sounds like a good deal.

"Say what?" says Mateo. "Me 'n 'Rafico gotta pay for what we eat!"

"You two steal twice that when you think I'm not looking," says Mr. Wang. "If I don't charge you for it once in a while, I go broke. Besides, if someone doesn't show some support for this young lady when she's trying to get her life straight again, then what's supposed to stop her from going right back to what she was doing before? It sure as hell pays more than what I can afford to give her."

This is no, "No tickee, no washee" Chinaman. He's first genera-tion all right, but his English is better than Mateo's, and he has been around a lot more, too.

"Thanks," I tell him, in all sincerity. I really am thanking him. For still believing in other people after thirty years in Hell's Kitchen.

Of course I don't really need his help, but the next person who comes along just might, and I don't want him to lose faith. Ever. For the next person who comes along, this man might be the last chance.

That's the thing about a place like New York. There are people here who would slit your throat for a five-dollar bag. Then there are people like this. People who don't know you from nothing, but they'll help you all the way to the city limits. For no reason at all but they're good people. And thank God for them. When we lose them, I'm giving up.

All this—plus a shot of caffeine—brings my thoughts around to Jean-Luc, and gives me the courage to try to contact him.

"Can I make a phone call?" I ask Mr. Wang, who is wearing a stained white apron that for me is shining brighter than any armor Sir Launcelot ever wore.

"Local?" he asks. Ever practical, too. He may be a good Samaritan, but he ain't crazy.

I joke with him: "What do you think, I'm going to call South America?"

"Don't laugh. These guys have tried it."

"Of course it's local."

"Right through there." He shows me the phone back behind the freezer. The back door of the deli is open to let the air in. It opens out into an alley—which is a rare enough thing in Manhattan. This is not Chicago. In a town where living space can be sold for $1,000 a square foot and climbing, alley space gets taken up pretty fast.

I dial Jean-Luc's home number, and after five-and-a-half rings he answers.

"Filomena!" says the voice. "I was beginning to think you 'ad forgotten about me."

"I had the same fear myself. I tried reaching you yesterday morning."

"I was still asleep, *ma chère*. Where 'ave you been?"

To the moon and back, honey.

"Let's just say I got hoist on my own petard."

"Oh, Filomena, I love it when you are literary. Why are you in such a beastly profession—?"

But I don't hear all of this last sentence. There is the unmistakable sound of scuffling around the corner in the alley. A garbage can gets knocked over with a distinct CLANG! And a man who sounds Black is telling someone to lay off.

"Sorry, what was that?" I ask Jean-Luc. But I'm not listening.

"Yeah, you're all alone now, nigger!" someone says out in the alley.

Jean-Luc is saying, "Someone with your intelligence should be doing something more productive than chasing muggers and rapists—"

But someone out in the alley is saying, "Yeah, where's your friends, now, *nigger?*" I hear a body being shoved against a wall.

"What's going on out there?" I ask Mateo.

"Whatever it is, it's not my problem," says he.

I cut Jean-Luc off in mid-sentence: "Could you hold on a second?"

Then I put down the phone and look around for something to grab. There's a pencil, a broom, and a big stick propping open the back door that was made to order. I pick it up in my two hands and march out into the alley.

"Yeah, what you gonna do now, *nigger?*" says the voice, in what I now recognize as a North Jersey accent. And you thought this sort of thing only happened in Natchez, Mississippi after sundown.

I round the corner and two big white guys from the Jersey suburbs have got a satisfactorily-built Black guy against a wall. He looks like he could fight his way out of this, but the others have both got knives out, and he's just waiting for the chance to make a break for it. They feel me coming, but a little too late. I do my ice-breaking, life-of-the-party impression of Sheriff Clark on one of the knife-wielding hands, and a switchblade falls to the wet alley floor. The guy I hit is howling in pain, and I pick up the switchblade before the Black guy can get to it and take out his anger in human flesh. The knife is one of those cheap Taiwanese copies of the West German switchblades that fall apart on you. It figures. It probably comes from a novelty store in Bergen County. Instead of running, the other Jersey guy turns his knife towards me. Oh come on. I can see this ape wants to learn the hard way.

I hand my stick to the Black man. "Here, hold this," I tell him, and I rotate the switchblade in my hand the wrong way around so that the blade is pointing towards my elbow out of my clenched fist, for that unconventional edge. It works. The Jersey kid has never seen anything like this, and he comes towards me with his blade ready to stab up. I punch him in the face and cut across his cheek at the same time, making a very shallow cut. But face wounds bleed like the devil, and the next second the guy's face is awash with blood, and the two of them are beating their tails out of there.

I can tell the Black guy's pride is damaged that some skinny female had to come help him out of this. "Two against one is a crock," I tell him. "They just weren't expecting me to be practicing my forehand around the corner is all. Can I have that back?" I ask him, holding my hand out for the stick. "If my boss notices it's missing I'm liable to get in trouble."

The Black man hands me the stick as if it were the most natural thing. He's been in worse jams than this, and doesn't seem a bit put out by it at all. But a minute ago he was sweating.

I hand him the knife, which is tinted with a thin trickle of blood now. He wipes the blood off on the bottom of his sneaker, closes up the knife and puts it in his pocket, and he walks a bit jauntily away from me down the alley. I turn around and Mateo is standing at the corner, arms crossed, and smiling.

"Just all sweet and innocent, huh?" he says.

"Yeah, so what?" I say, walking straight past him.

Back inside the rear of the deli, I pick up the phone.

"Hello?" But there's no one there.

"He hung up, babe," says Mateo coming in behind me. "Must of got tired of waiting."

* * *

It's pretty easy to figure out that Wilson was planning a well-publicized exhibit, certainly unfriendly, possibly extremely damaging to Morse, Inc. and its subsidiaries, using U.S. Government data and stolen materials, and that he just happened to croak right before the installation could get mounted. Pretty convenient for Morse, Inc. If there's any connection, it must be among the East Village circle of artists who knew about Wilson's work-in-progress. Maybe an overly greedy gallery owner who didn't want to ruin a good thing, although there's no such thing as bad publicity in that world, so I put that theory on a back burner for now. My only other hairline connection between all these separate events right now is the man with the big, brawling laugh. I figure my protean crazed-vet-turned-lizard-king skinhead friend must be the one who dosed me, too.

In spite of swearing to myself to stay away from the scene for a while, I've got this unquenchable urge to find him and nail his ass to a moving train. The Punk clubs don't open until way after dark, but there are plenty of liquor stores and bars that do business from ten a.m. on. Trying to describe a skinhead with a bandana or a guy wearing leather would normally bring laughter, but the guy I'm looking for happens to have just switched quite visibly from one look to the other, and it doesn't take long for three different proprietors to tell me that I'm probably looking for a two-bit panhandler named Bud Wiegand.

I'd better not confront Wiegand directly. If I'm right about him, he's been tipping his mitt to *everybody*, and I don't want to end up as an abstract study in bright red and black like Wilson did. No thanks.

I don't want to go directly to Snyder's precinct. But I know a young recruit named Betty Nichols who's wearing out her first pair of shoes in the West Village. Through an unofficial women's network, I helped mentor her through her first six months on the beat, and it's time to check in with her anyway. She should be coming off shift now.

They've got one of those beautiful, landmark brownstone precinct houses that used to have a horses' stable and a full-time blacksmith. I ask around and find her washing up in the women's locker, which used to be the stable, I think. She's still in uniform. Good. She's patting her face dry with a towel when she sees me. I actually get a hug, then she says, "Must be a favor if you're here."

"And I always told them you were a fast learner. Keep your uniform on."

She looks at me with those bright blue eyes and fresh, youthful skin that belong in an Irish soap commercial.

It doesn't take her long to pull up a few Wiegands from the system. No Bud, though. But only one has a recent record in the East Village: "Wiegand, Artemus."

"Artemus?" I say. "Let me see his mug."

A few minutes later and we've got a positive I.D. I'd know that vacant stare anywhere. The rap sheet shows a few parking tickets and a summons for disorderly conduct. No drug convictions on record, which is odd, because he sure seemed to know a thing or two about drugs. I say, "You'd think a nice guy like him and drugs would have clashed with the law more often than that. Pull up the long view of that disorderly summons."

"That's all there is: Just a date and a charge."

"Hmm . . . You ready for that favor?"

"I thought this was it."

"Then there are still a few things I need to teach you."

I take Betty over to Snyder's precinct. She goes in while I wait in a coffee shop around the corner nursing a yogurt and an herb tea. It takes her longer than I expected, but then maybe I should have expected it. She's got some photocopies for me.

"Something weird about this all right," she tells me as she sits down. "First, the original arrest report was missing, then the desk duty officer got irritated as hell when I asked him to help me find it. Turned out it was 'misfiled.' Now look at this—" she turns and asks the waitress for a plain soda.

"Good girl," I tell her. "You'll live longer."

"—The arresting officer's report says Wiegand was brought in on 3/19, but there's something about the '9'—"

I look at it. The top is quite flat. "It's a seven changed to a nine," I say. When you're collaring a perp, you don't always have time to write everything down at that exact moment. My reports certainly have their share of strike-overs—but getting the date wrong by two days—*that's* a bit unusual.

"So I asked real nice to see the March log, and guess what?" Betty continues. "There was a full line of white-out on the evening of the 17th, and Wiegand's name was crammed between two entries on the 19th at 11:45 A.M."

Again. There's plenty of white-out corrections in any log, but usually a letter or two or a couple of words, not the whole entry. It could be nothing. Or—

"Who's the arresting officer?" I ask.

"Officer Delacosta," she says, reading it off the sheet.

"Where is he now?"

"I don't know."

"Find out."

"Fil, I just got off my shift—"

"So did I, and I'm going on another as soon as I'm done here. Just give me one more hour."

She sighs. I've been getting a lot of sighs from people lately. "Okay," she says.

Officer Delacosta turns out to be a three-year veteran who's working a patrol car near Tompkins Square Park, keeping an eye on the Christadora building, A developer bought it to subdivide into $1,000-a-month studio apartments, and many of the local families, artists and anarchists are upset that such a prime piece of local real estate is about to get priced out of their range. That's what we need cops for: To protect this upscale slumlord's investment. Officer Nichols stretches her credibility to the breaking point getting Officer Delacosta to leave his squad car so he can spend ten minutes with us in the dark recesses of one of those all-day bars where none of the drinks cost more than $2. I'm waiting there with a pitcher of beer and three glasses. I nurse mine through the whole thing.

"So what's this all about?" asks Officer Delacosta, after draining his glass in one shot.

Now that we're all apparently violating Departmental regulations against drinking on duty, I figure I can jump right in. I plop down Betty's photocopies and ask him, "Why was Bud Wiegand charged with disorderly conduct two days *after* he was brought in?"

He stiffens a bit, but I'm already pouring us all another glass of beer, and he relaxes. He's smooth, well-practiced. And after only three years on duty. "Oh, he copped a plea," he says.

Betty opens her mouth but I get it out first: "It took him two days to cop to disorderly conduct?"

"Look, you got my report. It's all there." He's about to stand up.

I block his path with my arm. "Officer Nichols, go tell Officer Delacosta's partner that he'll be another ten minutes."

Betty gets up and leaves. I wait for her to get back. A nice long wait. I pour the last of the pitcher into his glass, and continue nursing mine. When we're all together again, Officer Delacosta says, "All right—I was busy and I didn't get around to him for a couple of days, and I didn't want it to look like I had kept a suspect in holding for so long for nothing, so I—"

"—So you falsified your report," Betty finishes his sentence for him.

I keep my eyes on Officer Delacosta. "It took you *two days* to 'get around' to him?" I ask.

"Yes."

"So he copped the night you brought him in?"

"Well, yeah."

"So what did he give you?"

"Huh?"

"Oh, come on, you don't cop a plea *to the arresting officer* without a very good reason."

Silence.

I go on: "Look, I don't give a flying fuck what kind of deal you made, Officer Delacosta, I'm trying to solve a fucking murder. So don't fuck me up here."

Now I'm talking a language he understands. Officer Delacosta lets out a breath and runs his hands through his hair. I think I've finally broken some of his nerve. He's worried now. You can see him deciding to come (relatively) clean.

"Okay," he says, finally. "It was a drug bust."

Surprise, surprise.

"He didn't have any volume of the heavies, you know, coke, smack—"

"—We know, we know," says Betty.

"—Get on with it," I insist.

"It was acid. Only about thirty-five hits, but thanks to the new carrier laws, the weight of the paper would have sent him away for fifteen years."

"So after sitting around for a day or two thinking about spending fifteen years in Attica he paid you off to drop it down to disorderly conduct. How much?"

More of the heavy-breathing-hands-through-the-hair-stuff.

"Look, I really don't care what you did," I tell him, putting the photocopies away. "I just want to know about Wiegand." I think he believes me this time, because he answers.

"Five thousand dollars."

"Jeezus," says Betty.

"Where did he get that kind of money?" I ask.

"Well, drugs," says Officer Delacosta.

"You got to sell a *lot* of acid to clear that kind of profit, Officer Delacosta. Like a couple of thousand hits. You picked him up with thirty-five."

"So he was at the end of a shipment."

"Maybe," I say. "But he didn't seem like the entrepreneurial type." Now there's an understatement. "A cheap con-man, sure. But not a big businessman."

I throw that "cheap" in Officer Delacosta's direction.

"Thank you, Officer Delacosta, you've been very helpful."

He picks up his cap and gets up with the same sheepish shuffling any street grifter gives you when you've got him on the hot seat. He heads out, adjusting his cap as he goes. By the time he opens the door and steps back into the light of the street outside his old swagger is back.

"He's all cop, that guy," I say.

Betty nods. Then she says, "Thanks, Fil. I learned a lot watching you work."

"You want to learn more?"

"Uh-oh, here it comes."

"Relax. Just call Detective Snyder for me and tell him you want him to put a tail on 'Bud' Wiegand."

"Oh. Okay. I guess I can do that."

"Now."

She shakes her head, but she takes his number and goes outside to find a pay phone. Five minutes later she's back.

"Can't do it, Fil. Detective Snyder says he can't justify putting a man on Wiegand on suspicion of simple possession, plus you've got no proof *he* did it to you."

Silly little girl. She told him the truth. Oh well "I've got no proof we evolved from an ape-like ancestor, either, but they're still teaching it at Harvard."

"And how would you know?"

"All right, I'm guessing."

For the first time all afternoon, we are able to share each other's laughter.

Then I ask her for one last favor:

"Could you possibly spend a few nights watching the SlapDash Gallery for me?"

"Now?"

I nod.

"Stakeout or undercover?"

"It's up to you."

"Whoo*pee* . . . "

* * *

On my way east along 110th Street just short of Amsterdam a bum stops me with an outstretched hand and asks, as I'm reaching for a quarter, if I can spare him a handful of twenties. I look at him.

"It never hurts to ask," he says. I shake my head, and hand over the quarter, which seems to satisfy him, despite his request for several hundred dollars more. The unfinished Cathedral of Saint John the Divine towers big and black over 110th Street. This is the second construction site that I have seen today, but there is quite a difference. Kids from the neighborhood with no futures have grown into men working in the shadows of the Cathedral in the apprentice stonemason program. From switchblades to chisels. From robbing liquor stores to turning blocks of Indiana marble into tapering Gothic columns. That's cutting in the right direction.

The window to the workshop is opaque with limestone dust. They're not going to let just anyone in here. I knock and show my badge. A man who looks like he might be the Reverend himself opens a door and asks me how he can be of service to me. I tell him I'd like to see Leon, if he's available.

"He's available," I am told, and the Reverend lets me in.

I stand there looking at the ten apprentices, all pounding away in their masons' aprons. Every one except the master craftsman is Black, *latino,* or that mixture of both.

"Uh, which one is Leon?" I ask politely of the Reverend, who looks at me with a hint of surprise before saying, "He's over there, working on the ashlar."

Call me stupid if you wish, but if I ever knew what an ashlar was, I forgot it along with the rest of the lies we were taught back in that dirt-floor public school in the Andes, where some of the Quichua-speaking students had to be taught Spanish first before they could be taught anything else. I thank the Reverend, and worm my way between massive slabs of uncut marble to the man who the Reverend pointed out. He looks up as I approach, and straightens up from his hunched-over position. He stands head and shoulders above me, which isn't all that much of an accomplishment, and although he is not big enough to tote a barge all by himself, he looks like he could easily be one of the middleweight champ's sparring partners.

"How soon are you going to be finished so you can start work on *my* cathedral?" I ask him.

He smiles and tells me, "Oh, we should be ready by about 2084."

A man with a sense of humor. This could make the going a lot easier.

"My name's Filomena," I say, holding out my hand, open.

"That's a nice name, Filomena. Mine's Leon." He grips me with a hand that could rip the top off a keg of beer, if applied. "So what you want with me?" he says, without malice.

"Can we talk somewhere where it's quieter?"

He swings his hand up to look at his watch. That swing alone could knock someone my size to the floor.

"Give me ten more minutes and we can talk all you want."

I tell him that's fine with me. I go over and lean against a randomly grooved battered wooden table on which is lying a nine-foot-long John the Baptist who is trying to crawl out of the solid block of limestone that still imprisons the lower half of his unformed body, and watch Leon work. Leon is one of those big guys who can control his movements as delicately as any prima ballerina. I watch him using a four-pound hammer to tickle the coarse grain of the limestone into coming through with the velvety, veiny texture of entwined vineleaves. It's amazing to see this big man concentrate on such detail, channeling all of his energy into the fine tip of his carving tool. It's like watching someone parallel park an icebreaking tanker in a mid-town parking space. He moves swiftly, yet carefully. I guess he has to. When you're working in stone, and you make a mistake, you don't just pick up an eraser and rub.

Some of the other apprentices are working with wooden mallets. Two of them are RI-I-I-I-ing through a block of limestone that looks like it weighs five or six tons, with what must be diamond-toothed saws, while a third keeps the blades cool by pouring on water—TSSSsssss! The WHOMP!-ing, chink-chink-chink-ing, PTANG!-ing and RI-I-I-I-ing goes on around me until 6:00, when a crew of tired but creative, involved men arch their backs and start to neatly stack their tools.

Leon comes up to me, brushing the white dust off himself vigorously.

"Where you wanna talk?" he asks.

"Somewhere cheap," I answer.

He laughs.

We walk up a few blocks towards Columbia University. Today has been one of those hot, muggy days where even the pollution doesn't feel like moving, it just hangs heavily and listlessly in the air.

"Not going to be able to watch the stars tonight through this haze," says Leon.

"Are you kidding? If it's like this tomorrow, too, you're not going to be able to see the *sun.*"

"Try it under a leather mason's apron sometime," he says.

We sit down in one of those cozy places near Columbia U. where the tables are solid blocks of wood with an inch of glossy varnish on them, and there are enough hanging plants to open a nursery. Leon is in the process of ordering two beers when I hold up my hand and interrupt.

"I'll have chamomile tea, please." This place should have it, right?

Leon orders a beer for himself and looks at me, nodding his head. "Uh-huh," he says.

"It's a cure," I explain.

"I dig, I dig. Mind if I have a beer?"

"Why should I mind?"

"You'd be surprised. There are people in this world who refuse to understand that nothing but a tall cold one cuts through seven hours of limestone dust on a hot day."

"I understand."

His beer comes first. He drains it in slightly more than three seconds and asks to be brought another one. The other one comes with my tea.

I look down into my tea. Yellow flowers are floating around in it.

"We used to drink this all the time when I was a kid in the Andean provinces. We still do. Nobody trusted doctors. Probably because none of them were trustworthy. Nervous? Boil up some *ruda.* Gallstones? Have some *agua de sabila.* Upset stomach—*manzanilla,*" I say, pointing to the swirling yellow flowers.

"The Andes, huh? What stretch you from?"

"Southern Ecuador."

"And what brings y'all here?"

"You really want to know? 'Cause I get asked that an awful lot. You want the Regular Joe's Answer, or the Real Answer?"

"I asked, didn't I?"

I take a sip of the chamomile. It's still too hot to drink.

"I came to the U.S. when it was still relatively easy for a *latina* to do it. You ever hear of the 'Tuna Fish War'?"

"No. Should I have?"

"About thirteen years ago the Ecuadoran navy got tired of having their petitions ignored by the U.S. government, and they captured twelve American tuna fishing boats in our territorial waters. Washington responded by suspending all sales of military material. O.A.S. voted with us, but when has the U.S. ever given a damn about what the O.A.S. says? We had a military coup pretty soon after that, and I had the singular thrill of getting my education during the military's seven-year reign. Ever hear about any of this?"

"Tuna fish war with Ecuador? No, never."

"Nobody here ever has. When my Mom died there wasn't anything left for me back home and I decided to try coming here."

"A Spanish girl with only one relative?—Give me a break—"

"Look, you want to talk about my father who still hasn't accepted the idea of the twentieth century? Who still thinks that a good whipping is all the education a girl needs? Or the police who shot and killed my brother during a C.I.A.-sponsored military coup? I was only four years old. I hardly remember him at all. What I do remember is how I got the news. 'Your brother has died.' That's what the goddamned fascist asshole said. Not 'We blew six holes in his chest with U.S.-made rifles.' No. 'Your brother has died.' Like he died of lung cancer or something . . . I might as well tell you I'm a cop."

"I kind of figured that out half an hour ago, sister. You still ain't told me what it is you want from me."

"*Some* people I can threaten. Others I can buy, if they're cheap enough. I'm not here in my official capacity. I'm here on my own. Why should you tell me your story if I don't tell you mine?"

"All right," says Leon, nodding with his whole body. "What you want to know?"

"What are you doing up here? Why'd you move out of the East Village?"

Leon sips down about half of his beer, wipes his mouth on a paper napkin.

"You know the scene?" he asks. I say yes. "How many Black Punks you see down there? Not too many, huh? Never mind the Rastas and the Born-Again Muslims, how many Black *Punks* you see? About none, right? That's cause it's pretty much a white thing. Here. Now I hear over in England it started much more working class, and cut pretty good across color lines—they got Pakistani Punks, for Chrissakes—but here it's mostly white, middle-class kids who are rejecting the comforts they've already got, that most poor folk waste their whole lives trying to get. So right from the start I felt like it wasn't for me. I was also getting tired of the forced standard of poverty. I'd room with people who when it came time to split up the rent they'd tell me, 'Man, like how can you be such a money-grubbing capitalist?' What the fuck—? You know, you want a roof over your head, you gotta split the rent, dig? All these kids came from money. They was just playing at being poor. I also got tired of the Punks upstairs always coming in at about five o'clock in the morning from the clubs and blasting hardcore headbanging music through the floor.

"But I had this one art teacher—she ran the intaglio studio—she taught me some things. One of them she said was, 'Never be afraid to look at things from a different angle.' Well I'd heard about the apprentice stonemason program, so I decided to give it a shot. And I love it. This ain't no SlapDash Gallery buy-it-now before it goes out of style shit, honey. This thing's going to be here fifteen hundred, two thousand years."

"It's not exactly an indigenous Afro-American form of expression either—cathedral building," I say.

"It is now," he says.

I have nothing to say to that.

"Listen, the only work that makes it from one generation to the next—that is truly timeless—is work that is unconventional in its time. Right now being something 'conventional' is the most unconventional thing I can be."

I nod. He goes on:

"I mean, six or seven years ago Punk was so unconventional the British government was scared of it. But now you go down to the S.I.N. Club and it's, 'Hey, man, where's your Mohawk?' Like nobody's allowed in without a Mohawk. That's as bad as the 'Jackets Only' dress code at the Russian Tea Room. Just a different emblem is all. But you take this project here: Julio, the guy you saw cutting blocks? Three years ago he was a six-time juvenile offender, looking forward to life as an adult offender, or maybe—just maybe—if he got his act together, trying to provide for a family on the $3.25 an hour they dish out at McDonald's. Boss says pretty soon he'll be able to move up to artistic cutting, like I'm doing. That boy's an artist. A craftsman. He got a *reason* now. A purpose. He cutting with the grain, now—you hear what I'm sayin'? Working with people like that is bigger than any exhibit at some downtown gallery."

This is beyond my wildest expectations.

"Then you'll appreciate why I'm here," I say.

"I'm listening."

Two-heartbeat pause.

"Somebody was killing Wilson. The circumstances of his death could have been an accident, but I doubt it. In any case, there's evidence that someone was slowly poisoning him. It's possible that he realized it too late and tried to retaliate by sabotaging an insecticide factory."

"Now wait a—"

"I never met Wilson but once, and he was unconscious at the time. This is just my opinion, but it's also possible that someone wanted him dead so bad they didn't mind nearly taking eleven other people along just to get him. As it is, they got one guy for having had the bad luck to be standing too close by. That points to some real up-and-coming pigs who care about as much about who they step on on their way to the top as Ivan the Terrible.

"There's no money in this for me. In fact, it's getting me in trouble with my superiors. They just want me out there ticketing illegally-parked cars at $40 a pop so the precinct can buy a new set of baseball jerseys. But somebody killed a man. That ought to be enough in itself. And something tells me that whoever did it isn't likely to hesitate to do it again and again and again if they think it's in their interests to do so."

"I still don't know what I can do for you."

I lift up my cup and have my second sip. The tea is now cold. And it always tastes more bitter when it's cold.

"Do you have any idea what Wilson was into that somebody would have wanted him dead over?"

Leon waits. The last ounce of beer left in the bottom of his glass is stale and flat. Dried foam is clinging to the sides.

"We used to spend a lot of time sitting up nights," says Leon, "sharing our pain—you know, how tough it is to be an artist, where are all the decent women at, shit like that . . . "

"I'm not after mysteries, I'm trying to solve one. I'll get to the point: Did he ever talk about being poisoned, or the earth being polluted, or something like that?"

"Did he ever? Once he got started, you couldn't shut him up. Instead of saying 'Goodbye,' he'd say, 'See you tomorrow—if there's still any air left to breathe.' "

"That Wilson was obsessed with the subject of environmental pollution is plain. But did he ever mention any specific names in connection with all this? Anything?"

"He used to complain all the time about his job. How the contractors were such cheap mofos, cutting corners on worker safety to boost their profits, as if they weren't making enough profit already. I mean, aside from that Columbia Presbyterian job, they've got about eight contracts in Queens, four in Brooklyn, two in the Bronx, and about five more in Manhattan. He once told me, 'Stab someone and they put you away for twenty to life. Slowly poison a world and that makes you a millionaire. *Then* you can start stabbing people, cause when you've got that much bread, you can buy the rest: You can buy the law, you can buy whole governments if they're cheap enough.' "

"Now we're getting somewhere. Did he ever mention any threats?"

"You mean *specific* threats? No. Not to me, anyway."

"Who else knew about all this?"

"Only his friends."

Some friends. I ask him about Wiegand and he says, "Sure, he hung around. Knew all about Wilson's feelings."

Well, well . . . "Where else did he work for this contractor?"

"It's hard to say. A lot of contractors circumvent the laws by dissolving their subsidiaries and reappearing with a new name and address. Hell, all you gotta do is print up some new letterheads, and that don't eat all that much out of a billion-dollar budget."

Where has my brain been? Why haven't I checked to see if the Columbia Presbyterian contractor was a subsidiary of the big, bad, Morse Incorporated? I've been chasing after individuals instead of corporations. I've been thinking like a beat cop instead of a detective.

"This thing has smelled of corporate control since the beginning," I say. "But I've been too dumb to go after it."

"No you haven't, sister. I bet you knew of the possibility the whole time. I'll tell you what kept it on the back burner all this time: Fear. You do not just go up against a syndicate on your own. I don't give a damn what they say in the movies, it don't cut no ice on the street. They'll use you for bait on their private yacht, sugar. And you know it. There's no shame in wanting to stay alive. I do it all the time myself. 'Course I knew Wilson had something on the contractor. But it's too big for me. And it's too big for you, too."

"Maybe with your help—"

"Maybe with my help what?"

"Easy, Leon. You're a nice guy. I could get to like you—" The waitress flits by to check our orders, and her ears open when she learns this. I glare at her until she goes away. I go on in a lower voice: "—But your artist's imagination is a little over-active. I'm not talking about putting on long coats, ramming two shotguns each down inside our pants along with five hundred rounds of ammunition and riding into their offices for a showdown. I've got all the holes in my body that I need, thank you. But I do know a little bit about the legal system. If we can just get some substantial evidence of major wrongdoing, we can institute a federal investigation. And I don't care how big you are—you can't knock off twelve federal investigators without attracting just a bit of attention."

"You want it, you got it. But leave me out." He starts to stand up. "I'm a family man."

I follow him over to the cashier.

"Recently?" I ask, while Leon pays. He nods.

"Congratulations."

"You better believe it. That kid's amazing. Just turned two, and learns something new every day. Anytime you say a kid can't do something they make a liar out of you real quick."

We step out into the night and head for the uptown subway.

"Watching him grow. I'm not giving that up for anybody," says Leon. I can't argue with that.

We go down into the subway.

"Can I at least call you once in a while—or are you afraid to give me your phone number?"

"You really gonna go after it?"

"Yeah."

He gives me his home number, begging me not to call him there unless it's a case of absolute 911 emergency, and the number to call to reach him at the Cathedral. He says the Reverend should answer.

"I hope I won't be needing the Reverend," I say.

"It's a good number to have," says Leon.

The further possibility of conversation is temporarily halted by the incoming roar of the subway. It's rush hour, and even at rush hour, trains north are rare. This one has over two thousand people pushed against the windows of five short cars. Leon curses mildly. The doors open.

"How do you fit on a train like this?" he asks me.

"I make myself smaller," I explain, and demonstrate by squeezing into a hitherto unoccupied volume of space whose boundaries are defined by a pregnant woman's swelling abdomen, a Yeshiva student's bobbing elbow, and the sports page of somebody's *New York Post*.

"Yeah? I make myself *bigger*," says Leon, and he plows into the car with the same force as that of the Pacific plate undercutting the Continental shelf along the San Andreas fault. But he's on the train. The door shuts behind him, and this is the way we ride up north.

* * *

It's late when I get the call.

"You're not going to believe this," says Betty. "Three hours of watching every suit in the Village waltz in and out of that high-rent clip joint before the owner comes out, heads for her car, and guess who runs up to talk to her before she gets in?"

"Wiegand?"

"Leather studs and all. You'd think the schmuck would figure out how easy it is to spot him when he's dressed like that. What do you think it means?"

"It means they know each other."

"Well, duh—"

"I'm serious, Betty. It could mean a lot. What did they talk about?"

"I was too far away. So anyway, I tailed him."

"You didn't."

"I did."

"Get anything?"

"Yeah, I got bored watching this dirtbag bum drinks from his friends all evening and listening to his roaring bullshit act. What a jerk! Then, when he ran out of prospects, he walked over to First Avenue and withdrew $200 bucks from a cash machine so he could hit some new bars a few blocks away, where he paid for his own drinks. Nice guy, huh?"

"I won't even tell you over the phone what I'd like to do with him."

"That gallery woman's a cute one, too. I watched her park her car in an illegal spot, then she took the parking ticket off someone else's car and put it on hers so she wouldn't get ticketed. She threw it in the street when she drove away."

"You should've busted her for littering."

"Meanwhile the other guy's fine will triple when he doesn't send in a plea on time."

"What bank did he use?"

"What? Oh—it was a NYCE machine, Fil, could be any one of half a dozen banks."

"So? He's got an account. Get his record."

She starts to complain.

"Do it officially, Officer Nichols. We're onto something."

For a change.

* * *

I start off the day by getting yelled at.

"What the hell was that?" says Federal Agent Ryan, red-faced and blasting like a foghorn.

"They were going to stick the guy."

"You abandoned your post. One of our operatives in the area says that turd you work with was shooting his mouth off to everyone who came in about how he saw you intervene and break up an attempted mugging." Those *can't* be Mateo's own words.

"It wasn't a mugging, it was a racially motivated assault."

"Never mind that, you almost blew your cover to respond to what could have been a diversion away from the drop-off."

"Oh, come on—"

"Do you *know* for a fact that it wasn't . . . ?"

What am I supposed to say to that? What cop ever knows anything for a fact? It's all just a feeling you have.

"How soon do you want me to hand over The Plumber?"

Now the agents look at me as if I've just offered them a terrific trade-in on their stone axes towards a brand-new controlled-nuclear-explosion-powered laser anti-satellite weapon. Then cynicism steps in and tells them it must be a bluff.

"How soon can you deliver him?" asks Matthews.

"Come by this afternoon at three," I say, and I turn and walk out of there.

Then, for a change of pace, I decide to get yelled at. I'm on the job, slicing the ham, for fifteen minutes—Rafico having gone on another of his frequent and mysterious missions—when who walks into the deli, raging mad, but Detective Snyder.

"Well, Miss Buscarsela," he fumes. "Can I speak to you for a minute, in private?"

"There's an alley out back," I tell him.

Snyder pushes past Mateo and walks into the storage area.

"Who are you, her parole officer?" asks Mateo, but Snyder is already standing out in the alley waiting for me.

I leave half a slice of ham dangling in the machine and walk through the storage area to the alley.

"Why didn't you tell me you were a cop, for shit's sake?" says Snyder.

"Paradoxically, I thought we would cooperate easier if you didn't know I was a cop."

"Why the hell not?"

"You know how it is, Detective: If a policewoman tries to help out, she's a pushy bitch trying to take over your job, and if she wants to work closely with someone, that means she wants to fuck her way to the top. Frankly, I thought I could get more cooperation as a citizen than as a fellow cop."

"I get what you mean. But you realize what it cost me? I go in to my Lieutenant, who's screaming for a report, but I got it covered, this fabulous contact—McCullough's ex-girlfriend, to be exact— has put me on to these tapes he made. Well, the Lieutenant loves the tapes, but then he asks me about this girlfriend, and I start telling him all about her, and the Lieutenant starts laughing in my face. He tells me that's not any ex-girlfriend, that's a lady cop who's so addicted to solving this case single-handedly that her Lieutenant had to have her transferred out of precinct work just to cool her jets, but it looks like she's fooled the two of you."

"Sorry about that. This isn't going to make matters any easier with my Lieutenant, either, if that means anything to you."

"Why should it? You screw yourself up, that's your problem. You screw *me* up, you gotta make it up to me."

"How?"

"You could start by telling me everything you've done since last Friday."

I tell him. I tell him everything: The gallery, The Amy Anxiety

Show, Wiegand, my nine hours in Sidneyland, followed by a "random" drug test and an ultimatum, and all—but I mean *all*—of the pharmaceutical-insecticide-possible building contractor connections. The only thing I leave out is Leon. It sure changes Detective Snyder's attitude.

"Shit, you *have* been doing your homework. It's a crime you don't have your bronze shield yet."

"Find me Pepe Gonzalez and it's mine," I say.

"It sure clicks with the tapes. This Wilson guy is being intentionally obtuse, as if he knew somebody was going to be listening to those tapes some day, trying to solve his murder."

"I bet he made copies. Have you checked safety deposit box records?"

"Yep."

"Private storage?"

"Yep."

"The Tape Vault down on Fourth and B?"

"The what?"

"It's a four-track studio in somebody's basement. A punk band can cut a single there for under $200. And they store all the copies you want on cassette in a fireproof vault."

" . . . Shit . . . " He gets out his notepad and I give him the exact name and address.

"What say we forgive and forget and work on this together?"

He holds out his hand. We shake.

"Great. Now you tell me what you've been doing, Detective."

Now he gets this cagey look that any veteran cop gets who has about one lead only, and isn't too anxious to let anyone else in on it. But he gets over that in a minute,

"Like I said, it clicks," he says. "But there's still a whole bunch of references that I don't get. We'll have to sit around and listen to them things together. How about later tonight?"

"Fine with me."

"I'll see if I can dig up any more tapes by then. What's your next move?"

"Well, I checked out the two contracting firms—the Columbia Presbyterian one and this one across the street here—and *of course* they're twin subsidiaries of Morse."

"That settles it. Lets go in and arrest all twelve thousand employees of Morse, Inc."

I smile. One joke can absorb forty-seven thousand times its weight in excess stress. Snyder and I need to turn to each other, not *on* each other.

"How's about one of us goes for a job interview at the parent company's headquarters?" I suggest.

"And I suppose you've already got the address and telephone number of their personnel department?"

I must admit that I almost giggle as I reach into my back pocket and hand Detective Snyder a slip of paper with just that information scrawled on it, in my handwriting. Snyder looks at it, shaking his head. Then the tension breaks completely. He starts laughing.

"Boy, you are something else, Buscarsela."

"Call me Filomena. What's yours?"

"You don't want to know. But ever since I wracked up the police van two years ago chasing down a perp on the Manhattan Bridge they all call me 'Van' Snyder."

"All right, Van, what do you say?"

"Infiltrate the home office? Hmm, ... I guess without a smoking gun, it's the only thing open to us; without probable cause, I can't do it legally. It'll have to be you. Unofficially, of course."

"Of course."

"I'll never be further than a scream away."

"You better not be."

"Are you up to it?—And I don't mean going through their file cabinets. I mean playing the part of an ambitious young barracuda, because that's the only kind they're going to hire at the head office."

"It'll be tough, but I think I can handle it. Once you've driven over the rim of the Andes in a rattling heap that's threatening to give out at any moment and the nearest replacement fuel pump is in Osaka, Japan, you can pretty much face anything."

He slaps me on the back.

"You're a brave woman," he says.

"A brave *cop* to you, Detective." What I mean is both.

"All right, all right, sue me. Tonight, then?"

"Where?"

"My precinct. Know where it is?"

"Yes, I know where it is."

"Gee, ain't there anything you don't know?"

"Oh yes. Several things."

He gives me a go-on-get-out-of-here hand gesture and walks inside the deli and sidles out onto the street and away. I smile with subdued amusement, but this feeling is immediately dispelled by a Manic Mateo.

"A lady cop, huh?! Jesus, I should have known! When I get out, I'm going to cut your fucking throat, bitch!"

This is the third time I've been nose to nose with a red-faced man in the last forty-five minutes, and I've had enough of it. I get Mateo to back away from me with a sharp up-cutting jab from my knee. While he's recoiling. I grab him, and bang his face against the cutting board—just to get his attention, you understand. A customer comes in and sees us this way.

"He swallowed a fish bone," I explain, as the customer nods understanding and beats a swift exit.

"Listen, you stupid shit," I say when we're alone again, "you're so dumb it'd serve you right to send you up, but lucky for you I'm one cop who happens to think busting street dealers as a way of solving the country's drug problem is a bunch of crap."

"Then why are you holding my arms down?"

"To keep you from hurting yourself. If I was going to bust you, why didn't I do it yesterday?"

"I don't know. Why?"

While he's answering this, I reach down inside his upper pocket and pull out five packets of coke.

"I knew it!—I knew it!" he says, breaking away from me.

I keep a hold on one of his wrists.

"Look, Mateo, what's this? Evidence?—Whoops!"

With that "whoops" I toss the packets into the deep-fryer. Mateo's eyes nearly bounce onto the floor as he watches $500 sizzle up into nothing.

"Gee, I lost the evidence." I go on. "No evidence, no crime. That's how it works, Mateo. You still don't understand? I'm letting you go, schmuck."

"Why?"

"Ah—a breath of intelligent thought from one of your three active brain cells. Because you're going to help me catch a plumber."

"Oh, no—"

"Oh—look what I found!" I open my hand to show Mateo that only four of the five packets I took from him went into the hot oil. I hold it up where he can see it. "I guess I didn't lose all the evidence after all! Now: You help me and this can disappear up your nose for all I care. Chicken out like you're doing now and *you* disappear—for about two to five. It's your decision."

"Some choice."

"I know it sounds corny, but, take it or leave it." Mateo pushes his white paper hat back on his head and leans perilously close to the boiling French-fry fat. He lets out a long breath of air.

"I want you to tell your man you need another ten grams, but Rafico's sick, and you can't leave the store, so he has to bring it to you here at 3:00 on the nose—so to speak."

"Only one thing wrong with that: I'm $500 short."

"I'll get it for you. You game?"

"What choice I got . . . ? What if he won't come?"

"Then tell him you want thirty grams. I don't care. Tell him whatever you have to to get him to come out of the woodwork."

"And what happens to me when they find out I squealed?"

"I don't think you'll be too popular for a while, but when The Plumber starts squealing they'll forget all about you."

"What if he doesn't squeal?"

"If the Feds catch him holding an ounce of coke, he'll squeal on his mother."

"Where are you going?"

"To get your $500. Don't go away," I say, sounding like a gameshow announcer.

I step back behind the freezer and call the Hartley. Eddie answers. My God. Now he has to talk to me.

"I need $500 flash money by noon to bring in The Plumber."

"Whatsamatta," is Eddie's first word to me, ever. "Your magic wand break?"

"You want the guy or not?"

Eddie stuffs the phone against his shirt to muffle it, but not well enough. I can hear him telling his cohorts that "This bitch says she needs five dollars by noon or her fairy godmother turns into a pumpkin." There are some muffled responses, then Eddie gets back on the line:

"Be ready at 11:45 sharp. He better have our five C's on him when we pick him up."

"That's your headache. Tell one of your 'operatives in the area' to shadow him. I've got my hands full with my end of it."

"Yeah. I bet." Eddie hangs up.

I go out to Mateo, who looks as if he has lost ten pounds since I last saw him, all in sweat.

"Okay, Champ," I tell him. "Action."

* * *

It's a quarter to three, and I'm back on the phone asking a receptionist at Morse, Inc., "To whom do I send my resume?"

She answers, "I'm sorry, but that's confidential."

"The name of your personnel officer is confidential?"

"I'm afraid I can't give that information over the phone."

Jesucristo en el cielo, What is this, the fucking State Department? These places kill me.

"So what should I do, just send it to the Personnel Office?"

"That's the best way to go about it, yes." Click.

I'm surprised she told me that much. That must be some fun place to work. The way she sounded you would think that the entire conversation was being tape-recorded and transcribed so that ten security officers could scrutinize it to see if she made any fatal slip-ups, because if she did, the mad doctor is going to chain her to the back of his submarine and take her over to his evil island fortress somewhere where it's tropical enough for the women to be wearing that sexy swimwear that's such good box office. Learn this, and you shall prosper, my son: Ass sells. Yea, and it is written in letters of silver and gold upon the high places that he who learneth that Ass Sells shall prosper and shall not know want. Amen.

All this from twenty seconds on the phone.

I go back out front, draw myself off a cup of warm battery acid, tempered to ingestibility with an equal part of milk, and step out onto the street for a moment to watch the traffic. I've just taken a nice, long sip and am turning my face up to catch some sun, when a well-dressed businessman passes by and drops a quarter in my I ♥ NY cup. He must have thought I was begging. I look down at my cup in mild astonishment, watching the dirty bubbles rise up from the sunken quarter. Forget it. No one would ever believe me, anyway.

I step back behind the counter, and check my watch. Zero hour minus two minutes. Mateo is as nervous as an astronaut who is about to be the first one to try out the new space-walk apparatus that so far has only been tested on monkeys, two hundred miles above the surface of the planet.

"Take it easy, kid," I tell him. "It's in motion. Besides, if he walks in here and sees you shitting bricks like you are now he just might get wise enough to scram before he makes the exchange. And if he splits, all our previous arrangements will go the way of the crossbow, dig?"

I might as well be talking to him in Chinese. I switch into street Spanish: "*Desahuevate chingazo de pendejo o te mando a la mierda.*"

Which might translate roughly as "Get a fucking grip on yourself or I'm kicking your ass from here to the state line."

That gets through. He lets out an expressive Spanglish word that you will have trouble finding in most dictionaries of the Spanish language. Then he straightens up as if someone's just goosed him with a cheese grater.

The door swings open and in comes The Plumber. I am casually slicing salami on the big machine. I have never actually seen The Plumber close up. He's one of those wormy little guys who the word "runt" was invented for. He glances over at me. I'm busy paying more attention to slicing the salami than a diamond cutter with a sixty-carat stone. He and Mateo exchange noncommital greetings. Then:

"How's the fried chicken today?" asks The Plumber.

Mateo wraps up a whole barbecued chicken in tin foil, puts it in a bag and hands it over the counter. I'm using the extra eye that I had put in behind my right ear a few years ago for just such an occasion. When I hear that second crinkle of paper that means The Plumber has taken hold of the bag I jettison the salami out of the slicer and onto the floor—sorry, Mr. Wang—and lunge for The Plumber's other hand—the one *not* holding the bag of chicken. With adrenaline-amplified speed I yank the hand towards me that's holding the cash and something else and stuff it on the tray of the meat slicer and slam the metal-spiked jam in place on top of his hand, holding it there with all my weight. Needless to say, the guy is in pain, and also would like to know what the hell I'm doing.

"I'm going to slice your hand into neat, thin strips if you don't stay right where you are," I tell The Plumber.

The big circular blade of the meat slicer is rotating at top speed, and there's just enough room between the guard and the blade to fulfill my threat. The Plumber knows it, and stands there, his other hand uselessly cradling the bag of whole barbecued chicken.

"How long are we gonna stay like this?" asks The Plumber.

I tell Mateo: "You want to go out and see what's taking them so long?"

Mateo deflects a look from The Plumber that has teeth in it. He has some difficulty opening the big glass door, which, after all, has hinges and a handle, unlike other doors, but eventually he manipulates it open and goes out into the street. He looks both ways and is nearly knocked off his feet by three federal agents who batter down the door looking like they're ready for the charge up San Juan Hill.

They grab The Plumber six different ways. I release his hand from the meat jam, which raises three sets of eyebrows. But the hand opens and ten dollars in small bills fall to the floor, along with the fifteen grams of cocaine they were camouflaging. The eyebrows drop and the Feds are all action. They get the guy cuffed and advised of his rights in under eight seconds. Then they start to lead him out.

"What about me?" I call after the retreating Feds.

"Get back to your precinct," says one, not turning around. "We don't need you anymore."

SIX

"De price of your hat ain't de measure of your brain."

—The Book of Negro Folklore

Mr. Wang was sorry to see me go. But he wished me good luck, and tried to make me take $20 tide-me-over money for making such a noteworthy effort to lead an honest life. I told him that I absolutely could not accept it. He finally said Okay, but that I had to come back when I got a better job and let him know that I am doing all right. He said there was a free sandwich in it for me. I told him I would come back to collect as soon as I got that better job. He's still waiting.

* * *

Betty chased down Wiegand's bank account for me. It was with Citibank, which I found somewhat ironic.

"Between January and April Wiegand got $15,000 in four separate cash installments."

"Cash?" I ask.

"Yeah. They're untraceable."

"I don't know, we could ask Wiegand where they came from."

Stunned silence.

"It's beginning to look like Wiegand sold Wilson to Morse," I explain. "He knew that Wilson was planning to expose some aspect of their illegal operations in a major public installation, so he told them exactly when and where to find him."

"Scumbag."

"Or else Schnelling put him up to it to get his paintings, and the 15K was just his cut."

It's also beginning to look like Wilson could have sabotaged Lilliflex for some pre-show publicity, then ran into the food stamp center when the vents refused to cooperate. Or maybe Lilliflex set up the whole sabotage angle on its own in order to be able to deflect the blame when the real shit hit. Or maybe they were just trying to get Wilson?

"Call up Detective Snyder. Ask him if he thinks suspicion of accessory to murder is sufficient grounds to put a man on Wiegand."

"Sounds like the right move. Of course, if I bounce it to Snyder's precinct, I'm officially out of it. Not that I was ever officially in it."

"I understand. Thanks, Betty, you've been a big help."

"Just remember that the next time I ask you to get out of bed on a cold, rainy night to come downtown and help bail me out."

"It's a date, sister."

* * *

It's a couple of weeks later and it's getting hot. I mean that TSsssssssss!-fry-an-egg-on-the-sidewalk New York in summer hot. I'm sitting at Detective Snyder's desk in an office that has been air-conditioned by the time-honored and efficient process of opening a window. At least he doesn't have to worry about brown-outs. Of course nothing substantial could be found against Wiegand or Schnelling, so Snyder had to drop all further investigation of where a loser like Wiegand got $15,000 in cash. Whoever did it covered their tracks well. People don't leave notes lying around saying, "Received: $15,000 blood money."

Snyder only turned up one new tape after going though a vault filled with over 5,000 Punk tapes and he hasn't quite gotten over the experience yet.

We've just gone over the tapes for the 80 millionth time, and it's getting us nowhere. I've proved myself useful by filling in several gaps in the logic of the tapes—particularly where the East Village Punk scene is concerned—but there are a whole lot of obscurities that are stubbornly staying obscure. There's one passage I make Detective "Van" Snyder play over and over:

"February 17: They're having poison for breakfast in Zone Three, but they get us back for it. They send it right back to us. It's in my morning coffee. And it serves us right . . . "

"I don't know why you bother, Fil, this one sounds just like the last one."

"There *is* a difference. He keeps mentioning coffee. It's the one constant in a sea of free association. And 'Zone Three' has got to mean something. It was handwritten on that barrel."

"You call that evidence? McCullough could have written that himself for that art project."

"Hmm. Still he's so sparing with concretisms that when he uses them, they must be significant."

"So you say," says Snyder, snapping off the cassette player.

We sit there and stare at each other for several minutes without saying anything. A hot breeze is blowing in off the asphalt basketball court outside where a group of big city kids are working off some frustration. Finally Snyder opens this morning's paper and starts flipping through it absentmindedly.

"Yanks dropped two," he says.

I stare out the window at the firm Black bodies jumping and coordinating plays that some big-league coach will make famous in a season or two.

"Will you look at this?" says Snyder. "NBC is spending two million dollars on a TV remake of 'The Greatest Story Ever Told.' "

"There are worse crimes," I tell him.

"Whoa!—They got Laurence Olivier to play Pontius Pilate. That should be awesome."

"I don't know—the greatest actors on earth can't make a turkey fly. Sounds like two million *lost* dollars to me."

"Ah, they'll make their money all right . . .—Now why do you suppose they always have British actors playing the Romans?"

"That's easy: Rome influenced the course of history for a half-dozen centuries, then fell with a crack heard round the known world. Just this century England's four-hundred-year empire has gagged and died. They still haven't gotten over it. Making Brits always play the Romans is our way of saying, '*Your* empire fell, suckers, so *you* have to play the Romans, and *we* get to play the Christians! Nyaah, nyaah, nyaah.' "

Detective Snyder laughs at my impression of a TV executive. A vulture-eyed Detective Sergeant passing by with an armful of case reports gives the two of us a sharp look.

"I'm tellin' yer wife about all this overtime with the pretty young policewoman who ain't even from this precinct, Van," says the Detective Sergeant.

"That's not funny," says Detective Snyder. He has to say that. You can't tell a superior to fuck off. I try to distract Snyder away from such foul thoughts.

"Reagan is always going on about how Rome fell because they were all decadent pagans who didn't believe in God. Somebody ought to get that guy a ninth-grade history book and show him the part where it says that the Rome that fell in the 5th century A.D. had been Christian for a hundred years."

"Then why did it fall if you're so smart?"

"Snyder, you can't conquer and enslave the peoples of one-and-a-half continents forever. Eventually it's got to give."

"I wonder what it would have been like to be a legionnaire," ponders Snyder.

"Probably a lot like being a cop: A pretty easy job, between barbarian invasions."

Snyder laughs. That fixes his head a bit. But his laugh turns sour, and he puts his hand to his mouth.

"What's wrong?" I ask.

"Ah, I went to the dentist yesterday with a toothache. Damn crook took out the tooth and left the ache."

"Hey, we ought to go on TV with all this great material we got between us."

"I'm tellin' yer wife—" The Detective Sergeant lobs this one over the partition into Snyder's lap. Snyder looks like he's counting to ten before continuing.

"Just once I'd like to see him have to work with a female partner—I'll fucking mail doctored 8 x 10's to *his* wife." Then he raises his voice to shout over the partition, "Don't criticize anyone until you've walked a mile in his shoes, Sergeant." He looks at me. "It's an American Indian saying. I forget which tribe," he says, apologizing as if he were insulting my ancestry. Actually, most Ecuadorians have some Indian blood in them. We didn't get pioneer families looking for a better life for themselves down in South America. No, we got the unwanted dregs of a collapsing society, who came and populated their newly formed bureaucratic, oligarchal dictatorships with the bastard children of the Indian women they raped. But that's another story . . .

"Jean-Luc says that judges should be required to spend at least one night in jail before becoming judges and being allowed to sentence people—just to feel what it's like," I say.

"Sounds good to me. Who's Jean-Luc? Your boyfriend?"

I raise my eyebrows high and give Detective Snyder a desperate, hopeful look.

"Never mind," he says. "Off limits."

"It's not that," I explain. "I don't even know myself. Between the two of us we speak Spanish, French and English—which makes *three* languages that we don't communicate in."

Snyder rustles the newspaper violently to accentuate his desire to shift away from taboo personal topics.

"What time's the interview?" he says.

"Two o'clock."

"You better go change into your Power Suit."

"I've got time. Today's my day off."

"Some day off . . . I sure wish they'd assign you with me officially, if only to shut up the office snoops."

"It's been hell going back to the beat, let me tell you—"

"Don't you think you'd better go get ready?"

All right, Snyder, I get the idea. My presence is damaging to your reputation as a loyal, married man. You can't escape it. And some of the strongest objections to the idea of recruiting women for regular duty came from the officers' wives. I hate it.

"Okay, Detective Snyder. I'll call you with the results of the investigation."

We shake hands, then he blurts out, "Check this out: 'Electrical equipment in the White House was found today to be leaking a coolant that contained polychlorinated biphenyls, or PCBs, which are known to produce cancer-causing chemicals when burned.' "

"Serves him right," I say, and my eyebrows collide with one another. Seems I've been listening to Wilson's tapes so much that I'm starting to use his expressions.

* * *

My interview with Morse, Inc. is at their midtown location, in a neighborhood where everyone walks around looking like they're in a detective movie. All the suits, ties, attaché cases and dark glasses make me think I'm in one of those *Twilight Zones* where everyone turns into automatons except for one person. Then I catch a glimpse of myself in a plate glass window and get the same shock the heroine of the TV nightmare gets: I've become one of them.

You wouldn't recognize me if you saw me. Gone are the leather jacket and black jeans, and all the tough-gal tableau-ing that goes hand in hand with them. The gal I see reflected in that sun-drenched mid-town window that stretches from the sidewalk up to the seventy-fifth floor is a young career woman, whose hair is styled according to this week's fashion section, her face is made up to appear at its optimum best under office light, and her salmon-and-white business suit accurately reflects her hunger for power. She also has a phony resume a mile long.

A woman walks out of the building dressed in an outfit that looks as if it cost her as much as the entire GNP of Ecuador—and she *spits* like a big-league coach on the sidewalk in front of me. The building must have left a bad taste in her mouth, too.

I take a good look at myself in the window: five-foot-seven-inches, one hundred and twenty-five pounds, and an Incan nose that someone once told me might get me work doing poster ads in the subway—if I got it narrowed (it's not really wide, just a bit blunt)—but only if I also bleached my hair, straightened my teeth, and lightened my skin by two shades. Then, maybe, I'd get work as a model, they said. Too ethnic, they said. Maybe I'd get work, but I wouldn't be *me*. I like being the person I grew up with. I like my impossible, frizzy hair, my thick, Iberian eyebrows and olive-tan skin (we call it *canela*). My lips full enough for a French guy to go for, which I got from my Indian grandmother, although they're not as thick as hers. Maybe my face is a bit gaunt now from overwork and undernourishment—all right, too much partying—but I wouldn't change a thing. Blue-eyed blondes have been told all their lives how gorgeous they are. Us dark-eyed, dark-souled *latinas* have to work so much harder to get there in this society, but it's worth it.

You know, this dress really shows off my figure. Too bad I could never wear it to work. Damn those blue work shirts.

Now I've got butterflies in my stomach. Don't I get enough brushes with terminal ulcers during work hours? Why am I putting myself through more? Why am I doing this? I better get moving before I try to answer that,

I step inside the building, which is easy enough. Then the fun begins. There's more security in this building than at the El-Al terminal at JFK. An (armed!) guard guides me into a maze of glass partitions that leads, after several twists and turns, to a reception desk that looks as though it could hold out for six months under siege.

"You had an appointment with—?" asks the gatekeeper.

"Mr. DeCharmant." I pronounce it "De Shar-mon," more or less, the way Jean-Luc taught me.

The gatekeeper corrects me, pronouncing his name with a hard "Ch," to rhyme with "Charred plant," with plenty of home-grown American nasal on the second "A." Nothing French about it. Then she keys his name into a computer and waits for the data to come up. After a few seconds my name appears reflected backwards and distended on her glasses in cathode-ray green glowing letters, and the hunchback starts lowering the drawbridge and raising the portico with a heavy iron chain. I turn to go.

"Wait," she says. The guard nearly goes for his weapon. She punches a few keys and somewhere behind the blast-resistant desk a machine starts printing something out in that high-pitched dot-matrix whine. Then she tears something along its perforations and hands an adhesive-backed nametag down to me. Dutifully I put it over my heart, and start to leave.

"You must surrender that pass upon departure from the building," says she.

Jesus, why not just set up the electrified barbed-wire fences and guard towers with searchlights already! Why wait? The nametag has my name on it, of course, *plus* the name of the person I'm supposed to see, and what floor he's on, followed by a space for my company affiliation and the date. It's clear that if I'm caught on any other floor there's going to be trouble. Sheesh!

A button is pushed somewhere and glass doors slide open noiselessly. I go through them before they get a chance to slice me in half on the rebound, and step into an area where a battery of elevators is being overseen by another guard—this one dressed a little less like a commando and a little more like a waiter. All the same, he stops me from entering just any old elevator.

"Who are you going to see?" he asks me.

"Mr. DeCharmant in Personnel," I answer like a shaved-headed conscript responding to his drill instructor's questions about what the four quickest ways to break a man's neck are.

He double-checks what I've just told him with the information on my tag, and directs me to the appropriate elevator, pressing the button for me, as if letting me see the secret of how the floor buttons operate would be revealing classified information potentially harmful to our national security.

A yellow "48" lights up on the board, and the doors SSSssss! closed with the same sound Amazonian snakes make while constricting around a suckling pig. I'm not just trying to be clever when I say that the elevator makes the trip in seven seconds, and I have to wait until my stomach stops fluttering before I step out of the elevator onto the plush scarlet carpet of the forty-eighth floor of the Morse Building.

Imagine my surprise when I encounter another steel-and-glass-enclosed check point with a metal door separating me from the office area that's thick enough to keep a crew of three acetylene torch operators busy for half an hour trying to cut through it. Once there I have to go through the routine all over again: Who do I want to see? Let me verify that—Yes, yes . . . So much for the idea of infiltrating this place undetected. Next time I'll stick to the soft jobs, like knocking off the Bank of England.

After I've been stamped, sealed, tattooed and fluoroscoped they let me inside, where I am told to wait. It's 2:00 on the dot.

At 2:23 (on the dot) I am shown into Mr. DeCharmant's office. He is anything but *charmant*. Maybe we can institute proceedings to have his name revoked.

The bearer of this misleading moniker is one of those overbearing people who thinks a suit and a job title give him semi-divine powers: The very tides shall recede at his command if he just orders it loudly enough. He's wearing a three-piece battleship-gray suit that's only missing the yellow call numbers to complete the resemblance to the prow of a dreadnought, and he's talking on the phone with his broker when I come in and sit down without being asked to.

I can see halfway to the Delaware Water Gap out the window behind him. Mr. DeCharmant is evidently a man who is used to getting his way, although he only appears capable of accomplishing this by the tried-and-true method of not letting his opponent get a word in. I've met this kind before: They're called "bosses."

I sit there for several more minutes, while DeCharmant castigates his broker. It is clear that Mr. DeCharmant has so much of his money tied up in stocks that I can't resist hoping for the market to crash and wipe this sleazebag out. Sorry, Wall Street. This is strictly a personal vendetta.

I use this time to have a look around his office. His specialty would appear to be real estate, judging from the framed photos of various New York scenes comparing the views of fifty to a hundred years ago with the same views as they look today.

I have to say it is one of the most depressing things I've ever seen in my life. It certainly has the reverse effect on me, rather than the desired one: Quaint, tree-lined streets with livable, four-storey brownstones turn out to be Lexington and 48th Street, looking downtown. This is juxtaposed with today's view of a narrow-walled canyon of featureless monoliths trailing off into infinity; something that looks like a Victorian manor surrounded by a snowy landscape is identified as Central Park West in 1895. And look at it now. The Gulf and Western Building rises up, defying all human proportions, dwarfing poor Cristobal Columbus, who in a previous photo dominated the skyline. Now he looks like a lamppost. The juxtaposition only serves to heighten the frightful contrast between a city built for people and a city built for megalithic corporate office towers such as the one I am now imprisoned in.

I just can't be at ease forty-eight floors above the sidewalk. Sometimes I wish I could forget my old physics lessons: I feel forty-eight floors of potential energy tugging at my innards, just itching to be turned into kinetic energy; forty-eight floors of energy telling me, "You've got to come down sometime, honey, and when you do, we'll be waiting!" Silly, isn't it?

My imaginings are cut short when Mr. DeCharmant slams down the phone and says, "Now!" looking up at me like a bored Roman Emperor who has just watched fourteen Christians get gobbled up by lions, and is wondering what could be done differently with *this* one.

"Miss Bus-car-sel-a," he says, struggling with the effort to read a word that's longer than the Amex abbreviations. I'm amazed they're even considering me. Usually resumes with names of more than two syllables go right into the garbage.

"Tell me what you did for the Housing Authority."

"Well, um," I begin brilliantly, clearing my throat, "I started there as a trainee in building inspection, where my duties included revision and evaluation of blueprints, stress and structural analysis, negotiation of air rights and landmark status, which also involved bringing landmark buildings up to current fire code standards without compromising the integrity of the original architecture, then after a year I was promoted to assistant inspector, which made me accountable for worker and pedestrian safety, which I particularly enjoy, because I feel I'm helping save people's lives that way—last year alone there were seventy-three construction-related fatalities that could have been avoided with proper—"

I go on like this for a while, putting Detective Snyder's coaching into practice. Snyder helped me create the resume, and for each reference on there, there is a collaborator in the Detective Bureau ready to answer the phone and swear to my outstanding service record in some fictitious function. Mr. DeCharmant stops me shortly. He obviously isn't accustomed to allowing people in his presence to speak for more than twenty-five seconds.

"No," he says. "I mean, tell me what you *did* there."

I look at him. Isn't that what I have been doing? Are we speaking the same language?

"What's the matter? Are you afraid of telling me?" he says.

"I'm not sure I know what it is that you want me to tell you."

"Listen: We hire all our own safety inspectors, and right now there are no openings in that area. What I'd like you to do is go take a typing test. Okay?"

I tell him sure, if that's the way they work things around here.

"Why shouldn't that be the way we work things around here?" he says, giving me a look that says my application is going straight into the shredder as soon as I'm out the door.

He punches a button and calls in a lackey. The lackey enters, a sweet-looking young woman straight out of college, with dimples that you could comfortably sleep three in, who was probably being grilled on this very hot seat less than a month ago. Oh boy, my first "real" job. So who cares if the boss is a lizard? I had to work for an octopus once . . .

"Give Miss Buscarsela a typing test and a job application form," orders DeCharmant.

"Yes sir," she says, and I get up and follow her out past rows of desks at which distracted, underpaid women are moving green numbers around on IBM screens. The few men working there look up at me as if they've never seen a woman before. Behind the glass partitions, they look like caged animals. I smile and nod back at them. They may be my only ticket inside this place.

My Judas Goat leads me into an out-of-the-way cubicle with four shiny electric typewriters on long tables, and sits me down. The walls are covered with propaganda about the virtues of selling your soul to Morse, Inc., preferably at a speed of 60 words per minute.

Welcome to the power structure. I've made it this far, I might as well go through with it. Other cops get to spend their day off washing the family car and drinking beer along with a ball game. What the hell am I doing here?

The young woman sets up a page of printed text on a tabletop stand next to the typewriter, and I roll an extremely blank sheet of paper into the machine, while she sets a timer for three minutes. I'm supposed to do the whole page in three minutes, eh? And I'm used to the precinct's coal-burning manual typewriters that Gutenberg would have considered old-fashioned. All right . . . .

I check the margins, the tabs, the line spacing, all that jazz, then I set my fingers in position and get ready. Mike Hammer never had to do this.

The kid just out of college says, "Go!" just a wee bit too much like a kid just out of college, and she starts the timer. I begin typing, reading the text in clumps, then looking at the keys to assure my accuracy, which you're not supposed to do, but since all of this has the quality of an absurd dream anyway, who's making the rules?

My fingers are flying over the keyboard, a tad detached from the rest of my being, like a bomber pilot whose inner defenses protect his sanity by severing the ties with the nerves of his fingers at the precise moment he obeys the command to push that button.

I try to make the information travel from my eyes to my fingertips without passing through my conscious mind, but ever since that Buddhist sect in Tibet turned down my membership application I've never been able to suppress the sensation that I *am* surrounded by matter that has weight and meaning.

The text that I'm typing is an exercise in the ridiculous. It's a rah-rah battle-cry for Morse, Inc., urging me to type faster for the greater glory of monopoly capitalism, compelling me to burn up every ounce of my creative energy so that my boss can make even more money this coming quarter.

My eyes are scanning the text continuously, and my fingers keep racing along the keys, but words are being imprinted in indelible black ink on the page, by my doing only, that are completely at odds with everything I stand for; and I'm going along with it, with nobody to blame but myself. After all, no one's holding a gun to my back. Not yet, anyway.

My fingers are raising a cloud of dust on the straightaway as the timer's buzzer shatters my concentration and my young friend slaps down the alarm button and turns the power off on my typewriter in what seems to me to be the same motion. She unhinges the carriage lock and liberates my tired, poor, typing test yearning to breathe free from the jaws of the insidious machine, and tells me to begin filling out the applications while she goes over my test.

I have to come down from my high first. Who needs drugs when we've got job interviews with high-pressure multinational corporations? I shut my eyes and breathe deeply of the pasteurized, processed company air, trying to clear my head. Then I blink them open again and look at the job application.

Sweet Jesus on the rocks! This job application asks for more security references than the Police Department! I look up at my young friend.

"Not bad," she says. By some miracle I have completed the required ordeal with the exact limit of three typographical errors. Now I get to wait some more, while she takes the results of my test back to the Caliph. While I'm waiting I look over the job application form again. I'm not exaggerating. They want a record of every

address I've lived at during the past six years, three security references, three character references from my place of residence—who
must live on the same block: What if I live on a farm in the country, I
wonder?—my political affiliation (I thought this sort of thing was
illegal in these United States)—ah! yes, down below in infinitesimal
print it explains that answering that question is optional, but if I
refuse to answer it, they will refuse to read the rest of the application—and (get this) they want the complete addresses of every
school I've ever attended, down to and including grade school!
Good luck trying to telex the *Nuestra Señora de la Nube* one-room
adobe schoolhouse in Solano, Ecuador—a town that *still* doesn't
have more than one telephone or reliable drinking water—to see if
I'm telling the truth or not!

I hate these standardized forms with all of their built-in, institu-
tionalized racism. Oh, I know, you native-born North Americans
will scoff, There she goes again, but I'm serious: It starts at the very
top with the standardized spaces for "Last Name," "First Name,"
and *one* stupid box in which I'm supposed to cram my "Middle
Initial," because all God's chillun got a first name, a Christian
name, and dad's last name; but what if you're like me, and you come
from a different culture, and you have *two* first names and two last
names 'cause we backward Ecuadorians think your mother's identity matters as well? Like the wicked stepsister in "Cinderella" (the
real Cinderella, not the Disney version), I'm expected to cut my toes
off in order to fit my foot into the glass slipper.

And that's not all. At the very bottom there's a space where I'm
supposed to sign a declaration that I will never reveal anything I
have learned about the company's practices to any person who does
not work inside the company. Whew!

I have reached my fourth incredulous gasp so far in two minutes
when my young friend emerges and informs me that, "If you'd like
to follow me, Mr. Faber would like to see you."

Oh, he'd like to, would he? To do what—Check the souls of my feet for The Mark of The Devil? (Can't have anyone working for us who's fornicated with the Devil, now, can we?)

I follow her past the leering eyes of the stable of males, past my inquisitor Mr. DeCharmant who looks at me as if he could get fined just for having let me out of the elevator, into a long glass corridor, one wall of which is nothing but floor-to-ceiling windows that look down into an abyss as heart-stopping as anything Mr. Hitchcock ever thought up, and into the transparent office of Mr. Faber.

Mr. Faber's office is not to be entered by people suffering from a heart condition. Three of the four walls are clear plate glass, forty-eight storeys over New York. If his desk were glued to the flag-pole jutting out from the fiftieth floor of this building, it wouldn't be much different. My feet are succumbing to electrostatic waves of cold wetness as I am led over and told to take a seat in front of the monument to modernism (a two-ton slab of black marble) that is Mr. Faber's desk. I sit down and try not to look out the windows, but how can you when the only solid wall is the one you came in through? We have thousand-foot drops all over the Andes. Solano itself can only be approached from the south by a road that is not so much a road as it is the hair stretched across the Pit of Hell that my Incan ancestors believed this life to be. But the drops are tempered by hills, valleys, and gradations of all kinds that leave you a chance of slowing yourself down and surviving should you go off the road. We have nothing like this. This teetering platform, seemingly defying gravity, six hundred feet straight up from the unfriendly concrete down below.

I close my eyes and rub them a bit. When I open them, Mr. Faber has materialized behind his desk, and is looking over my resume, typing test, and application. Mr. Faber isn't anything like that iguana, DeCharmant. I could go on and on describing him, but I'll just risk your wrath and tell you, unobjectively and as a woman, that Mr. Faber is younger, smaller, and *much* cuter than Mr. DeCharmant. He just looks like a nicer guy. It's hard to believe that he has more power than DeCharmant. I would think a snake-oil vendor like DeCharmant would have pushed a guy like Faber out the window years ago to get his position. Hmm . . . Mr. Faber may turn out to be slicker than I thought. I'd better be on my guard.

Mr. Faber places my documents neatly before him, one, two, three, and sits down, He looks directly across the desk at me, which is also a step up from DeCharmant, who couldn't muster more than a sneaky sideways peek. I focus on his face. Not to flatter him, but because I can't bear to look over his shoulder out the windows. The cold flashes have traveled the length of my body to my hands by now. I try to warm them up by sitting on them in the most ladylike, power-hungry career woman way I can.

"Well, Miss Buscarsela," he begins. Nicer voice too. "I must say I'm very impressed with your qualifications. But I'm sure Mr. DeCharmant informed you that unfortunately we are not hiring any safety inspectors at this time."

"Yes," I say, my voice weak and shaky. Lifting a piano would be child's play compared to trying to carry on a casual conversation in this pressurized space capsule.

"And I'm afraid that the only positions currently available are secretarial—for which you are immensely overqualified. I wouldn't even think of insulting you by suggesting that you take such a position."

Oh? DeCharmant did.

"Morse Incorporated possesses a vast network of international interests. In addition to your extensive experience with the Housing Authority I see you also have a knowledge of French and Spanish."

"Spanish is my native language," I fill him in.

He looks surprised.

"But your English is impeccable—"

"Right down to the Bronx accent. I've been living in New York

City for eight years."—And I single-handedly caused the fiscal crisis, too.

"Hmm!" he says, and flips over my job application. Then he starts. "You've forgotten to fill in the back of the application."

"Have I? Oh, I'm sorry. You know, job interview nerves . . . "

I am trying to shrug it off, but a sheath of hardness has coated Mr. Faber.

"Please fill it in," he says, without much warmth.

More stupid questions. I take up the pen from his 24-karat gold display set and slide the application towards me. It asks for a list of every country I've ever visited in my life, with the exact dates of departure and arrival of each visit.

"This will take a week," I say. Travel is cheap in South America. I've been to the Andean countries a half a dozen times, to say nothing of the early, frequent trips between the U.S. and Ecuador, and those two weeks in Spain.

No answer from Mr. Faber. I start writing, cursing inwardly. You can dress them up and put them in glass offices in the sky, but inside they're all brutal swine who get off on watching other people squirm. I can feel his eyes on me as I'm writing. What, has he got X-ray vision? Is he peering into my thoughts, because Morse, Inc. knows no limitations of earthly power? Is he learning that I'm really an impostor, that I'm *not* part of this set?

He keeps staring at the crown of my head, and I keep bent over the application form so as to avoid his seeing my eyes. He keeps looking and I keep writing. It goes on like this until I've reached my exodus under the Military Triumvirate (I'd like to see this guy get along with a nine p.m. curfew and a Colonel reviewing his books once in a while), and I'm picturing DeCharmant back home under the *junta;* a guy like him would probably have a nice, cushy job ambushing congressmen with a machine gun, when Mr. Faber says to me, the malice gone from his voice, "Actually, it's really just to verify if you've ever been to any socialist countries."

But I'm drenched with my own bile now, thanks to him and his company, and I don't cool off as easy as some of these docile North American secretaries.

"Well, I once went out with a French man, and France has socialized medicine," I say, nastiness seeping out in spite of myself. I can't keep up this act much longer. I'm saturated with this place and its deceptively spic-and-span computers that contain more raw sewage than the Gowanus Canal.

Mr. Faber says, in all seriousness, "Well, I don't think that would count against you. The fact is that we could use someone with your outstanding capabilities, and with our worldwide concerns, something's bound to turn up sooner or later. What I'm saying is, there may be nothing now, but I would like to keep in contact with you."

"All right," I say, not looking up.

Mr. Faber says, "Excellent. I'd like to begin with tonight, at dinner," so smoothly and unexpectedly that the effect is genuinely disarming.

I look up at him, and when the feeling comes back into my jaw I realize that it's hanging open. I practically have to use my hand to close it.

"That is, if you would be kind enough to accept my invitation," he says.

Someone in the room says, "Yes," and it must be me, because his lips haven't moved, and I left my stunt double at home. "What time?" I add. Yep. It's me talking all right. I know the voice.

Mr. Faber smiles a deep, satisfied smile, and removes the application from under my weightless hand. I leave the building in a daze.

* * *

I have one hell of a subway ride home, disguised as I am in the uniform of the territorial enemy; I am subjected to death-stares from industrial workers coming off shift, who are looking at this decked-out young businesswoman with the same benevolence as the Welsh looked upon the invading Saxons. I am the hereditary adversary. I want to get up and scream, "I am *not* a rich, successful businesswoman! I am one of you!" Naturally, I can't. But it's a disturbing feeling to be listed among those who are going to die first when they finally get their acts together and take over this city, just because of the costume my role requires.

And this is only my costume for Act I. The hardest scene is still to come. Now I must dress myself up as a scheming career-conscious woman who is going out to party with the elite few, to whom the mantle of rule will be passed, just as soon as they learn how to drink a beer without yielding to the urge to howl like a dog and smash the bottle against a wall.

I telephone Detective Snyder about it, and he thinks it's terrific. "What an opportunity," he says, "you see, I'd never have gotten a date with Faber, and he's likely to take you into his confidence and tell you all kinds of inside secrets once he's off his guard. It's a terrific breakthrough, and exceptional police work."

Then why do I feel like a whore?

It takes me a very long time to get the right look for Act II: Later That Evening. My greatest task is taming my untamable long, frizzy hair. But eventually, after the sun has been down long enough for darkness to be creeping out of its daily hibernation to hide my treachery to my *barrio,* I slink out into the night and catch a less-crowded, post rush-hour subway downtown, attracting fewer razor-sharp glares this time.

I come up out of the subway at Bryant Park and walk over to meet Jim Faber (yes, I've learned his first name) in front of the Public Library's uptown lion. He's already there, waiting for me, and he hooks his arm around mine to walk me down Fifth Avenue to a restaurant about which he could reveal nothing earlier this afternoon, for security reasons.

On the way downtown, we talk about nothing at all. I learn what college he went to, what kind of car he drives, what kind of move he's thinking of making to a better co-op than the one he's in now. Well, I guess you can't expect a corporate magnate to open up right away. No, the necessary stimulation must be supplied. The catalyst. Liquor, my grandmother used to say, talks quite loud once it's out of the bottle. Mata Hari never felt so dead inside.

We turn east on 33rd Street, and he wants to know about me now. Should I tell him what kind of ill-equipped university I went to, what kind of subway I ride, and what kind of apartment I'm renting in the heart of a neighborhood that's probably his worst nightmare?—Nah. . . .

I tell him about how the administration of the University of Guayaquil refused to cancel classes, ever, because the military government (correctly) feared any chance for the students to mobilize, and that, one season, when we had particularly heavy rains, and the Daule River overflowed (Guayaquil lies about half-an-inch above sea level), we had to wade to class in water up to our knees. Once inside, we had to sit on the desks, because there wasn't a classroom that wasn't inundated; after class we had to pile into somebody's pickup truck because the buses were filled beyond capacity—like you always see in those photos of *other* countries—with thirty people hanging from the windows, and taxis were refusing to open their doors.

Jim Faber laughs and tells me that they used to have some pretty wild parties in his fraternity, too. Don't ask me what the one has to do with the other.

Our destination turns out to be one of those chrome-plated Mexican restaurants in the Murray Hill area where the same plate of rice and refried beans that 100 million peasants survive on goes for $17.95. My escort leads me inside, and we are shown to a table over by a stone hearth that has never known a fire, and handed authentically hand-written menus in English with very American prices.

Jim Faber breaks our first brief silence:

"Burritowise, this place has the rest beat."

Burritowise? *Must* he talk like that? I guess my reaction shows, because the next thing he says is, "Oh, am I embarrassing you?"

"Hell, yes," I answer back, kindly. He laughs.

"Sorry. You're the first Spanish girl I've ever gone out with." This is supposed to be justification. What am I, International Conquest Number 1003? You know; Italians—12, French—4, Japanese—1,—But—but—but—Sir, we have no acquisitions yet from Latin America.—Well don't just stand there, do something about it!

So we order some peasant food at a price that would keep a typical peasant family fed for three months, and I have to suffer through Mr. James Faber's Theory Of How The World Works, Volumes 1-24. Staying alert through the whole thing and pretending I'm intrigued—and responding occasionally with attentive questions that indicate that I have been paying attention—is about as hard as spending six hours in the tank trying to break a fourteen-time offender down into confessing, and believe me, I've had to do it.

I catch frequent glimpses of the other diners. I wonder how many other imposters there are. Not many, I imagine—at least not in the same way that I am. The place is filled with people for whom Mexico is a column label on the little screen they move numbers around on. Buy today's rice from Ecuador, sell to Brazil, buy tomorrow's corn from Nigeria, sell to Korea. Never mind who *needs* the rice and corn the most. Buy at the cheapest, sell at the highest. What other way is there?

When the check comes Faber pays it with the nonchalance of a televangelist faith-healing a non-believer in front of a live audience, and who expects something in return from the healee. He slips the receipt into his inside jacket pocket, no doubt to show it to me later as proof of ownership when he tries to claim his property.

But the ordeal is still young. Faber whisks me outside and into a cab with a flick of his wrist, and we start heading downtown. I always seem to be heading downtown.

He talks the whole way down, gesturing animatedly with his hands, continually touching me in a way that's light and quick enough to be "permissible." One of his favorite spots has been measured, mapped and located precisely half-way between the relative neutrality of the top of my knee and the part of my thigh where it starts getting sensitive. Quite a diplomat, this Jim Faber.

We get to where we're going. It's one of those ugly-but-beautiful 19th-century brownstone churches that was threatened with demolition before a rich-kid speculator bought it and converted it into a high-class, by which I mean expensive, disco. There's a crowd out front (of course) waiting to be among The Chosen few who get to go inside. Faber walks past the 6'2" doorman with a hand-held metal detector as if the crowd weren't there, trailing me behind him. I can feel resentful gazes burning into the back of my head. I'm incurring a lot of those resentful gazes today. Must be the company I'm keeping.

We have no coats to check, it being hot enough to incubate some terrific penicillin in any available garbage can, and we walk down an eerie green and red pin-spotlight-lit hallway to the main area, which is the interior of the church. Stained-glass windows are partially obscured by state-of-the-art sound equipment and a video projection screen so oversized it might strike Caligula as just a bit excessive. A stone statue of St. Anthony looks down on the bar and blesses it.

If you haven't figured it out already, I'm a practicing Catholic, although time and experience have led me to ignore the sacrament of confession through a priest—I prefer to talk to God directly—and a number of other doctrines (and I'm not mentioning premarital sex just to boost the ratings). The point is that I hear Mass frequently enough, and read a fair amount of the Bible, particularly those ever-radical words of Christ about devoting yourself to helping others with little thought of reward, forgiving, and coming to the aid of those who are the most in need. I particularly like the part where Christ says it is better to worship in the privacy of your closet, because going to church carries with it the danger of going just to be seen going. And in my profession, there isn't always the time and space to hear a complete service. I like the idea of each person being his or her own mobile church: Able to get down and communicate whenever and wherever you are—say, pinned down behind a packing crate in a warehouse shootout.

I just mean that I'm no Bible-thumping proselyte, but there is something deeply perturbing about this former House of God having been turned into an overly chic rock club. You don't have to be a seminary postulant to know that Jesus got kind of pissed when he saw the all-powerful rival God of Mammon being worshipped in His stead in that temple in Jerusalem.

And I inwardly ask for forgiveness, God, but you know why I'm here, and if you happen to call Judgment Day within the next three hours or so, please take into consideration that I am only doing this because of my insatiable desire to see some sort of justice served.

We walk around the dance floor to where the tables are. I watch as couples dry hump to a throbbing bass line, under lights that probably wouldn't stop flashing if you took an axe to the dimmerboard. I've seen enforcement killings in Colombian neighborhoods where eighteen-month-old babies have been found nailed to the walls, but I must confess, this shocks me.

Faber spots a table full of friends, and leads me over to present me to three men and one woman. The men are all sitting in hot spots of incandescent light, but the woman has had the bad luck to be placed in a lozenge-shaped shard of green light that makes her look positively dreadful; a grotesque reflection of her soul in hell after being caught here. Everyone says hello to me as best they can through the ninety-odd decibels that are emanating from speakers that are far too near to the spot that's obviously intended for socializing.

Once we sit down, we can lean a little closer and shout into each other's ears, if that's your idea of enjoyable conversation.

"We're drinking Margaritas," one of them yells into my ear. "You want one?"

"No!" I shout back.

"What do you want?!"

"Nothing!"

I get a look like, Which spaceship did you say you came in on? followed by one of, I must have heard wrong. What am I supposed to say?—I no longer trust drinks in public places? I never drink on duty?

"I'm taking antibiotics!" is the answer I give, which seems to excuse my peculiar lack of interest in getting quickly blasted like a good little party girl.

"Jim says you had a French boyfriend!" says the one on my right. I didn't realize my resume had been passed around. "I don't like the French!"

"There are fifty million of them," I say. "Which ones don't you like?"

"They're all a bunch of snobs," is the answer. Oh.

The conversation turns to the hot topic of Manhattan real estate. The one on my right is a commercial real estate broker who lives off commissions. He explains that this is *the* time and Manhattan is *the* place to make a bundle.

"Land," he explains. "It's under all of us."

I ask him how he feels about destroying the character of ethnic neighborhoods by driving out the low-income families.

"Gentrification is integration," he tells me.

Yeah. Like when I flatten a roach on my stove with a rolled-up newspaper, you could say that I was "integrating" the roach and the stove. I mention that we could stand to learn from the way the Japanese conserve space in order to house 90 million people on those tiny little islands.

"The Japs!" he says. "Fuck them." I see that alcohol has brought out the real estate broker's humanitarian inner self. "They don't play fair. You know, some of us still remember Pearl Harbor."

I excuse myself to go to the bathroom. I have to dodge a lot of panting petting partiers with big bodies and small hands and ask directions three times before I am allowed the privilege of waiting in line outside the women's bathroom. When is somebody going to design a public place with more facilities for women? Must there always be a line?

I judge a place by its bathroom. All the phony glitter up front doesn't cover up for the putrid piss-hole in back of the balcony stairs that smells like any sewer back home in Ecuador, or the cheap toilet paper that's tough enough to inscribe all five acts of *Anthony and Cleopatra* on three sheets with an iron stylus. Also the place reeks of pot. Not that I'm hypocritical enough to look down on it, but it's worth mentioning.

This temporary lull in the confusion only serves to make it all the more striking when I walk back out into the middle of it. There are simply too many things happening in this place: Drinking, dancing, music, lights, Brobdignagian video screen with remote TV monitors in all kinds of alcoves that probably served as prayer nooks in the edifice's original design. Old gods replaced by new. They should eliminate at least two of the elements in this sensory-overloading experience.

I find my way back through the stroboscopic light-show that is starting to make me feel just a touch epileptic, to the table where Jim Faber stands up and invites me to dance, using sign language to get his message over the wall of sound. I signal back that that's fine with me, and he escorts me out into the middle of the dance floor. Couples cavort all around us, wearing designer-shredded T-shirts and other trendy accessories, to the latest in musical product from the Lowest Common Denominator Factory—that uniquely American institution where they make watery beer, bad sit-coms and all those movies where the hero is invincible and the dying criminal repents on the steps of an old-fashioned neighborhood church such as this one . . .

The disc jockey segues into yet another drum beat that is not made by human hands, and the crowd roars with ecstasy, and starts bopping to the computer-generated rhythm of a perfectly banal synthetic song by one of those groups that always have their picture in the papers because the lead singer dresses in baby clothes or some such gimmick. Shocking, huh? The Velveeta of the music world, and everyone seems to love it, too. I don't want you to get the idea I'm a strict-construction Latin-musicologist. You already know how much I appreciated the chainsaw music at A7. It may not do anything for you, but at least it tries. By contrast, this music sounds like it came out of a spray can:—Pfffffffffffff! Adding to my dilemma, the accompanying video is assailing my eyes on a screen forty feet high and forty feet wide. That's kind of hard to avoid. Couples are dancing as though mesmerized, not looking at each other, the magnetic appeal of the great god video is so irresistible. As I said, there are at least two stimuli too many in this place.

Twenty minutes of gyrating to this fluff and they finally put on a decent song—with a human drummer! Now hear this: It's Elvis singing "Jailhouse Rock," a song that is well into its third decade, by no means my favorite, and unchallengably the best of the lot so far tonight. Future archaeologists will marvel that we should have fallen so far in under thirty years.

I cut loose like a thoroughbred who has been penned up with the plowhorses. At last a tune with some electricity. Screw everybody, I'm dancing. I barely look at Jim, and the rest of the crowd is a blur as I go into my demented jellyfish roll, shaking out all the unspeak-able strain on my overworked personality filters. I bump into some people but I can't be bothered now, I'm engaged in some therapeutic hip-grinding. It feels good to undo the bones; helps remind me that I have muscle and blood, heart and soul, that sort of thing.

Unfortunately Elvis only lasts about two minutes and thirty-five seconds like all classic rock songs of the period, and my session with the rock and roll doctor ends. Jim is looking at me with renewed admiration, and I feel myself grow hot from the closeness of all those bodies. Suddenly a sting of remorse pricks my conscience: I have been dancing in the House of the Lord. Well, the Bible *does* say salvation is kind of a positive thing, and that we should all enter His house singing and dancing. What makes "Jailhouse Rock" any less divinely inspired than the *Missa Solemnis,* aside from the immortal pelvis?

Jim takes me back to the table where his friends are. One of them has just returned from the second floor balcony with a two-inch wide zip-lock baggie full of white stuff. Oh, that white stuff.

Busting these people is not a priority right now. On the other hand, wouldn't it just blow their minds if I whipped out my badge and my .38 and cleaned the place out? I assure you the temptation is strong.

But my own mind is blown slightly when, instead of stashing the baggie away like a normal member of a society which allegedly frowns on such things, he dumps some of the contents out on the glass tabletop and starts drawing lines for everyone at the table. I Watch them all take turns snorting up the party favors, thinking how entertaining it would be to arrest everyone just as soon as the high starts to kick in. Finally the "host" gets around to me and offers me a sterling silver inhaler.

For the second time this evening, I refuse the libation offered, and the natives are getting restless. Various comments are made about my maturity, of all things, and I actually catch the tail end of "fraidy cat,"—something I was, up to now, convinced that no one over the age of six or seven ever used. I announce again that I am taking antibiotics. It doesn't go over as well as the first time I used it, but the ever-practical host shrugs and snorts up "my" line, smearing his fingertip in the residues and applying them to his gums. At $120 a gram, you don't waste a speck. To think that *gold* is presently worth about one-eighth of what this stuff brings in.

Cocaine affects different people in different ways. Some just sit back and stop contributing to the conversation. Others it makes very psycho very fast. In still others, it shoots right towards the sexual membranes, giving an instant hard-on to the men, and the equivalent in a suffused clitoris to the women. The trappings of the drug are not entirely devoid of their attraction. Of the five participants at this table, I'd say we have one representative of each of the first two categories present, and a total of three of the last. A good deal of alcohol helps, too.

"Man, coke is the *ultimate*," says the one to my right, leaning in close enough for me to feel the bulge pulsating in the crotch of his pants. I shift away from him.

I reflect for a moment on this interesting linguistic polymorphism. "Ultimate" means both "last," as in farthest, and "first," or superlative. Going to have to get in touch with my old linguistics professor and chart this one out.

They are now trying to make the other woman chug a boilermaker, apparently in expectation that upon finishing it, she will tear off her clothes and dance naked on the tabletop. No wonder my abstinence is viewed with such derision.

I'm thinking too much. On the other hand, one of the only courses available to one being assaulted by auditory eliminators is regression into an introspective trance. Either that or getting the hell out of there. Maybe I should give in and order something to drink. I'm looking around for one of the elusive waiters in this place, and the broker on my right practically rips my nose off my face trying to get me to turn towards him so he can engage me in some of his meaningless gabbling. The others all groove on the broker's implied profundities, and I can't take this crap anymore. They start telling sex jokes, and I stand up in the middle of a punch line. The psycho lets out one of those *Reefer Madness* giggle-chokes that swallow themselves before they get past the front teeth.

Who invited the skeleton to the banquet? But nobody's really listening. It's all part of the joke.

There's more nervous laughter, and I want to go. Jim Faber manages to pick up on this, gets to his feet as if he were climbing a ladder, and makes some ritual departing gestures to the others, some of whom kid him openly about not over-straining himself when he's humping me later. How nice. As we're leaving, the remaining partyers, now bordering on a state of numbness, raise their newly bought round of drinks in a toast:

"To being young," declares Larry. "Isn't it great?"

The Weight of Doom is lifted from off of my shoulders when we shoot out through the door that is far too narrow to accommodate my desire to split that dump *now,* and hail a cab,

"Nice friends," I say, sliding inside the cab.

"Aren't they?" he says, getting in next to me, unaware of the real meaning of my words. "The salt of the earth."

I can't help laughing at this one, but it fits with Jim Faber's mood (or rather, his condition).

He gives the cabbie an Upper East Side address, and we pull away from the House of Sin and Sensation, heading uptown, for a change.

"You wanna come back to my apartment?" he tells me after the die has already been cast.

"Really I'd just prefer to go somewhere for some coffee."

"We can have coffee at my apartment." End of discussion with Mr. Faber of Morse, Inc.

The man is already floating, banging his head on the roof of the cab without appearing to notice it as we go over the bumps and potholes that mark the route north. I'm asking myself, should I go for the old, *old* routine of getting the guy plastered enough to loosen his tongue? Is it too stale to work? But I recall the words of a certain Ethiopian slave in ancient Greece who was freed from bondage when his astounding story-telling talents were allowed to see the light of day: "One good plan is worth a thousand that are doubtful." That settles it. Back to his place for the Delilah Treatment it is. When among Philistines . . . This guy's halfway gone already, I've had none, and the liquor in his apartment shouldn't be laced with hallucinogens, now should it?

I'm wondering if a guy like this will ever make the discovery that his friends are going to age right along with everybody else, when we pull up in front of a swanky co-op in the East 60s. Dis must be da place.

The doorman lets us in and helps us find the elevator as if we were a delegation from the U.N. rather than two decadent partyers. He doesn't flinch as the elevator door closes on the two of us. And why should he? It's his job to cater to the wasted children who had too much Hi-C during play time, and I bet he gets paid plenty more for doing that than I do for being a moving target for rapists, drug dealers and roving bands of discontented, angry youths during riot season.

Faber succeeds in opening all three locks without inflicting any serious injuries on either of us. I take one step and I'm inside. He closes the door and flips on a light, in that order.

"Make yourself at home," croons Faber, throwing off his jacket and loosening his tie.

I go open up a window, and look out. It's only six storeys up, but there's no fire escape. That puts jumping through the window out of the question. No, the only way out is back the way I came.

"What'll it be?" he says, opening his liquor cabinet, having completely forgotten about my original suggestion of coffee, which is so much the better.

"Well, let's have a look," I say, walking over to join him. He has a respectable collection of the finest in hooch. Now there's another word: Hooch. I know it's slang from the twenties, but I like it because it fits, especially under these circumstances. Because I am not the least bit interested in a quiet nightcap. I'm calculating the number of drinks I saw him have over how long a period of time, figuring his alcohol-to-body-weight ratio into it in milligrams per kilogram, plus the fifteen minutes he just spent hydrolizing that ethyl alcohol during the cab-ride up here, and I'm deciding that he's probably dangerously close to sobering up. And I don't feel like going fifteen rounds with this *dreckrammer* (that's "shitraker" to you). Better go for the loaded gloves.

There's some genuine Danish Akvavit (not the green-bottled importation, the brown-bottled, *stronger* brew) gathering dust in the back. That's the right size iron for this sand pit. Smooth enough to go down without feeling it all that much, with a wallop like a three-balls-two-strikes-bases-loaded-bottom-of-the-ninth-with-two-men-on and the pitcher lets Hank Aaron have one right over the plate, if you get what I mean.

He pours two shots over ice, and we drink.

"Mmmm, good choice," says he. I hope so.

Three drinks later and he's still coming in loud and clear. While I have been using the simple but devastating strategy of tossing my entire drink down in one gulp, then going to get more from the bottle—my mouth still full of the stuff—only to spit it all into the kitchen sink without him noticing, which is a neat trick in itself (may the Danish gods forgive me). I come back with Round Five.

"Boy, you sure know how to hold your liquor," he says. "I admire that in a woman." I'm flattered.

"My grandfather raised us on *aguardiente* that could take the enamel off a refrigerator," I tell him.

We toast and this time I swallow some. I mean, What the hell? It is pretty good stuff. Then something magical happens. My prayers are answered. It's as if the previous four drinks have been caught in his esophagus, and this fifth one has slid down and knocked them all in, because upon finishing this drink, he's suddenly quite drunk. This calls for a celebration. I pour us both another round and I drink all of mine this time.

Now. I slip my shoes off and rub my feet against his ankles. He soon has a hard-on pressing against his leg and he makes no effort to hide it from me when he reaches into his pants to adjust himself. Good. If he's that far along, it's time to drop the Delilah bomb big time. I let him slide over and kiss me. He gropes me a little, but I've been through worse. I let him start unbuttoning my blouse. He's having a lot of trouble with it, and I don't help him. He gets one button open and starts nuzzling my neck, but that's hardly enough to satisfy him so he leans back and starts to work on the next one.

I ask him, ever-so-gently, "When was the last time you saw Bud Wiegand?"

His head jerks backwards in mild shock. He stares at me a moment, then he shakes this unromantic nonsense out of his head.

"Whaddaya wanna talk about that creep for? Bleah!" He leans in again, gets the second button open and buries his face in my flesh. He slobbers on me. Charming. But he's still got a couple of buttons to go to really get at me, so it's back to work.

"What about Erika Schnelling?" Nothing.

I let him slobber on me a bit more and then I ask, honey dripping coolly from my tongue, "What about Wilson McCullough?"

He gives a shiver—although I suppose it could have been a hiccup—but no answer, just a hollow and fake-sounding "Who?"

It sounds so phony even he seems to notice how phony it sounds. That's enough of an answer for me. I pour another couple of drinks. "You know, that hot new artist down at the SlapDash. I thought maybe you'd have some hot investment tips for me," I say, sipping my Akvavit.

Faber shakes his head in bewilderment, sips the drink I put in his hand, out of reflex, and says, "Ssome date!—You get off and talk about invessments at th'ssame time. You're a ssmart babe." He wants to know more about my grandfather and the—what was it?—the *agua de fiesta?*—that he raised us on.

I tell him yes, my country has a lot of famous products—most notably bananas, rice, chocolate and coffee, and What does he know about coffee?

Now the guy is slurring his words and wavering unsteadily from side to side like I've been waiting for, and he tells me with liquor-enhanced pride that he knows all about coffee, Morse, Inc. *imports* coffee, for Chrissakes.

"Where do you import it from?"

"All'lover th'world."

"And where does it go?"

He smiles an all-knowing, cockeyed smile: "Sa secret."

"Oh, come on, you can tell me."

He winks at me. It takes most of his coordination skills. "Y'wanme t'sshowya?"

I'm saying, "Sure," when he takes my hand in his and puts it on his crotch. I realize that I'm wasting my time now. I've learned all that I'm going to learn from him. I start to rise. He throws his arms around my head like he's going to kiss me, and he tries to direct my face towards his hard-on. He's stronger than I thought.

"What the fuck do you think you're doing?" I say, angrily breaking free from him. And maybe blowing my cover.

"S'okay, baybee, allmy dates gimme blowjobss."

"Oh. Great." I sit there for a second, wondering what I should do next. To my surprise, he seems to forget what just happened, and his mind skips a groove backwards to what we were talking about before.

"Mos'of th'coffee comes from Zone Th-three," he says. Boom.

Of course: The Third World.

"Zone Three?" I ask, waiting for more.

But there is no more. My friend Mr. Faber is on his way out. No matter. I can take it from here. I continue my interrupted act of standing up. Jim Faber grabs for me.

"How'bout it, honey? Less go t'bed."

"Some other time," I say, buttoning up my blouse and heading towards the door. He tries to raise himself up, but only succeeds in receding deeper into the upholstery.

"Like when? Gimme a date," says the lonely voice behind me.

"September 45th," I tell him. "No, don't get up, I'll let myself out."

I've got a long subway ride home.

SEVEN

Opiate, n. An unlocked door in the prison of Identity. It leads into the jail yard.

—Ambrose Bierce, *The Devil's Dictionary*

"Woke up this mo'nin', found myself dead."

—Jimi Hendrix

I decide not to cross the park to the A train, but to take an East Side train north to the Bronx, get out and walk across the Harlem River to my neighborhood. I go down into the subway at 68th Street, let my hair out and loosen some of the knots in my costume. It's still early enough for the revelers to be returning home, but the first train that pulls into the station is one of those battle-scarred, unmarked trains that moves slowly through the station, without stopping. All is dark on board. Pray, Who is on board this Mystery Train? People frozen in time? Is that the Flying Dutchman? Or Aeneas? Odysseus? Gilgamesh searching for the secret of eternal life? The train keeps moving and slowly passes into the tunnel leaving my Eternal Riddle unanswered.

The next train has living people on it. Quite a collection, too. It's nearly 2:30 A.M. Saturday morning, and the mixture at this hour is very telling. There are basically three groups: Fatigued, Black and *latino* workers who are just coming off the late night shift, Bronx kids who *own* the party car, and packs of rich white kids cavorting as if the middle car were their private playpen. There are only two people who don't fit in. The guy sitting next to me reading the *National Enquirer,* who looks like Colonel Khadafi, and me.

The white boys are entertaining the white girls by swinging on the poles and aping themselves. The girls giggle. The elderly Black worker across from me sees through my disguise, responds to me by looking into my eyes, and then rolling his eyes heavenward in reaction to the white kids, I nod, smiling in agreement. He has recognized that I am not One Of Them.

Then one of the great transitions in the Northern Hemisphere takes place. At 96th Street the train disgorges each and every one of the rich white kids, leaving a train full of janitors on their way home from cleaning out the rich white kids' dustbins. Three more stops and we're at East 116th Street, one of the most uninhabitable stretches of charred brick and broken glass in this neck of the universe. Two stops more and we're in the South Bronx, and the only passengers left are the holdouts too stoned to move or care, and a handful of working-class *menschen* (that's Yiddish for "people") trying to survive the ride to their homes around 180th.

There's a rush of cooler air, and the train goes elevated. But the fresh air is the only symptom of our being above ground. I stand up and look out the open window, the wind blowing my hair. There is a darkness outside that I instinctively sense is unnatural in a city of nine million inhabitants. Then the coupling between the first two cars hits a switch, and one by one the other couplings ignite sheets of sparks as they cross the switch, lighting up the night like a gigantic strobe light, capturing the stark and ghostly faces of the hollow-eyed, dark, empty buildings that line the elevated track on both sides, for blocks.

* * *

The next morning I'm up bright and early reporting to work. It feels good to be once again wearing clothes that I can sprint in, if I have to. The fruit is bubbling up out of the Korean grocery store like the goddess's own horn of plenty. I can't resist those rich, red colors, and I buy myself a pint of cherries. In winter, the fruits and vegetables that are shipped to New York aren't fit to play racketball with (they're too tough), but in season, it's every bit as good as what we used to pick off the trees all year round in Solano. The male half of the young Korean couple has just washed them in front of me, so they're absolutely ripe and ready to be devoured. And they're heaven.

I've eaten the third part of them by the time I climb the stairs to the precinct. I put the wet, glistening carton down on the first desk and announce that they're here for the taking. A number of fellow cops take advantage, and crowd around, grabbing a fistful each and emptying the carton in no time at all.

Carrera comes around and there are none left for him.

"Come on, guys, give," I plead.

"That's okay," says Carrera. "In fact I was going to ask you all to give—"

He flips over the clipboard he's holding, He's collecting names and donations for a halfway house, a neighborhood drug-rehabilitation center that just had its budget hacked in twain by a President who claims to be waging a war on drugs. Hmmm . . .

"Sorry," Dorset begs off, "you got me flat broke: First of the month and Con Ed and the landlord have all my money."

The others give similar excuses, except for two who chip in $5.00 each with cherry-red-stained fingers.

"How 'bout you, Fil?"

"Actually, the *best* time to hit me up for a charitable donation is when I'm paying all the bills," I say, digging into my pocket. "As long as I'm giving all my money away, I might as well give some of it to somebody who really needs it."

I give Carrera $20. My company whistles.

"Thanks, Fil," says Carrera, and hands me the clipboard to sign my name and fill in other pertinent statistics that these places need to claim nonprofit status—something which the President has just made more difficult for them to do, by the way.

Who should walk in just this moment but my belated backup from the rape detail. He makes a point of saying hello to everyone but me.

"It must be the camouflage I'm wearing," I confide to Carrera. "It makes me blend invisibly with the file cabinets."

"*¿que te dice la patria?*" says Carrera.

"*No sé nada, hombre.*" I haven't had any news from Ecuador in months.

"*Oye,* we're going to have a baseball game Sunday to benefit the shelter," he tells me in Spanish. "We're still short a third base coach."

"*Confía en mí. Estaré allí.*" I'll be there.

"*Gracias, hermana.*"

"Don't worry about it."

Carrera gives me a pat on the shoulder as I turn and walk towards the stairs to the locker rooms. Halfway down the stairs and the smell of what *could* be somebody burning last October's leaves—but probably isn't—wafts up to meet me. I descend to the women's locker room and lean inside. This is the source all right. There's a cloud of marijuana smoke in there thick enough to be sniffed out by a guard dog crossing the Hamilton Bridge. It's not even good pot. I can tell it's some of the elephant reef that we routinely confiscate from the schoolyard nickel-bag vendors—though they always come back with more. I try to wave some of the stuff out the door, but the place is full of it. Besides, where's the smoke going to go besides upstairs? I decide to get to the bottom of this, and I think I have a pretty good idea where to start. But I don't even get past the door.

My proxy rapist is standing there, blocking my way with a few of his cronies.

"Pee-yew!" he says. "Whadja do, Buscarsela, burn up a whole bag full?"

"It certainly smells that way, doesn't it?" I answer.

"Jeez, check out her eyes, man, they're bright red!"

"You want to see bright red, one of these days I'll make sure you see plenty of bright red," I say, trying to get out of there. He won't let me.

"I'd hate to have the Sergeant hear about this," he says. "Oops! Looks like it's too late—sorry, Buscarsela, this is the last time I cover up for you."

He steps out of the way, only to let Sergeant Belasco fill in the void. Sergeant Belasco is not amused.

"You know I just got in," I tell him. "I was upstairs until twenty seconds ago—which is not enough time to smoke up the locker room like this."

"I don't want to hear it," says the Sergeant, mad at everybody, including me. Why me? "Whatever it is, it isn't funny. Destroying state's evidence to commit a prank like this—"

He stops. What's the use? He knows there's no way to make it stick to these guys, and worse, that they'll only have it in for him for the next twenty years if he tries. But he won't even take *one* step over to my side. That's a cop for you. And he leaves it at that.

"Officer Buscarsela, would you kindly step up to the Lieutenant's office? Now?"

I follow Sergeant Belasco up the stairs past a men's glee-club chorus of random potshots about my drug problem. Yes, it is a problem. But sympathy? Encouragement? Help? Try the Red Cross, baby. This is the Police Department. One time in the Academy these beefheads make a tape loop of Cher's "Half

Breed" and played it one hundred and thirty-seven times before I found the power source and disconnected it. That was in the women's locker room, too.

Once again I sit encased in the Lieutenant's insufficiently sound-proofed cell, waiting for the latest installment in the continuing saga, Let's Drive Filomena Crazy.

"You have lucked out, Officer Buscarsela," are the Lieutenant's first words to me.

Exactly when did I "luck out"? Did I miss a week of my life in there somewhere?

"The policy review committee read the Feds' reports of your part in that bust. Even the way the Feds loaded it, it was pretty evident that you brought in that guy on a platter. They were impressed."

"How about you?" I ask. Pause you could drive a beer truck through. Then:

"I'm impressed with the fact that you seem to have taken my words seriously about trying to keep yourself clean. Well, how about it?"

"I'm keeping myself clean, Lieutenant." Forcibly.

"Good. I hope so, for your sake. It wasn't easy burying your last drug test, I'll have you know."

"I appreciate your efforts on my behalf," I reply.

"I just don't want to lose a good cop."

My God. A compliment. Somebody call the SWAT team. I'd better not acknowledge it, or he'll start screaming at me to save face. But it was a compliment just the same, my second in just about five years here.

"You didn't call me in here to tell me that," I say, leaving him an out, which he takes.

"The track panel has elected to assign you to a probationary undercover. They're doing this because as of this moment, the Department has no further need of Detectives with your qualifications in any of the three categories you requested. But in recognition of your dedication in the field of Rape Crisis, among others, they have awarded you this temporary status, rather than an official transfer, so that you won't have to wait the minimum of two years before another request for transfer can be submitted. Whaddaya say to that?"

"I'm honored. What's the assignment?"

He swallows. Pause you could back a convoy of beer trucks through.

"On account of the lack of Hispanic Detectives, you have been selected to be the Department's official undercover liaison with the U.S. Immigration and Naturalization Service."

Now it's my turn to swallow.

"You got some crappier clothes at home?" he asks.

"I've got some older things."

"Good. Go home and change, and be at this address by twelve noon."

He hands me an open file, isolating an address in Long Island City, Queens, by making circles around it with his index finger.

"It's a garment factory," he explains. "We need to start cracking down on illegal hiring procedures."

"You mean illegal aliens?"

"Yeah."

Strength-gathering pause.

"Can't they assign someone else to this job?"

"Are you kiddin'? You're perfect! What, am I supposed to send O'Shaughnessy down there to pose as an illegal alien?"

"It's not that, it's—"

"Oh, not this again: You can't ask to be reassigned every time you land a detail that cuts into your social register. Let me tell you something, Fil—we know all about your letting that kid in the deli go on account of you said you didn't believe in arresting street vendors as a way to solve the city's drug problems."

That bastard. When he squealed, he squealed on *me*. I resolve to perform a tonsillectomy on him with a rusty penknife the next time I see him.

"I had to promise him something so he would lead us to the other guy," I say.

"Granting Federal immunity is a bit different from letting the guy have back a gram of his confiscated dope to party up with."

Oooooh!—Never mind the rusty penknife, I'll just use my teeth!

"I'd say you've used up all your free spaces, Fil. It's time to play the game the way we tell you. *Capisce?*"

Resigned sigh. I look up:

"Let me see the file."

* * *

After an unsatisfying coffee break I check in with Detective Meehan, ask him about the toxic leak.

"Still under investigation. But you know it's pretty tough going when your primary suspect is dead."

"And how's *that* investigation going?"

He says: "We're closing the case."

"Yeah? What'd you get?"

"Nothing. It was an accident."

"It *was?*"

"Don't sound so disappointed."

"—But what about—Oh, never mind. Okay, thanks."

"Don't mention it."

He asks me, "By the way, what are you doing next Friday?" I say I don't know and he says how about going out with him? I say let me call you back. I'm about to call Meg but my superior points out rather gruffly that my coffee break is over and I'd better get back to work.

And I'm wondering what the payoff is to throw over a murder investigation. I could use a new yacht. The old one leaks.

* * *

Saturday afternoon begins an experience that I would rather forget. The garment sweatshop I'm investigating for the I.N.S. lies in the shadow of the Queensboro Bridge, in an industrial neighborhood that in most cities would be the proud, job-producing center of town, but that in the Financial Capital of the World is relegated to the seedy, as-yet unrenovated factory district across the East Channel. It's a low-lying, squat building with rows of upward jutting window shafts on the south slope of the roof that earmark it as dating from no later than 1910, and possibly twenty or thirty years earlier. I never did have the time to take that History of Architecture course.

Why doesn't the I.N.S. just bust the place flat if they're so sure of it? Well, the file says that some bright boy downtown set forth some elaborate equations that led to the conclusion that the I.N.S. was wasting too much money with not enough return to show for it—too many of these firetrap sweatshops have too many back exits, through which too many illegals are always escaping—and they thought it would be worth their time and effort to try a new system: A designated agent infiltrates the targeted joint, learns where these exits are, and makes sure they're plugged when the *migra* drop in. And they got me to do the plugging.

Somebody phoned ahead and told them I was somebody's cousin, just in from El Salvador (which I guess sounds *sort of* like Ecuador), and could they find a spot for me? They were told, Sure.

The ground-level entrance leads to the storage and shipping offices. I am sent around to the loading dock in back where a wrought-iron staircase takes you down into a real hell hole. The union derrick operator who showed me in here abandons me at the bottom of these stairs, in a low-ceilinged room that must have the surface area of a football field, and the breathable air of a good-sized suitcase. It's getting on into the real dog days of summer, in the 90s every day up on the street; but it must be at least 110 degrees in here, and I don't see any fans operating, just seventy-five to a hundred men, women, and—yes—children working fabric cutters, sewing machines, steam presses, and lord knows what else. I can't see beyond the wall of steam that rises up from the presses. For all I know there's a funny little red dude with horns and a barbed tail keeping things in order on the other side.

I'm almost right. Through this haze steps a barrel of a man, with *schweinhocks* for arms, salivating into a cigar, and wearing a raggedy tank-top T-shirt that does for his gray-haired and flabby roll-top chest what a carnation might do for an oil spill.

"You Maria?" he says, bearing down on me.

I almost answer, before I remember that I'm not supposed to know English. So I just look at him like your average scared rabbit.

"Never mind, come here," he says, grabbing me by the arm and toting me into the melée. What? No W-4 forms to sign?

He hauls me past the wondering eyes of dozens of olive-skinned women with black hair who are sewing men's white shirts together at a fantastic speed under conditions that Henry Ford would have found oppressive, and drops me in front of an unoccupied sewing machine.

"Know how to work one of these?"

I shake my head rigidly.

"Oh, great. What the hell can I have you do?" He's not talking to me, but to himself. "Chees I thought all you spics knew how to sew . . . " My love for this guy is improving by the minute. "I got it." Here he snaps his pudgy fingers, and crooks the index for me to follow him. We walk past tired-eyed men who look like they are used to getting whipped for not jumping fast enough, and young women whose natural beauty shows through even this grime, who should be washing clothes in a mountain stream somewhere near a village that no longer exists because it was carpet-bombed away in the search for rebellious subjects and their sympathizers.

The guy walks ahead of me as if he's weighing down the building, keeping it from drifting away. We stop in front of a battalion of finished pieces hanging closely-packed from eight free-standing clothes poles on wheels, and the human ballast tank picks up a bottle of industrial stain remover in one hand, and holds out the besmeared sleeve of a shiny synthetic blouse in the other. He shakes the two as if trying to train a seal, showing me that I'm supposed to use the one on the other, let it dry, and scrub out the stain with some dry brushes. I nod to show understanding. He spreads an arm to encompass all eight units. I nod again.

"Good," he says and points to his watch. "You work 'til four o'clock. *Sí?* Four o'clock."

I nod again, stiffly. He hands me the bottle and the brushes.

"Get to work," he says, and gives me not a pinch, but a solid, full-handed grab on the ass. I don't have to do any pretending. My startle is genuine enough. He chuckles and moves off into the fire and brimstone. He should be the one going to jail.

I'm already sweating just from standing still. This place is oppressively hot. What can I do? I get to work applying liquid stain remover to the ladies' garment. The smell that rises from the stuff as it evaporates is enough to make me feel faint. I take a look at the "CAUTION" label that I'm not supposed to be able to read. It states very clearly that this product should only be used in a well-ventilated area, and that prolonged exposure without a breathing mask is hazardous to one's health. Oh, goody. There's something else below that's just too ironic to keep to myself: The small print says that this is made by Scynthia Chemical, which is a division of Morse, Incorporated. Jesus, what *don't* they own? Is there anything left? Some hand-operated orange-juice press in the Northwest Territories that they haven't taken over yet? Some unconglomerated Eskimo who still fishes with hand-carved deer-antler spears, and not a nylon rod and reel manufactured by We Own Everything, a division of Morse, Inc.?

I look around for a clean scrap of fabric to wrap around my nose and mouth. That ought to be easy enough in a garment factory, shouldn't it? But there's nothing near my section of the floor besides *Night of the Lepus*-sized dust bunnies, so I skip over to the cutting tables to ask for a spare scrap.

I don't even get the second half of *"Hóla"* out of my mouth when a fat hand clamps around my elbow and yanks me rudely back towards the clothes racks, and the overseer lets loose with a stretch of curses relating to the unusual characteristics of my reproductive system, as well as my mother's reproductive system, which I won't inflict on you just now. The basic idea is that I'd better stay where he told me to stay and do what he told me to do.

He stands and watches me for a few minutes while I squirt on some of the liquid brain-cell-corroder-in-a-drum, blow on it to help it dry—which is not easy at 110 degrees Fahrenheit and a humidity approaching total saturation. It's hard to catch my breath given the presence of noxious chemicals and lung-searing air, and I feel dizzy as I start brushing away the crusty powder to reveal the spotless fabric beneath. The troll is satisfied, and leaves me alone to my fate.

I get busy with my two jobs. One for the sultan of this tar pit, the other for the Federal Government. I start looking around while I work, checking the place for exits as per my instructions. I am also looking around at some of the faces, hoping to spot some Ishmael who I can warn of the pending storm. From where I stand, I'd say they all qualify. This is going to be rough.

The President's abstract rhetoric about these people does not give color to the daily, blood-shot reality of life in those strips of fertile volcanic land where spreading the true Word of Christ is persecuted far more violently than it was in the Roman Empire, as recorded by the Apostles. Christ was nailed up to die in destitution by the side of the road, but not buried in a mass grave along with 20,000 of his "sympathizers." Oh dear, I'd better watch myself. Thoughts like these could lose me my shot at the Medal of Freedom. Forget it. Forget I ever said anything. I have a job to do.

But it's not that easy. When we break at four o'clock and pile out to the street and some fresh air greets us that contains the active ingredient oxygen for a change, I am instantly surrounded by a throng of motherly refugees who have seen the new girl and want to help her out.

Not all of them are here fleeing bloodbath repression. Admittedly, some of them have snuck in from reasonably democratic countries such as Venezuela, Guyana, Trinidad, and Costa Rica, looking to better themselves economically. But they are illegal nevertheless, and are paying the price for it. One woman's husband lost his hand in a workplace accident that was caused by the company's negligence. If he had been a resident, he could have dragged them into court for that. As an illegal, he has the right to remain silent. One guy wants to go back, but knows that he will never be allowed to return here, even if he voluntarily gives himself up.

The grandmothers want to know where I'm from. I tell them the truth. That puts me in the economic refugee category, which is less urgent than the life-threatened refugee, but they are still just about knocking each other down to be the one who offers me the place to stay for the week until I get my bearings. I thank them all profusely, but tell them I am staying with some cousins in the Bronx, A young couple tells me that they're heading for the Bronx, too, we can all go together.

We catch the RR train to Manhattan to change there for a Bronx train.

"You want to go out to a movie with us?" invites the woman, in Spanish.

I give the excuse that I don't have any money.

The man laughs and says, "Who does?"

I explain that it's not that, but that I'm already spending money that isn't mine, and I have to live very frugally until I pay off some debts. They understand that all right.

The man tells me he has a great second job that brings in a bundle. He works for a cable TV company, drumming up business.

"How?" I ask.

"They pay me to drive around the neighborhood using a CB and jamming the airwaves."

The young couple laugh. They are happy. For them it has been working out all right after all. They are on their way to a better life here. My head hurts from thinking about what's going to happen to them, with my help. I want to tell them. I want *so much* to tell them. But they would have to tell everyone else, for the very same reasons, and the word would get out, and the Lieutenant promised me that if that happened, my ass would be grilled until the fat sizzled into the fire. In those words.

I excuse myself from their company when we get out at the 59th Street station, telling them I have to meet a cousin downtown. They wish me well, and I go down into the pissy underpass to cross to the downtown side of the platform. When my train pulls into the station, the young couple are still standing on the opposite platform, waving at me, their arms around each other.

I get out at City Hall and find a pay phone. I dial Detective Snyder's precinct. After a few relays, he gets on the phone.

"Where you been, Fil?"

"'Don't ask."

"I've been waiting for your call."

"The place I was in didn't have a phone."

"Izzatso? So how'd it go with Faber?"

"Fair to middling. I think the best way to move is after the coffee. I'd like to locate where they send their coffee after it comes off the boat."

"So get on it."

"Can't you do that?"

"With what?"

"You do work with a whole bureau full of people, don't you?"

"Fil, I can't tie it legally to the official investigation. You know that."

"Yeah. So what am I supposed to do?"

"Call them up and ask where their warehouse is."

"Dream on, Snyder: They won't even give out what brand of toilet paper they use in the executive washrooms over the phone."

"So go back and see Faber."

"And do what? Fuck him on his marble-top desk while I crack their computer access codes with my feet?"

This is met by silence. That means, in a word—Yes.

"I'm a married man, Fil," is what he says. And I'm not. So that's it.

"I'll get back to you." And I hang up.

My fingers are cold and shaky down in this sweltering subway station as I reach for another dime, drop it into the slot and dial Jim Faber's home number. I don't know what I'm going to say, and I don't know why he should talk to me at all. Ring. Ring. Ring. Ring. Ring. No answer. I try his office number. Score.

"Sorry about last night," I begin after the greetings.

"*You're* sorry! I got so plastered I let you slip away. I oughta be whipped with a wet noodle. Give me a chance to make it up to you?"

He obviously doesn't remember shit. I can't believe my luck. Or his stupidity.

"Sure, when?" I ask him.

"How about in an hour?"

"I've got a meeting now. Is two hours all right?"

"You've got a meeting at five o'clock on a Saturday?"

"Hey, you're in *your* office."

"Sorry. Where do you wanna meet?"

I take a blindfolded swing at the piñata:

"How about your office?"

"You can't get in, the building's locked."

"So come down and let me in."

This option has apparently not occurred to him.

"Okay," he says, betraying the fact that he never thought of such a bizarre thing. "Seven o'clock?"

"Between seven and seven-fifteen. You know how meetings are—"

"Sure, right. See you then."

I heave a deep, nervous sigh after hanging up. Now what? A little voice inside me says, I'll tell you now what—now you've got to walk up to Federal Plaza and talk to the folks from the U.S. Department of Justice.

Ten minutes later I'm in the Assistant District Director for Deportation's blank-walled office, giving my report.

"Nice work," says the Assistant District Director for Deportation. "We really need some numbers to get that budget increase. We pull off a few of these and we'll finally be able to update our equipment and increase the number of agents. How are the exits?"

"There's only one. Barely big enough for a rat." Like me.

"Great. You be on that exit. Right?"

"Right."

"Then it's set. We make the sweep Monday morning at eleven A.M. Good job."

Good job? If you say so. Now let me have those thirty pieces of silver so I can go hang myself.

* * *

I'm still in my sweatshop clothes, and there isn't enough time to make the long haul to my apartment and back by 7:00, so I have to go into a store and buy a new summer dress and some make-up supplies so I can look the part for Mr. Faber. This money comes out of my own pocket. If I were officially on the case, the Department would supply me with a whopping twenty bucks. But still it's something. As it is, I'm working a cross between a cop and a private eye, and getting the worst of both. The New Me struts out of the changing room and heads for the street past salespeople who, even in this town on a Saturday, cannot help but be taken aback by the transformation.

* * *

Faber's office hasn't changed since yesterday. He welcomes me with a kiss that ends up on my cheek after some evasive maneuvers that I picked up watching Mr. Sulu pilot the *Enterprise* every night at midnight. Hooray for reruns.

"I hope I wasn't—uh, sexually aggressive last night," says Jim Faber.

"You tried to be."

"Sorry. I bet our immoral American ways are kind of shocking to a small-town Catholic girl like yourself."

"You're forgetting that I've been in New York for eight years."

"Oh that's right—"

"But what you say is still true, to a certain extent. My town didn't have any year-round roads linking it with the outside world until the early seventies. It's still a place where it's more acceptable to be an unwed mother than to use birth control. Because, the reasoning is, we all sin, and it's okay to sin, as long as you repent, but birth control means you're doing it over and over, and *liking* it, and *that's* bad, if you can picture that sort of community mindset."

"No, not really.—Excuse me," he says, going over to answer his phone, which is making the muffled chirping sound of a dying cricket.

While he's talking on the phone about holding out on some price fixing until after the rainy season to see what kind of a crop they're dealing with, I wander around the office, taking in all those details that I missed on my first breathtaking visit to this high tower. There is a bookcase displaying cigars, framed photos of Faber and some fishing buddies, two standing college track and field trophies, in fact, everything but books. There's a freshly unpacked box on the floor in front of the bookcase with some brand-new brochures that must be stockholder's reports, because I can't imagine Morse, Inc. soliciting investment from *anybody*.

I kneel down, which is a long-forgotten challenge in a clinging summer dress, and lift out a sample copy to flip through. Faber has his back to me, talking on the phone while looking out the window. I stand up and try to stroll around the office looking casual as I glance through the brochure. There are pictures of the interior of this building (the photographer probably had to sign a blood pact never to let the negatives fall into the wrong hands), then there are pictures of some nice stucco branch offices in Stamford, Connecticut; the proud flagship of their importation fleet, foreign offices, logos, and—small and unassuming, because no matter how you try, you can't dress up a warehouse—a photo of their "Intermediate Waste Management Facility in Mahikatinuk, New York." Well, well. Things are looking up.

Faber gets off the phone and turns towards me. He's got "What are you doing with that?" written all over his gaping mouth, but he doesn't say it.

"Can I keep this?" I ask. Innocence personified.

"Uh—sure, why not?" He can't very well tell the woman he's hoping to screw that he doesn't trust her with a copy of the company brochure. So it's worked. But at what price? Now I have to go out with him and listen to volumes 25-50 of his Theory Of The World, including The Index and the Supplements.

I ask him. "What is this, anyway?"

"Oh, that place. I don't even know why it's in the brochure. It's just a storage facility."

In upstate New York?

"The boss is sending the V.P. for Waste Management up there in a week. Search me what for. That place is the asshole of the universe."

Well, then maybe the universe has two assholes . . .

All through the evening I keep things cool, doing everything I can to indicate that I'm not a "fast" American girl, but that if he treats me right, eventually, maybe . . .

In reality I'm thinking about getting to Mahikatinuk, New York. If it's not too far, maybe I can go tomorrow—no, tomorrow I'm committed to being the third base coach for the rehabilitation center. All right then, maybe Monday, after—God, no—after the immigration raid.

It's only by way of the severest threats to myself that I stick to three drinks, overcoming the tremendous scream within my warring breast to drink myself into oblivion. In fact the only safety catch that keeps me from it is the knowledge that I could end up in bed with this creep. Someone else and I just might go over the edge. It's that bad.

* * *

Of course there was no ball game the next day. You might have seen it in the papers: Officer Francisco Carrera of the 34th Precinct was shot and killed late Saturday night while answering a complaint about the dope dealers gathered on the corner of 173rd Street and St. Nicholas Avenue.

There was no heroic fight to be the first in line to donate blood. Officer Carrera was declared dead at the scene.

The word went around to all the street dealers: We are going to bust every one of your asses from now till Doomsday until we turn up the motherfucker responsible, so it's to your benefits to smoke the guy out for us.

But that doesn't make any of us feel any better. An NYPD cop's chances of being killed in the line of duty by some scum are a lousy 1 in 3,744, which is just too damn low for comfort given the fact that people win Lotto every week against odds of 1 in 7 million.

Officers in the precinct are expressing their deepest sympathies for a guy most of them didn't care about while he was alive. I was one of the ones closest to him, but none of the others will admit that. I still remember his last touch—that "thank you" pat on the shoulder just the day before . . .

So instead of a ball game we have a funeral, which is packed to the rafters with high-level officials and the like. The priest chooses a passage from Samuel:

"But truly as the Lord lives, and as thy soul lives, there is but a step between me and death."

I'm standing near the back (because all the seats are taken), confronting my greatest fear—Isn't it anybody's? That of sudden, violent death. Or the worst variation on that—painful, violent death that is not sudden *enough*, the kind that leaves you able to feel your personality draining out of you; that horrible, irreversible way that transmutes you from a unique human being into just another jangle of ganglia, an anonymous heap of bone, flesh and blood, a jungle of twisted, still-warm entrails, slowly leaving the realm of the quick, fighting for life that is going forever, and feeling it going; maybe even seeing other forms blurrily standing around you gaping down as you recede unstoppably into the emptiness of that last level—Level 23, step down, please—the only one from which no one ever comes back; a quivering mass of protoplasm, while sidewalk observers look on saying, Tsk, tsk, what's the world coming to? And that you should be rendered into this woeful condition by the remorseless lashing out of an ignorant ape. But the most dreadful is that feeling of losing everything that makes you *you*, and becoming nameless pulp, just another tagged stiff for the first-year forensics to play practical jokes on the women with. To think that one minute you're eating a jelly donut and the next you're flat on the sidewalk with a very large hole in your heart . . .

And for the second time in twenty hours I must suppress the urge to drown myself in alcohol, with all I've got in me. I have to face tomorrow straight, or I may never face another day straight for as long as I live. I go home and throw up. Tears mix in with it.

* * *

Monday morning and all's rotten. I'm perched by the clothes racks near that one route to freedom, like a carrion crow waiting for the old coot to keel over and breathe his last already. Why don't they just shoot me and be quick about it—Why do I have to sit and watch while they clean and load the rifles?

Exactly eighteen minutes late, the *migra* raid the place, and I execute my orders. When the flow of desperate refugees gets to the metal door that leads to the street, I'm there blocking it, with my badge out and gun drawn, pointing it straight up. I might as well put it to my head. It'll be a quicker, less agonizing death than being torn apart by the eyes of my brothers and sisters, as they are doing now. The young woman from the Bronx wipes away her tears and slaps me across the face with the same hand, leaving my face wet with her tears.

And I deserve it.

The *migra* lick the place clean.

What have I done?

＊　＊　＊

I try calling Meg for moral support. It takes six tries but I finally get her.

"Fil?"

"Don't sound so surprised. I know I haven't been in touch for a while, but my job's really been dragging me down lately."

"Yeah, some days my job doesn't quite fill me with joy, either," she says.

It's nice to hear a sympathetic voice. It's nice to hear a *voice*.

Then I say, "Did you ever come up with anything more on the McCullough-Lilliflex connection?"

"No, McCullough didn't have any friends at Lillifiex."

"But you said—"

"I was wrong."

"Well, give me the names and I'll check it out."

"It was a bum tip, Fil. There's no story."

"Give me the names and I'll check it out."

"I gotta go—"

"Meg!"

"What?"

They got to you didn't they?

"Make it quick," she says.

"Look, you want to pull out, that's fine, as long as you didn't tell them about me."

Click.

Her too. What the fuck is going on around here? What am I supposed to do now? Never mind what the books and movies say, I can't pick up *all* the angles and investigate them myself. All I can do is pick one and hammer away at it. And that one is Morse, Inc.

* * *

"Hello, Jean-Luc?"

"Just a moment," says the voice of a woman.

"—Oui?"

"Jean-Luc, it's Filomena. I know it's been a little—"

"What do you want?"

"Well, there's a party in my neighborhood tonight, going to be some friends who I haven't seen in a while—I've been busy all week with this awful undercov—"

"No. I'm not sure—"

"What: You're not sure about going out tonight?" Or you're not sure about us?

"I do not theenk that we should see each other any more. *C'est fini entre nous. Bonne chance.*" I hear the woman asking what was that all about and him telling her, Oh nothing, before we get disconnected.

And I streak my face in a silent primal scream.

* * *

It's still light out when I walk in to the party, which is already in full swing. I have set myself a strict limit of one beer every hour and a half. The hostess, a fattening Peruvian woman with a boring husband and three kids under six, kisses me, plants a cold bottle of American beer in my left hand, and grabs my other hand to lead me into the fray.

There's a nice crowd there, and dance music manages to get selected with a minimum of nationalistic interference. Sure, the Dominicans want to play *merengue,* the Colombians want *cumbias,* and the Puerto Ricans and Cubans want *salsa,* but two diplomats who have positioned themselves by the stereo are keeping themselves busy by insuring that each faction gets the floor in equal allotments. I should have brought my armadillo-hide *charango* and bamboo *rondador* and insisted that the Ecuadorian sierra have its representation as well. Maybe next time.

Some of those who know me come up to greet me and ask me where I've been. I tell them I'm being given a trial run as an undercover, but I can't talk about it, which is true enough. I hear that most of the crew of that plane that dropped the atomic bomb on Hiroshima had a pretty tough time coping afterwards, too. (All except the Captain. He thought it was just great.)

One man mentions Carrera—I knew him, didn't I? I say yes. Gee, that's rough. I say I'm recovering. But his family never will.

He asks me to dance some *cumbia,* which is good to get the circulation going, and then some *merengue,* which is for when you're ready to get *hot.*

An elderly man with an Argentine accent to his Spanish complains that there are no *tangos.* The two diplomats go into conference over this international crisis, and manage to dig up a scratchy record of *tangos* from the 1950s.

The *argentino* clutches me without warning, and whisks me out into the middle of the living room, barely giving me the chance to put my beer down. Now I can *cumbia* with the best of them, and the Caribbean beats are similar, just faster with more African flavor. But I don't know a *tango* from a hole in the ground, and I am reduced to being a rag doll in the *argentino's* hands, falling when he trips me backwards over his leg, stopping where he catches me, and landing where he throws me. The living room rug has been pushed back in a disorderly mass behind the kitchen chairs, and I find myself wishing it were back in place. I could use the friction.

The *tango* finally ends and someone from the Puerto Rican contingent requests *salsa*. I wriggle away from the *argentino* and go to find my beer, which has disappeared. I'm going to start another, but I've been here for less than an hour. One side of my brain argues that I was only halfway through with the first one, so it doesn't count as a full beer. The other half of my brain says to Shut up.

I have the second beer at 10:00, by which time a number of people who don't have long rides home or can afford baby sitters are already getting drunk. I have to limit my dancing, which makes you sweaty and thirsty, which makes you drink. Also when you're always moving to the rhythm, you don't notice how unsteady your gait is becoming.

There's a group of people talking politics, and I have to stay away from them too. Politics always makes me want to drink more as well. It occurs to me that if I'm not going to dance or talk politics, Why am I at a party? To keep me from wallowing in my own solitary despair, says a voice inside as my hand brings the beer bottle up to my mouth and tips it straight up, to chug it down fast and silence that goddamn voice already.

The voice says, Whoa—Slow down, girl, slow down . . . I listen to it, put the beer down.

The group talking politics moves away from the noise of the hi-fi speakers, nearer to me. I go over by the window and look out onto the hot summer night outside. I can hear a car stereo playing louder than the stereo in the apartment, in front of the *bodega* on the corner. I can also hear the politics. A reactionary Cuban is defending the President's policies, explaining that cutting taxes would increase federal revenues and pay for the military build-up. Some of those around him are trying to tell him that he's full of it, but people are either getting too foggy from drinking to argue seriously, or they just don't have the ammunition necessary to provide the antithesis that would put the Cuban on the defensive. Telling someone that they're full of it is not an antithesis.

I've got an antithesis, all right, but like I said, I'm staying out of it.

One of the women—I don't know her, but she's a *dominicana* who talks faster than most people listen—counters the Cuban by bringing up the Administration's latest declaration that the nation's homeless are basically "Not their problem."

"They're not," says the Cuban. "That's a problem for the state and local government, not the federal government."

"But if they weren't building all those bombs, there'd be money to help those people," says the *dominicana.*

"Let me ask you a question: How many homeless do you think there are in the United States?"

"Well—I don't know, exactly," admits the *dominicana,* which seems to satisfy the Cuban. "But it must be at least two or three hundred thousand."

The Cuban laughs at this and tells the *dominicana* she doesn't know what she's talking about, and that the only reason she holds such naive opinions is that she doesn't know all the facts, like he does. I start towards the group to tell him that 300,000 homeless is a *low* estimate, but—well, you know the story. I empty my beer and head for another one. There are no more out on the table, so I go into the kitchen.

There's no one in the kitchen, so I take the liberty of looking into the refrigerator, where a few dozen beers lie on their sides, having temporarily usurped the territory that would normally be occupied by food in a family with three small children. I'm helping myself to a beer when the hostess walks in, and starts yelling at me.

"That's right, just come for the beer, what do you care about talking to the guests or dancing?!! No, you're just here to drink my beer! I should hide it from you, you *maldita ecuatoriana!*"

She has obviously been drinking more than her capacity, but that shouldn't be enough to produce this outsized raging.

"With friends like you, who needs enemies!" She grabs the beer from my hand and throws it into the sink, where it shatters.

Now everyone is looking at us. I don't hear the music. A song must have stopped and now we've got an audience. Please put on another song and go away, please? But no, everybody hears what my inebriated hostess says next:

"Dirty *perra* of an ecuatoriana, get out of my house! You who turn in your own people to the *migra! ¡Perra! ¡Puta! ¡Marecona!"*

I think I'd better be going.

Frankly, I feel like I've got a broom handle all the way up my ass as I walk out of the apartment, all eyes following me. I walk down three flights of stairs and out into the hot night. It's still early, many parties are just starting, but I decide to go home and go to bed.

But I stand on the sidewalk, unable to turn in either direction. Going home alone right now might only make it worse. I need to be with people. I need a drink. I head for a nearby bar and order a straight shot of whiskey. My hands are shaking. I spill some of the whiskey on my chin as I gulp it down. I make myself pay for the shot right now and move away from the bar. It's okay. I can stand it.

Alcohol is more dangerous than the worst illegal drugs. One bottle is a lethal dose. Much less will make certain people crazy. But alcohol is not just dangerous because of its unpredictable effects. It's dangerous because it's so accepted. Tell people you've tried pot and they run to hide their children from you. But alcohol?—Drink, drink! What's the matter, you a snob or something? Don't want to drink with me? Don't be a baby, drink! As far as I'm concerned, it's pure chance that has landed marijuana under the stigma of illegal, while alcohol gets served as breakfast "eye-openers" on commercial airlines.

I try to distract myself by looking up at the television. It's the news. A group of elderly Jews, many of them concentration camp survivors wearing their fifty-year-old striped uniforms, are being dragged by West German police away from a protest demonstration in the parking lot of the Bergen-Belsen Memorial. I tuned in too late to learn what the protest is about, but not too late to hear one of the tall, blond policemen explaining, in good, German-accented English, that he is "just following orders." A shiver runs through me. So it's the same over there, too. I'd like to invite this policeman over for a drink. I think we'd understand each other. Handsome, too.

Then the scene switches to more protests, this time anti-government, anti-American protests in South Korea. The police fire tear gas canisters from behind a wall of metal shields. Then I watch glassy-eyed as a student from Seoul National University sets fire to himself and jumps off the top floor of a four-storey building that looks like the library. Somebody sitting at the bar says, "Hey, Paco, change this, will you?" thus saving me the trouble of asking.

Paco changes the channel to one of those fake mafioso movies where everybody walks around in sharp suits with white shoes and ties, blowing people away whilst hollering Brooklynese at each other. And the network censors are having a helluva time splicing away at every third word of the "dialogue."

Why do they bother showing a movie like this if they're going to have to chop it into incoherent shreds like this? If you ask me, there's a little too much inbreeding among TV executives.

The ads interrupt, and they're no relief either. First some pretty member of AFTRA gets a few thousand for trying to convince me that it's actually *fun* to wrap meat in plastic. Then they try to sell me some products by *telling* me that the products are artificial: One big brand name emphasizes that an envelope of chemicals "is not soup when you buy it: *You* make it soup." They actually go out of their way to tell me that their soup isn't soup! How strange, this America. Next, someone makes the selling point of their ad the fact that they have made a salad dressing that doesn't separate. Now everyone knows that oil and vinegar separate if you don't shake them, so what these people have done is add some chemical that binds the two together, and they're proudly telling me, though not in quite so many words, that this is the case.

And what genius did it take to come up with the circular dustpan? Oh God, these late-night ads offering a better life through mail-order plastics are so depressing.

I decide to take a walk.

Out in the street it occurs to me to head up to Inwood, which is a neighborhood where they don't know me, it's only a few stops away, and some of the bars up there have great live Irish music on weekends.

I can appreciate the soul music of any oppressed people. No matter what angle of the world it comes from, it's all got the heartbeat of truth in it.

I take the M100 up Broadway to 204th Street, get out and start walking. A bar called the Warthog seems to attract a clientele who favor the use of motorcycle chains to end discussions. I decide to avoid the Warthog. Kelly's Piano Bar looks like it has the same clientele, only a generation older. McCafferty's is the place. White-haired men with bright pink faces and cardigans that three sheep provided the wool for are up on a small stage singing Irish Republican songs. I walk inside, and nobody takes much notice of me. Everyone is singing or tapping their feet along with the music, except for a few of the younger ones there, who talk about sports. Fine. This is a nice crowd. At least I'm not likely to get gang-raped on the pool table, which I'm not sure I could say for the Warthog.

The third-generation American Irish are singing a stirring collection of classics like, "The Rising of the Moon," "The Men of the West," and "Kevin Barry," with its refrain, "Another martyr for

Old Erin, another murder for the Crown," that raises the hair on the back of my neck.

I order straight Irish whiskey. I can't help it if the stuff—the music, that is—gets me in one of those moods. It doesn't matter that I'm not the least bit Irish. The music of an enslaved people crying out for rebellion kind of gets you—no matter what color the passports are in the country God slapped you down in. At the end of this song, there is rousing applause, accompanied by the rhythmic pounding of beer bottles against tables, and the musicians start playing the deceptively sweet opening notes of "Tipperary So Far Away."

When they sing:

The moon it shown down on old Dublin town
When the deadly fight was o'er
Thousands lay on the cold, cold ground
Their lives to claim no more
The moon it shown down on O'Connell Street
Where a dying young rebel lay
With his body gashed and his arms outstretched
And his life's blood flown away . . .

—There's a lump in my throat and I'm fighting back the tears. I order another whiskey. And another. And another, before I realize what I'm doing. I tell the barman to cancel that last one even as he's pouring it out for me. I pay my tab and leave McCafferty's, prepared to go home and cry myself to sleep.

I come home to the silent walls of my apartment. I put on some Ecuadorian *pasillo* on my pitiful but adequate cassette player, but the mournful harmonies are worse than the silence. This is going to be some night to forget.

So I put on some jazz instead, turned way low and go to get down the bottle of whiskey, promising myself that I'm going to have just one to knock me out so I will sleep. But I've hidden the whiskey. I laugh at my own foolishness. I can handle it, I'm assuring myself as I open the closet, drag out the ripped storage boxes and pull out the whiskey. The box the whiskey is in is full of papers. The one on top is a note Jean-Luc left here once during happier times. I read it:

Dear Filomena,

I hope you have had a good day.

I have got up quite late! I feel sorry for you who must get up so soon.

We should not work 40 hours a week for pay. In fact a French study has shown that 2 hours a week would be enough. I really want to believe that, since everybody could earn a living & life could be much more interesting for most people. The sad reality is that we have not reached that wisdom.

I'll call you tomorrow at your work. Have a very good night and day.

See you soon.

Love

– Jean-Luc –

Reading this was a mistake. Today was a mistake. My life was a mistake. I start flipping through the papers, all the things I've done wrong in my life flashing before my eyes: My acceptance into the Police Department, my application for citizenship, my application for a visa, my transcripts from the University of Guayaquil, and there, near the bottom I come across some family pictures of us all as children in the mountains. Stuck to the back of one of these is a washed-out photocopy of my brother's death certificate. It's one of those absurd vestiges of that cruel era, hand written, with stamps, seals, and illegible signatures all over it. But I read the text. I should know better than to do that, but I do it. I can be that way sometimes. I read the death notice and there's no stopping it this time.

I had shed some tears of sympathy for Carrera and for my own mortality, but now it just comes flowing out, ceaselessly.

It's coming now. All the accumulated pain of all the bad, stupid, selfish things I've ever done, which happen to be counter-balanced by all the good, intelligent, caring things I've done—or at least have tried to do—but there's no one around to remind me about them now.

I uncork the bottle and upend it, swallowing about two big shots' worth before a spontaneous shiver forces me to stop, and whiskey dribbles down and stains my shirt.

Such a colorful world and I have to deal with so much black and white. Drink.

Suicide statistics say that more women try, but more men succeed. Drink.

It's like riding a brakeless go-cart down a mountainside. Once it starts it just gathers speed until it hits bottom. I come up for air, then dive back down for another dunk. I put the bottle down on the floor with a much heavier Klunk! than before.

I think about my brother. I feel guilty for so rarely thinking about him, but you've got to keep on living. The past makes a lousy hiding place. I'm having a good cry, aren't I?—thinking how nobody I love is here with me, or alive.

Drink.

Where did my sensitivity go? Right now I would estimate that I have sunk down to about Level 17 out of the 23 available shades of black. Level One is black, but it's a glossy black, reflective surface like the glass top on the table I'm using to stand myself up with. Whhoops. Left the bottle on the floor. I pick up the bottle without banging my head on any of the walls and put it on the table, where I can see myself staring up at me from under the bottle. But the subsequent levels of black get duller and darker until you get sucked into the singular Pit of total blackness, from which nothing escapes, not even light.

Why does the basement always flood when the house is on fire?

Drink.

I'm almost—almost—not feeling the pain anymore, and a sinister thought spreads through my brain like an opiate, takes hold with hooked talons of iron, and the little voice is overwhelmed. I stagger over to the icebox and get out the bag of marijuana. I find the papers and commence rolling a joint, even though I'm barely able to stand. It's funny how reflex can keep you going after reason has gotten up and left. The rolled joint looks like a cheese doodle, which I find excessively amusing. I ignite one end of it, and begin trading off drinks for tokes, drinks for tokes, drinks for tokes.

By the time I'm finished with the joint and the joint is finished with me, the room is spinning so fast that the glass that I didn't even know I was holding flies against the wall and falls to the floor with a Clatter! Somebody has put my room in an ultracentrifuge. The centrifugal force is pushing all the objects in the room away from the center of spin, and they start climbing the walls. I try to go over and bring them back down, but the force pins me to the wall along with all of the objects. My feet aren't even touching the ground, as I struggle against the spin, but it keeps throwing me back against the wall. Finally, I muster all my strength, and hurl myself headlong into the eye of the storm. There's something reflective there and my face comes up and hits me.

I don't remember dreaming.

* * *

I wake up out of a blackness as in one of Wilson's paintings, and spend the whole of my day emptying every last drop out of all the liquor bottles in the apartment.

Into myself.

That night I pee in my bed for the first time in twenty-six years.

* * *

The next day I call in to claim one of the sick days I've got coming to me, and as long as I've got another day off, I head downtown to get blind drunk in a bar, for a change of pace. I figure maybe being in public will keep me within more reasonable limits. I'm only partly right.

After dropping the equivalent of a day's net pay in three, four, five different bars, I stumble down into the subway and stare at the pylons, waiting for the rattling roar of the train.

What I hear is quite different: TING!

"Ting?" That's an odd sound for a subway to make. But a large fleck of paint has just exploded off the pylon in front of my eyes, leaving a deep depression. How curious. Then I look across the platform to the downtown side and there's a man there aiming a long, silencer-nosed pistol at me.

I jump behind the pylon as this time more of a KRAK! chips a few knife-like shards of tile out of the wall behind me. Pylons and I have been developing quite a symbiotic relationship lately.

When you're really drunk, as I am, not even this will sober you up completely, but I sure as hell start paying attention. Is this happening? Or have I got the delirium tremens after only three days? I want to look, but to look is to stick my head into the line of fire. Shit, they even teach that at the Academy.

But *not* to look means maybe he's coming after me and I'm standing here waiting for it. I look. The man with the gun shoots. A huge dent gets TANG!-ed into the lip of the pylon as I duck back behind it. Where is everybody? Aren't there any people down here to help me?

There's a phone three pylons down. There's also the exit to the street at the other end of the station, but—it's at the other end of the station.

I run for the phone. Thank God this station has two local and two express tracks, so my assailant has to direct his shot through a forest of pylons, and the two shots he squeezes off don't even reach my side of the platform. I've made it to the phone. I dial Detective Snyder's number. He's not in, I'm told.

I look. The man with the gun has jumped down onto the first set of tracks and is starting to step carefully over the third rail to get to me. I can hear a train rumbling in the tunnel.

He's tall, thin, wearing a long black overcoat, with thinning slicked-back hair, two black dots for eyes and the pale face and long sharp nose of a vulture. I would definitely not have trouble picking him out of a lineup.

I tell them to radio Detective Snyder and have him or have someone send a car to the 23rd Street station, that an officer is in urgent need of assistance.

The train rumbling increases and it turns out to be the downtown express. So the man with the gun has to step back onto the downtown local track and wait while the express zooms by. By the time the downtown express whooshes out, the uptown local is pulling in, and I've made it. I suddenly realize that the line is dead. I hang up and jump aboard the train. There's no sign of the man with the gun down in the well. Then I see him running for the stairs to cross over to my side.

I don't even have the gun that I'm allowed to carry even when off duty. You don't head to a bar with the express purpose of getting drunk with a loaded gun in your waistband. I'm still woozy, and fear is bringing on a wave of nausea. Why won't this damn train start? Christ! You wait twenty minutes for it and then it just sits there!

Shortly before the millennium arrives the doors finally close, and I look out the window on the platform side. The man with the gun is running after the train—although I don't see his gun right now. But the train is pulling out. No matter for this guy. He runs up to the train at full clip and jumps onto the tiny three-inch ledge that protrudes from under the sealed doors, and rides into the tunnel that way. This guy is serious. And I'm scared shitless. Oh God, why did I drink so much? If only I were straight I'd have a chance.

The floor starts breaking apart under my feet, and I remember the Words of Christ, now burning into my conscience:

"Heaven and earth will pass away: but my words shall not pass away. And take heed yourselves, lest your hearts be overcharged with surfeiting, and drunkenness, and cares of this life, and so *that day* come upon you unawares. For as a snare shall it come on all them that dwell on the face of the whole earth."

Oh Jesus, God, forgive me and get me out of this. Please just get me out of this. I promise, I swear, to mend my ways if you'll just please, please, *please* get me out of this.

We pull into 34th Street, and the man with the gun steps off the ledge he's been using the principle of opposing forces to keep himself attached to, and he starts strolling along the platform, carefully checking each car, but mostly watching the doors. He moves up two cars before he has to hop on board as the doors close. We get to 42nd Street and the train just sits there. It sits there for all eternity. The man with the gun advances one, two, three more cars. Two more and he's got me. I can't hide on the train, and my reflexes are too fucked up to outmaneuver him. Normally my only safety would be in staying close to people, but he seems like the kind who could blow me away in front of 20 witnesses and still disappear into the crowd. After all, who'd stop him? Would you?

My heart nearly explodes when a grating, static-distorted announcement jars our ears and explains the reason for the wait: "This train is going express. This uptown local train is going express. Next stop, 59th Street."

The doors close and we pull out. I've got twenty or thirty seconds to live. I stop waiting for divine intervention and run to the end of the car. I open the door into the rushing darkness, and climb up on top of the train, keeping close to the roof, not lifting my head at all.

We get to 59th Street and the train stops with me lying spread-eagle, face down in six years' worth of seething grit. And I'm kissing it. The man hasn't found me. I'm thinking maybe being drunk was a godsend after all. I'd never have had the nerve to do this sober. "Next stop, 125th Street," is announced, and the doors close.

The tunnel rushes over me. I dare not *budge*. There is a hair's breadth clearance between death and life slicing by above me, and probably about *three* hairs' breadths from death grinding by below. I hear the interconnecting doors open under my feet. I'm clinging to the inch of grime, embracing it, hoping still another death is not approaching from behind in human form. The train races along through the darkness. How can Zeno have hypothesized that a flying arrow is motionless, merely based on the simple-minded assumption that at every moment it is only in one place? But that was before Gauss and continuum theory. Now, Gauss, *there* was a genius.—Gauss? Now I know I'm raving. But no, no, there is very definitely a man with a gun after me, who must have been following me and therefore must know I've just had ten—or so—drinks over the course of an evening that I left behind a lifetime ago. So she can't have gotten away, he's thinking.

I'm waiting for a bullet to come ripping up through the metal roof and disembowel me. No, there are too many people on the train.

The local stops are zinging by every so often in brilliant flashes of distant light, but I'm not moving my head for anything. What am I going to do at 125th Street? The man is in the car below me, and he hasn't found me yet. But he'll be ready at one-two-five. We go down the 110th Street station incline, disappearing into that utterly engulfing tunnel, devoid even of the light from the local stops, and ultimately resurface at 125th Street. I can't wait for the train to stop. I slide down and jump onto the platform. I'm still high on *something,* because no time whatsoever passes between the instant my right foot is set on the ground and the instant I find myself slapping flat on my side, rolling over and watching the train go by, with people looking down at me. I must be a sight, with six years' grime all down my front. I take far too long getting up, and when I do, the man is already coming at me through the crowd.

A janitor is cleaning gunk off the floor with a long pole that has a flat-edged razor on the end of it. I lunge at the janitor, who relinquishes the tool without a struggle, and stands back wide-eyed as I turn it upon my pursuer, who I am now getting sick of.

He reaches down inside his coat and is drawing his hand back out when I take a long sharp swing that slits his gun wrist wide open. I confess it's a welcome sight.

Clutching the pole, I tear up the stairs without looking back, careen through the mid-level arcade, and up the second level of stairs to the street, where it's raining, and a car's backfire scares the living hell out of me, and leaves me mad at myself for being so scared. My man has a silencer.

I dash between moving cars to a traffic island. The man with the gun steps out of the station, looking for me. He already has a bandage wrapped around his wrist as if he was expecting my move, seen it a hundred times. The index finger of his gun hand is glued to a trigger that looks like it still works very well. Only now he's *mad*. I don't wait. I jump into traffic. Brakes screech, sirens wail. Sirens? I turn to face the uptown traffic. A police van with sirens screaming and lights a-flashing comes bounding around braking cars and jumps the curb to the traffic island, splashing rainwater on some pedestrians. Van Snyder opens the passenger door for me and says, "Climb in, Fil. Cheesis, you look like shit." I slam the door. My attempted assassin has already vanished.

"Snap goes the third thread, Watson," says Van Snyder, but I'm too disoriented to catch the reference. The whole cab smells of alcohol. "Look, I'm not gonna lecture you now, but take a look at what you're doing to yourself."

I misinterpret him and lean out the open window to tilt the sideview mirror towards me. Snyder is right. I do look like shit. As the stone-cold fear leaves, bleary-eyed drunkenness returns. Not to mention enough blackface to make up a chorus line.

"That Carrera thing is just an excuse," he says. I look away from the death mask in the mirror.

"Tomorrow, okay?"

"Okay. Here, wipe your face off." He hands me a rag.

"Thanks." The rag is dirty, but it's cleaner than I am. I start cleaning off my face in the mirror.

"You want to tell me what was going down back there?" he asks.

"Someone was shooting at me. I climbed on top of the subway." I'm not sure he believes me. "How'd you find me?"

"I was cruising near 86th on the West Side when they radioed me with your call. So I dispatched a message to the transit cops to check the trains at 59th, and I drove up here on a hunch. When they reported no sign of you at 59th I floored the thing through thirty blocks of traffic lights. It was fun."

The transit cops!

"Well, the cop on my train must have been asleep," I say. Snyder looks like he's thinking, No cop's good enough to catch a hallucination, sweetie. I tell him, "I owe you a big one, Van."

"I got all the debts I need for this life—you can pay me back in the next one. Deal?"

"Deal."

I try to laugh, but it comes out a choke. Suddenly it's all catching up with me. I have broken out in a cold sweat and am feeling *very* ill.

"I'm gonna be sick." I telegraph this message along with visual cues, talking fists drumming on the dashboard, and knots tied in my intestines.

"Hang on," he says, swerving to the side and helping me open the door.

I fall down to the sidewalk on my knees and start retching convulsively, which in this neighborhood is no big deal. Oh—Look, the police van caught another junkie. Good, at least they're ridding the city of the scum. That's me all right.

I get rid of it all. It feels like everything I've drunk during the past three days is coming up. My liver may never be the same. When it's done, Van Snyder steps onto the sidewalk and scoops me up into the van. Now the sweat I'm covered with turns to ice, and I start shivering uncontrollably. Van Snyder lets slide a few oaths as he starts roughly massaging my arms and legs. The shivering won't stop, so he redoubles his efforts, concentrating on my legs only. His hands are filthy from touching me. The shivering diminishes, and he keeps rubbing, saying, "If I keep this up, does a genie appear?"

I laugh. Maybe I scream. The next thing I know I'm hugging him, but he carefully gets his arm between us and nudges me away. I have left black marks all over him.

"Sorry," I say.

"Forget it. I think maybe you could use something to eat."

"I don't know—" I'm starting to say as he pulls up in front of a dive that calls itself Rico's. "I don't like the look of this," I say.

"Hey, Rico's is the best Greek Tex-Mex pizza place in town," he says, climbing out of the van and coming around to help me out. "Besides, there aren't very many places where you can go looking like you do."

I spy myself reflected in the window of Rico's and I have to agree. We sit down at a table in a dark, unobtrusive corner. Nobody looks at me. Van Snyder orders two slices of mushroom pizza and two Cokes.

"I hate Coke," I tell him.

"It's good for an upset stomach," he advises me.

"Van, you're a real *mensch*."

"Say, where'd you come up with all them Yiddish words, anyway? Ain't you Catholic?"

"My first partner, Artie Lieberrnann. I was a rookie and he had seventeen years. He pretty much taught me everything I needed to know."

"What other words do you know?"

"Oh, the usual, *meshugga, kvetsh, schmuck*—"

"Aah, 'schmuck' is English already."

I laugh. Our food comes and we eat. I manage to have about half a slice before I have to push it away.

When we're back in the van, Detective Snyder asks me where he can take me.

"Not home," I say. I give him Doris's address.

He starts up the van and streaks off up Bradhurst. A couple of young Black men are walking along on the opposite side of the street, nearing a huge puddle. Snyder purposely swings the van clear across the street so he can splash into the puddle and soak the two men with water and drive away.

"You're such a fucking ballbuster," I tell him.

"Yeah, but you can depend on me to drive off my detail to come rescue you from attempted murder on the subway."

I have nothing to say to that. Then Detective Snyder's radio kicks alive. He responds. It's the voice of his Detective Sergeant, saying, "Hold please, Detective Snyder, your wife is on the line."

Detective Snyder groans.

"Leonard Snyder!" A woman's screechy voice assaults us from the crappy speakers, and doesn't let up for ten minutes, calling Detective Snyder every name in the book, including a few from the Revised Extra-Nasty Edition. What is he doing out at this hour of the night alone with that policewoman?

"—And without a chaperone," I say into the seat cushion. Snyder shushes me.

When his wife is finished, Detective Snyder promises her he'll be home in an hour and that he'll never see me again. Then he says, "Put the Detective Sergeant back on."

"Yes?" asks the Detective Sergeant.

"You supreme motherfucker," says Snyder, and signs off.

"Sorry I'm causing you so much trouble."

"That motherfucker. He's so stupid he cut his foot the other day."

"Anybody can do that."

"Shaving?"

I laugh again.

"But seriously," he begins, "this is it, Fil. No more from me."

'I understand. And I'm sorry."

"Me too."

We pull up in front of Doris's building. Out in front stands the super I busted for rape, having a party with some of his friends. I grab him by the T-shirt so hard I tear it.

"You got out already? You—" I say.

He doesn't seem to recognize me—probably because the one time he saw me I was wearing a sharp, cleaned and pressed, blue policewoman's uniform, and my face was washed. Snyder grabs me and pulls me away from the bewildered super and pushes me up the stairs to Doris's apartment. He knocks for me. When I see Doris looking at me through the half-open door, I tell her, "I need a place to stay."

* * *

Doris helps, rocks me to sleep. I don't give her any trouble. I pass out easily enough.

The next morning I discover that Doris's apartment has no gas, no hot water, and no electricity. The super, in revenge for not getting away with raping her, has spitefully shut off the utilities. I promise to fix it for her. She tells me not to.

I don't mind the cold shower, which actually does me some good, but I have to drink a cold cup of yesterday's coffee to start me up. Bleah!

"Would you want to go to Mass together later?" asks Doris.

"Yes."

"You know, I promised Saint Anthony a rosary to look after you."

"*One* rosary to look after me?" I say, feigning incredulity. "He works cheap."

Doris appreciates my joke, especially after my having told her some of what I've been through lately. I say we can go together when I get off from work.

I walk on feet of cracked glass all the way to the precinct.

You won't believe what's waiting for me when I get there: Surprise Drug Test #2. Needless to say, I don't do very well. My piss burnt a hole in the litmus paper. The Lieutenant gets me into his office.

"Just what drugs have you *done*, Buscarsela?"

"In my lifetime? Pot, hash, hash oil, coke, speed, LSD, mescaline, psilocybin, sucrose, dextrose, polysorbate 60, alcohol, caffeine and even tobacco."

"Sacred shit, woman, pot is *baby food* compared to some of those things!"

"Yeah, I didn't like speed."

"I think maybe you'd better take a week off."

"A week off?"

"Think of it as a vacation without pay."

* * *

Doris and I go to Mass together. The preacher gives a sermon based on the text of the Tenth Psalm. And a powerful psalm it is, too:

"Why standest thou afar off, O Lord? why hidest thou thyself in times of trouble? The wicked in his pride hotly pursues the poor. His mouth is full of cursing and deceit and fraud: under his tongue is mischief and iniquity. He sits in the lurking places of the villages: in the secret places he murders the innocent: his eyes stealthily watch for the helpless. He lies in wait secretly like a lion in his den: he lies in wait to catch the poor: he catches the poor, when he draws him into his net. The helpless collapse: they bow down, and fall into his power . . . As for all his enemies, he hisses at them. He says in his heart, Thou wilt not avenge. Thou hast seen it; for thou beholdest mischief and spite, to requite it with thy hand: the helpless man commits himself to thee; thou art the healer of the fatherless and the oppressed, so that none shall any longer terrify innocent men from the earth."

That fortifies the hell out of me. I haven't forgotten my promise to mend my ways if the Gods got me off that train alive. I gush thanks to Doris for having put up with me knocking on her door in the middle of the night. She says it was the least she could have done in return for all I did for her, and am I sure I don't want to go back to her place for dinner?

I tell her thanks, but I have a job to do.

I go home and trash most of my drug paraphernalia. You don't usually find out what your limit is until you exceed it.

Now I've got another job to do.

EIGHT

"There are two types of dangerous madmen: those who are kept in isolated cells, and those who rage against humanity as politicians and military men."

—Ernst Toller

"No one ever looks over their shoulder to see who lost their job because of protectionism."

—Ronald Reagan

"I need a second-floor man."

Vittorio looks down at me with his hard green eyes, eyes that are rare in color for a *Napolitano*. "Nope," is all he says.

"Vito, my testimony got your sentence cut from five-to-seven years down to two—the minimum, in case you forgot—and you were out in eighteen months."

"What's in it for me?"

"A reserved seat in heaven."

"Don't drag in heaven, Fila, that ain't fair."

I look up at him with my big brown eyes. Sometimes they're more persuasive than any blunt instrument. Vittorio shakes his head, resigning himself to the fact that I've got him morally cornered.

"Think of it as a day in the country. A chance to get out of the city," I say.

He asks me: "The place got dogs?"

* * *

On my way from the Rent-a-Wreck to Vittorio's workplace, I stop into a *bodega* to pick up some sandwich supplies and tomato juice for the road. The owner insists on joking with me until he gets me to laugh. Then he says, in Spanish, "Once your sense of humor is gone, forget this thing called living."

I swear I hear more profound truths in the *barrios* than I was ever taught in a university.

I'm driving up a narrow, curving street with cars illegally parked on both sides leaving an even narrower passage down the middle for me and the oversized van whose quirks I am not the least bit familiar with. The brakes are worn, there's enough play in the steering wheel for the Rockettes to dance through, and if you drive it faster than 45 m.p.h., the front wheels may fall off.

I'm driving up the incline, when a car in front of me pulls up to parallel park in the only available spot for blocks. So I hold off with the van, giving the guy room to back up. Now my van is blocking the street, but I figure it's obvious that I'm waiting for the guy in front of me to park. But then I always give Queens drivers more credit than they deserve. The guy behind me, who can't see the car in front of me, must think I've stopped in the middle of the street to catch up on my bird-watching, because he starts honking like mad. The guy in front of me, who can't see the car behind me, obviously thinks *I'm* the one honking like mad at him, because, once this absurd charade is over, and the guy has been honking like crazy for a full minute, the guy in front parks, and as I pull past him, he yells out his window at me, "Asshole!" I continue on for half a block and pull over in front of the bagel bakery where Vittorio works, and the guy behind now passes and yells out, "Asshole!" at me.

What can you do? This is my reward for trying to be nice. I'd like to say, "Only in New York," but the sad truth is that this type of random brutishness is *not* limited only to New York. So far I've encountered it in seven out of seven countries, on three continents.

I have to wait twenty minutes until Vittorio gets off his shift. When he does, he comes out of the bakery with a bagful of bagels for the road, and gets inside. He shakes hands hello, and his hands are warm from the bread ovens.

"You drive, I'll navigate," he says.

"We can take turns." I hand him the map. Mahikatinuk is about two hundred and fifty miles north towards Canada along Route 87.

"What do we do when we get there?"

"We ask around. If I know my rural America, this warehouse probably employs two-thirds of the town."

"This monster got a radio?"

"I brought my tape player."

"Oh no, I'm not sitting through five hours of that *salsa,* baby."

I'm currently navigating through Queens traffic, which is only a bit easier than engaging Baron von Richthofen in an aerial dogfight, so I'm in no mood to argue.

"There's a whole box of tapes. Pick what you like."

Vittorio starts looking through the cassettes. I go on: "And if you kick it just right, it'll play."

"Bach?" he says. "You brought Bach?"

"Hey, he's like the Chuck Berry of classical music."

"Yeah? If you say so."

Vittorio puts on a Bach partita for solo violin, and chamber music from this distant epoch sweetens our surreal journey across the Triborough Bridge to meet Route 87.

"Hey, did you know that Lake Erie is the twelfth largest natural lake in the world?" quizzes Vittorio, looking at the map.

"I was deprived of an American education. How's the new job?"

"S'all right. Better than that last one. I'll never get used to office work. You always gotta kiss somebody's ass. Here, I just do what I gotta do. Office work—sheeeit!—sometimes it'd take me 'til Sunday night just to unwind from the week before."

"I hear that."

"Also the commute was killing me."

"You've still got a helluva commute from Avenue U. Why don't you find a bakery on Kings Highway? There must be tons of them."

"Too many Blacks."

That's right. I had forgotten Vittorio's one flaw. He's a racist pig. Well, I spent a lot of time thinking about the Zone Three Intermediate Storage Facility in Mahikatinuk, New York, and decided that there was no way I was going to go up there alone. Intelligence and cunning are all very well and good, but they aren't much help in a pit full of hungry lions, and Vittorio is the only felon who owes me who I haven't tried to collect from lately.

"If it keeps up I'm going to move down to Avenue X," he says.

"I can't imagine living on Avenue X."

"Maybe you're right. I'll have to move to Rockaway or something."

"There's always the ocean."

* * *

Five miles out of Pottersville we get a flat.

"Aw, where'd you get this heap anyway?" asks Vittorio.

"Well, I asked for a Jeep, but you know how we *latinos* always pronounce our J's like H's."

"Are you shitting me?"

"I think so, yeah."

Of course the van has no jack. I tell Vittorio, "You hold up the van while I take the tire off."

"You crazy?"

"All right: *I'll* hold the van up while *you* take the tire off."

"While you're at it why don't you replace this biplane engine with a real one—you know, for cars?"

I flag down a rig and ask the driver to stop his engine. He looks down at me, making no effort at all to pretend he's not totally checking out my body.

"There's only three things I stop my engine for, babe," he says. "And that's cash, hash, or gash. Now which is it gonna be?"

"Sorry," I say, jerking a thumb towards Vittorio, "but my boyfriend castrated the last guy he caught me in bed with."

The truck driver throws his truck in gear.

"Don't you fucking dare!" I say, hopping up on his running board and dragging out my badge. "Or I'll run you in for failing to aid an officer of the law."

He looks at my badge.

"Aren't you a little out of your jurisdiction?" he says.

"Yes, but that won't stop me from putting six bullet holes in your carburetor if you don't help fix this tire."

I know I'm making a mistake, that any truck this size this far north stands a good chance of having a warehouse in Mahikatinuk as its destination, and truck drivers are not known for their extraordinary powers of keeping quiet in bars at the end of a day's work. But the wheels are in motion, and what's done is done.

He stops the truck, spits onto the shoulder and removes a jack from his tool chest.

"Where you heading?" I try to be friendly.

"Plattsburgh," says the truck driver. It's a place name, but it sure sounds like a curse the way he says it.

When we're back on the road again, it's another thirty-five miles to the turn-off for Mahikatinuk, followed by twelve more miles on a one-lane country road. But it's paved. Vittorio complains about the road.

"This ain't nuthin'," I tell him, sinking down to his level of English. "We've got roads in Ecuador that wouldn't pass for cow paths up here. And no guardrails. It's not for nothing that Padre Crespo used to perform the traditional Blessing of the Cars every Easter."

"You sure come from a screwy country."

"And you don't?"

"I'd like to check it out sometime."

"Don't forget to bring a bag full of anti-intestinal-virus tablets."

"Forget it."

Half an hour later we pull up the main street of Mahikatinuk, New York. There's a work crew digging a ditch by the side of the road that looks *very* odd to me before I realize why: They're all white.

"Boy, we *are* off the beaten track," I say.

"It's a small town."

"I was in a small town once. I didn't like it."

Some teenagers in a fifteen-year-old bright orange Mustang with silver racing stripes down the middle of it raise a cloud of dust as they rip up Main Street sailing past up. I stifle the urge to chase it down.

"Easy, lady," says Vittorio. "Once a cop—"

"It's just that there's nowhere around here worth rushing to that fast!"

"And how do you know?"

"Point taken."

"Let's get something hot. I'm sick of bagel sandwiches."

"Well, you got a choice between the Mount Haystack Restaurant and the Mount Haystack Restaurant."

We get out of the van and cross the street, into the restaurant. The waitress looks at me as if I'm from Mars, and won't even address me directly.

"Maybe it's the antennas," I tell Vittorio.

"Might as well be. Take a look at that."

He directs my attention to a bulletin board over the cigarette machine advertising baby-sitting services, second-hand farm tools, jobs available and jobs wanted. Right in the middle is a hand-written sign announcing tonight's meeting of the White American Bastion, to discuss the pressing problem of how to handle the threat to Aryan values posed by Blacks, Jews, and Federal judges.

"Jesus H. Christ," I say. "Federal judges?" But it gives me an idea.

I get up and walk over to the bulletin board. Vittorio follows me. I start checking the Jobs Wanted.

"What are you looking for?" asks Vittorio.

"Maybe one of these people is the proverbial disgruntled former employee of the Morse, Inc. Intermediate Waste Management Facility."

"That's a tall order."

"Maybe. But if the President managed to find a cabinet position for the one Black man on earth who's against civil rights, we ought to be able to find one employee who's pissed off at Morse, Inc."

"Uh-huh," he says. I'm writing down the names of all the people who are looking for work in Mahikatinuk, when our food arrives. I stick to coffee and the sandwiches we brought. There are probably enough toxic chemicals floating around this town to cause genetic mutation.

"What's the address of this place?" asks Vittorio through a mouthful of mashed potatoes and gravy. "The brochure says '1313 Twelfth Street.' Sounds fake, huh?"

"No way there are twelve streets in this town."

When we're back out on Main Street, I ask directions to the Morse warehouse. I'm told to take something called Nine Mile Road all the way to the end. I drive off in the direction indicated, and after less than a mile, see an unmarked turnoff. By chance a man happens to be walking towards town along the road. I lean out and ask him, "Excuse me, where does this road go?"

"It goes that away," he answers, pointing down the road with a gnarled finger.

Inside the van, Vittorio and I look at each other. We eventually manage to find the right road, and after a bumpy, dusty ride, come up on top of the hill that overlooks the warehouse. It lies on a dry plain, with a perpetual dust storm in the wind that seems to be left over from the stones this plain was leveled out of. The dust is slowly choking the life out of the vegetation in the vicinity, a visible radius of infertility spreading ever outward. My mind recoils to one phrase from Wilson's tape-recorded memoirs:

"It gets up the nose, in the food . . . Death comes in the form of a beautiful woman to my mind, who squashes me like a bug."

"We looking for anything in particular?" asks Vittorio.

"A signed confession would be nice. I just wanted to see the place during the day."

"You mean we're coming back here again at night?"

"I don't see any other way to get inside it."

"This is wicked beat to the max."

And so it is.

* * *

"What's the angle on the door-to-door?" asks Vittorio.

"We got a list of twenty-two names—"

"How about we're from the census?"

"Right: Only we're about six or seven years early."

"How's about the Board of Labor—?"

"No wonder you got caught."

"Bite me, Fil," he says.

"Hmmm . . ."

"I got it! 'We're with the IRS and we might have a refund for you if you could just answer a few questions . . .' "

* * *

We go around all afternoon, knocking on doors and presenting the *spiel:* Where did you last work? And where are you working now? Did you file your income taxes last year? Et cetera. Eleven of the first fifteen are working at the Morse warehouse. But they like it there. We score when we hit number nineteen:

"I hate the bastards!" says a wizened man in his late sixties, though he looks older. "They forced me to retire."

"Let's go out for a drink," I offer. The man eyes me with suspicion. "I'm paying."

"Let's go," he says.

His name turns out to be Lee Torrance, and he left a kneecap in South Korea. He wants us to go to—

"A branch of the Hartley, way up here?" I reply.

"It's filled during ski season, honeypie," says Lee. On the way over to the Essex County Hartley, he tells us that he returned from the Pacific to active duty in the desert, where he was stationed during the first H-Bomb tests.

"That's some story," I say.

We go inside the Hartley and sit at a table in some kind of night-club-style set-up. The last comedian on earth is on stage, and this is what his routine is like:

"You know, they don't allow alcohol in Libya—Maybe that's why they're always in such a bad mood!" Here he goes into a juvenile imitation of an Arabic language. "Well, that's my offensive joke for the evening—Hey, you gotta offend *somebody* to be funny, right? So keep those nasty cards and letters coming—Ha!Ha!Ha!"

"They should hand out vomit bags with this guy," is Vittorio's contribution.

After a few drinks, which I sit out, Lee starts to warm up to us. The comedian from hell keeps talking:

"Ever wonder why those Indian dresses are called 'Sari's?' Because the Indian women are so frigid that every time a man tries to take it off she covers up and says, 'Sorry!'"

"When he starts insulting the Latins, I'm leaving," I say.

"When he starts insulting the Italians, I'm going up there and bashing his face in." Guess who said that.

"I've got to go make a phone call," I announce, leaving the boys to their next round of drinks.

I am pointed in the direction of the pay phone, and have to change a fortune in quarters to call up Detective Snyder, via the operator.

"Thank you for using AT&T," she says, for some reason.

What choice do I have? Who else owns and operates pay phones? (I may be showing my age, but this was in the days before all those calling cards and things.) Snyder takes a long time to answer. All I want to do is tell him where I am in case I don't come back. Six dollars go by before he gets on the line.

"What kept you? This phone call is tomorrow's pay," I tell him.

"Why not today's?"

"I already spent that getting here."

"Where's here?"

I give him the story thus far. He manages to take it all in without screaming at me.

"Okay, call me tomorrow at nine a.m. to check in," he says.

I go back to the table, and tell the guys I want to leave.

"I want to keep drinking," says Lee.

"Don't you have a bottle back at your place?"

"Sure do."

"Okay, let's go."

I go to pay for the drinks. The bill comes and it's for $695.00. I think there must be some mistake. The waitress flushes a healthy and rather attractive shade of red while looking for the correct check. The jerks ran up a tab of $35.00 awful quick.

Back at Lee's place he pulls out a bottle of Death-By-Slow-Torture Whiskey—at least I *think* that's what the label said—and I warn Vittorio to take it easy, we've got a lot to do.

"What do you gotta do at this time of night?" asks Lee, perplexed.

I figure it's time to let him in on it. I tell Lee we're really newspaper reporters, and we want to break into the Morse warehouse to see if we can verify an anonymous tip that they're mishandling funds, or some such tangled yarn.

"Well, I knew you wasn't from the IRS, girlie, they don't never buy nobody no drink!"

Pretty in-depth analysis for a guy with no teeth.

"But will you help us?"

"You betcha! You can get inside the compound through a hole in the ground under the fence. I doubt they've fixed it up, the cheap bastards." Lee is chuckling as he goes over to his night table and opens the drawer. "I'll even lend you this." He pulls out an old nickel-plated revolver.

"Jesus! You win the West with this thing?" I ask him, scrutinizing this antique weapon.

Lee breaks into a toothless grin.

* * *

An hour later we're crawling along the perimeter of the Morse warehouse, having parked the van along a side road—"They all look like side roads to me!" says Vittorio—in order to approach the grounds from the blind side. And it works. Lee locates the hole, we slide under and now we're trespassing. We walk through what seems to be an open field, then huge low buildings loom up out of nowhere, spread out and humming. Lee takes us to just outside the main complex.

"Vito, this is where we split up. You take to the rear, and Lee and I'll go in through the front."

"What?" says Lee.

"Pretend you're my hostage," I say, pulling out my revolver. Lee chuckles. He thinks this is great. I haven't the heart to tell him it's really because I don't trust him to back me up properly, but I can use him to buy some time. Vittorio wishes me luck, and disappears into a shadow. Lee, chuckling all the way, leads me past nine dozen port-o-sans to the front entrance. Actually, I wouldn't mind using one right now, but it's pretty hard to stop a commando-raid-in-progress just so the team leader can take a pee. There's a guard there who starts to stand up when he sees Lee, then sits right back down when he sees me behind, pushing Lee along with the help of a police .38. I decide it's easier to have the guard come with us.

Very little persuasion is necessary to get the guard to forfeit his gun and take us inside. Chemical fumes permeate the inner galleries, despite a fierce, relentless mechanical pounding coming from the gargantuan air filters somewhere overhead.

Boy, doesn't everybody look surprised when we round a collection of fifty-five-gallon drums containing God-knows-what, and there, in a large open area, stands my slit-wristed assassin, and another man who's clearly the boss of the two. They look up when we come around into view. The assassin is smoking a cigarette that's hanging from one lip, now that his mouth is open. He's wearing a gray suit with a white tie. With the scar, the effect is complete.

"Hey, you look like a criminal," I say to the assassin.

"I'm sorry, Mr. DiAngelo," begins the guard, "but I didn't expect—"

"It's perfectly all right, Martin," says Mr. DiAngelo. "You're not to blame in the least."

"Thank you, sir."

"Hello, Lee," says DiAngelo, ignoring me. The assassin stays quiet.

"Good—uh—good evening, sir," Lee stammers. Retired two years and still unable to break the habits of a peon. I tell you it's shameful.

I say, "I'd like to know why you had Wilson McCullough killed."

DiAngelo busies himself by picking a nonexistent piece of lint from the sleeve of his $750 suit.

"Aren't you going to answer me?"

"Soon as I figure out what you're talking about," oozes DiAngelo.

"Oh, fuck this—" I say, pushing Lee and the guard aside, and showing both of the dangerous men my gun.

"Oh my, a gun," says DiAngelo, calmly. I don't like it. No one's That smooth facing down an angry cop with a loaded gun. I back to the side a bit so I can keep an eye on all four people, as well as the passageway we just came in through. DiAngelo knows why I'm doing this and starts to smile.

"This is the cunt who slashed my wrist, Mr. DiAngelo," says the assassin. Such language.

"Oh? And now she's staying sober long enough to come point her cap gun at the big, bad, Morse Corporation?" says DiAngelo. "We know about you, girl."

"Look, I don't know who you are, but finding you here with the guy who tried to waste me the other night is kind of a blemish on your character as far as I'm concerned."

"And since you're only a *half*-stupid drunken spic bitch, it only took you a week to find this warehouse after you stole the address and phone number from Mr. Faber's office. That's a first-class piece of detection, Officer," croons DiAngelo.

Great. They know everything about me and they're not a bit surprised to see me. They probably have thirty sharpshooters on the catwalks above just waiting for a clean shot. I wonder where Vito is. I go on, pretending I'm still confident.

"What is this, an insult contest? I'm supposed to be the one holding the gun here. And I'd like some answers before I take you in, if it isn't too much trouble."

DiAngelo puts a leg up and sits on the table, comfortably. Too damn comfortably. There it is again. I don't know what he thinks he's doing. I watch his eyes. It's something I learned to do with attack dogs and knife-wielding junkies. Watch their eyes.

"That McCullough kid was going to blow the whistle on one of our operations," says DiAngelo evenly.

"So you snuffed him."

"We've done it for less."

"I bet."

"And we'd do it again." They're all looking at me.

"Is that a threat?—Not that it needs to be: I already have everything I need on your pal here to send him away for twenty-five-to-. Forgive me for being curious, but I feel I have a right to know what you consider to be worth taking three or four people's lives for."

"Try $54 million in waste disposal."

"What?"

"We get $90 a ton for collecting the toxic wastes other companies don't want or are too small to know what to do with. Wastes you're not allowed to dispose of within the continental United States."

"So what do you do with them?"

"Ship 'em overseas, sweetheart. Out-of-the-way places that nobody cares a damn about like India, Nigeria, Zimbabwe, Ecuador—that's illegal too, but it's *less* illegal, if you get my meaning. McCullough got a hold of some of our records and he was going to turn them over to the E.P.A."

"Places nobody cares about, huh?" I challenge him.

"All those African countries are nothing but desert anyway," says DiAngelo.

"Nigeria is tropical forest and grassland, and Ecuador is not in Africa."

"Gee, does that mean I get a 'D' in geography, teacher?"

They all burst out laughing. That must have been the signal. It happens very fast. Four or five tough, professional hands seize my gun and pin my arms from behind; DiAngelo socks me in the eye hard enough to produce a red fuzz at the edge of my field of vision, then the assassin lands a full-body kick to my temple with a steel-toed boot. When confronted with this logic, I fall back sideways to the floor. I'm really not quite sure how many more times I get kicked, but when I'm next able to distinguish such details, I'm lying with my head propped against a fifty-five-gallon drum, and two guns are pointing down at me out of a reddish haze. I think one of the guns is mine.

"Wake up and smell the coffee, baby," says a voice above me.

And sure enough, I am lying on a hundred-pound sack of Ecuadorian coffee. Funny how I didn't notice that sooner. I move and someone tries to take the coconut milk out of my cranium with a machete. I belay all further moving for the moment. A laugh reverberates in the haze above me.

"Kicking a woman when she's down," says a different voice. "Shame on you." More laughter. Somebody's having a great time up there. Why aren't I invited?

"All right, on your feet," says the first voice, and I am lifted through a hallway full of razor blades that tear at my eyes and the side of my head where I must have been kicked. A door opens and I am flung against more fifty-five-gallon drums in a very small chamber. I hit the barrels with a dull Clongg! The barrels don't seem to mind. I notice a shape very like the assassin handcuffing me to a rail, then he handcuffs Lee to the rail. Don't ask me where the rail came from. Then the assassin takes a fire axe and breaks open the top of one of the drums. He uses a crow bar to widen the gash, then steps back.

A smell like an embalming factory extends from the barrel.

"You know what that is?" asks the assassin. "Methyl isocyanate.

Ever hear of it? We use it in our insecticides. A terrible accident, that barrel rupturing like that. Just like it's going to be a terrible accident when you get locked in here, and a terrible accident when we find you dead inside of an hour. Either that or permanently brain-damaged. How'd you like that? It's your own fault for getting involved, kiddo. But don't worry. We'll send a $200 condolence check to your family."

There is more laughter and the door closes, leaving us in darkness. Total, hellish darkness. I'm trapped, and I've *really* got to pee, too, which kind of puts a crimp in my efficiency. They must have kicked me there too. The bastards. The image of Lee's nickel-plated fossil of a gun flashes into my mind. I wonder if they thought of frisking him. But I never get that far.

In the darkness something more palpable than any natural gas starts to overcome Lee and myself. An acrid taste first stings my nostrils, then it singes, then it burns. The human sensory apparatus has a built-in warning system. I can *tell* that this stuff is extremely noxious. I close my eyes to protect them. There's nothing to see anyway. Every tip at the end of each one of my tiny air passages stabs into my poor little lungs like so many knives. It's not that I can't inhale, it's that I can't breathe. Breathing in is like swallowing hot knives. I try not to breathe, but I don't have enough air to hold on to. I'm expelling air instead of taking it in. I'm being constricted by an invisible gas. Every bit of air that I let out gets replaced by ten sea urchins that each choose their own individual alveoli to crawl into and scorch me. My lungs are punctured, and they start leaking. I can feel fluid building up inside of them in place of air. I'm drowning in a closed room thirty miles from the nearest body of water. I cough. Pieces of something come out with the cough, and ten million lit cigarettes go back in all at once. I cough. Out come my heart, lungs, liver, spleen, intestines, uterus. The white-hot core of a tungsten arc jumps inside me, sizzles in my air passages. I cough up all my arteries and start on the veins in my legs. Is there anything left to cough out?—that isn't all over the floor? I swallow an active volcano, cough up an earthquake. I swallow the sun, whole, and cough up a supernova. The universe gets torn apart colliding with the anti-universe. The explosions are deafening. The floor shakes. The door cracks then bursts open.

Vittorio rushes in, chops through our handcuffs with the fire axe, and drags the two molten humans to safety in the other room for us to cool off and remold into new shapes and forms. My legs are all wet.

When I can see again, when I can hear again, when I can think again, I try to talk:

"Mblgbmp!—cch!"

Blood splatters onto my hands from somewhere behind where my face should be.

Vittorio comes over and wipes some of it up for me, and strokes my forehead.

"I saw the whole thing from the second-floor catwalk," he says. "Talk about a reserved seat in heaven! You let the whole town know we were here. They've been waiting all night for us to show up. Then you practically turned your back on them. Your contacts are getting rusty."

I manage to reply:

"I left them soaking in alcohol too long."

NINE

"Life is a struggle, and this is it."

—Avram Chaim Wishnia

Of course Mr. DiAngelo doesn't stick around to find the corpses in his storage room. I was out long enough for him to go to a nice steakhouse to establish an alibi. Then they all joined him for coffee and dessert, while I got rushed to the hospital, where I peed red for five days straight. I spend five weeks in the hospital learning how to breathe all over again.

The Lieutenant pulls *ropes* to get me retroactively assigned to the case so the city will pay for my hospitalization. I have to say that much for him. My assassin gets ten years on two counts of attempted murder (maybe if he'd succeeded it would have been more), but he skips the country before sentence can be applied. They still don't know where he is. Maybe he'll turn up on my fire escape some day.

Lee recovers but is never quite the same after. His testimony and that of the janitor on duty at the IND line 125th Street station corroborate my testimony against the assassin; besides my being carried into the courtroom on a stretcher to testify, which really sways a jury, especially if you have to stop every once in a while to spit blood into an enamel bowl that's there for the purpose. And you can't speak more than ten words at a time. And breathing hurts. The Doc says I'm marred for life. No more smoking *anything*.

But DiAngelo gets clean away. They say there's no evidence linking him to the events. The defense does somersaults to get Vittorio's eyewitness testimony dismissed as inadmissible, and I have to admit under oath that I was incapable of focusing on who cuffed me in the chamber, and when I try to push it, Morse's lawyers drag in my record of drinking and drug problems. They really set to work on me and it gets relatively nasty. The jury actually buys the argument that I was trespassing and that I never announced myself as an officer of the law, so Morse, Inc. was acting within legal limits as the property owner. I try to bring up Morse, Inc.'s "trespassing" illegally in foreign countries with contaminated wastes, but this is loudly silenced as irrelevant.

And they never pin Wilson's murder on anybody.

They claim Wilson caused the leak to discredit Morse, but who knows? Maybe Morse did it to damage his own stock and write-off the whole dilapidated facility.

And whoever killed Kim Saunders got away with that, too.

For those of you who are wondering, What the hell were all those big shots doing up in Mahikatinuk?—apparently they knew I was heading up there and figured I'd be easier to waste 200 miles from nowhere. They also had a record office there where they kept most of the truly illegal stuff and Morse personally ordered it to be destroyed. They were planning to come back later. Vito scared off the two guards they left behind with a couple of gunshots that I did not hear, which is how he rescued us, and called the cops, which is how we got ahold of all the undestroyed data.

The point is that they get away, but that's okay, because I've got enough to go on now to instigate a formal *legal* investigation of the shadier practices of Morse, Inc., and if I make Detective—which seems to be in the wind—I can head the investigation myself.

I tried calling Meg a few times, but she was always "out."

My first day back on the job, the Lieutenant has two papers for me. One congratulates me for being promoted to Detective, the other tells me I'm fired for failing my second drug test. There's nothing else for me to do but shake a few hands, clean out my locker and take the A train all the way to the end of the line. They say you can pick up *anything* on the back roads at JFK Airport: Liquor, luggage, automatic weapons . . .

I find a dishonest-looking baggage handler and fish out $20 from my own pocket for some information. The guy looks at it as if it were a used kleenex, holding it loosely in one hand and blowing on it to show me how weightless it is.

"What is this, a twenty?" he says. "I blow my nose in these, girlie."

"What do you want, $200? Go inform for the FBI," I say. "Have a heart, I'm unemployed."

I show him my letter of dismissal, which has today's date on it. That impresses him. He says he read about the trial.

I take the shuttle bus back to the subway, where somebody's radio is announcing that the air quality today is "acceptable." My standards of what is an "acceptable" level of air pollution seem to be quite a bit different from theirs. I can hardly breathe. My throat is so tight. My chest hurts. I'm on my way to midtown to see Mr. Morse, and I don't know what I'm going to do, which scares me. But if it scares me, it'll scare *him*.

It's a long train ride, and I have plenty of time to ask myself, What the hell do I think I'm doing? I still don't know who fingered me for that A-train assault.

Faber? Wiegand? Meg? Any one of the 400 people in the front office of the corporate headquarters of Morse, Inc.? Does it matter now? As Leon said, one person can't go up against a corporation, that's the stuff of the movies. Or of legend? Call it the David and Goliath Syndrome. Think of Samson slaughtering 10,000 Philistines with the jawbone of an ass, Barabbas stopping a chariot with a pointed stick, James Bond Agent 007 versus 10,000 of Doctor No's loyal guards—who all seem to die so easily. Taking down the giant colossus with a sling, a peashooter, a spear, a pistol, it's part of our shared mythology—right down to Luke Skywalker and the single shot aimed at the Death Star's *one* weak point. Think of Achilles and his heel, Superman and his kryptonite, the Scarecrow in *The Wizard of Oz* and his one fear, fire: I can relate to that all right. Sometimes I feel like I'm made of straw myself. But talk about mass uprising against a collective oppressor and watch out! Can't make no millions thataway.

I don't mind telling you how cold my hands and feet are on this hot August day as I get out of the subway and walk towards the headquarters of Morse, Inc.—Aah, What the hell? Once you've played "Stick" with four adult male Filipinos you aren't afraid of anything.

* * *

The receptionist asks me if I have an appointment to see Mr. Morse.

"He'll want to see me," I answer.

"What name shall I say?"

I tell her my name. She calls Morse's office, and the word comes down to let me up. I wonder if he knows about my being fired. Who am I kidding? He probably knows what I had for breakfast.

I get through security because I realized in a brief moment of sanity that I'd never get past the front door with a loaded gun in my purse, so I stuck the package in a locker at the Port Authority Bus Terminal, then stopped off at a corner fruitstand to pick up three hard, green mangos and one overripe yellow one.

I step out of the elevator onto the seventy-ninth floor. A humorless security guard passes my purse through the metal detector *twice* and checks all the mangos closely before deciding I've got no offensive weapons in there, then he escorts me through a cordon of security personnel into the luxurious office of the oleaginous Mr. Morse.

A wild-eyed devil glowers down at me from a six-hundred-year-old oriental silk painting. An *original* Alphonse Mucha *Job* poster woman that should be on display in a museum, not this bum's office, catches my eye, above a pre-Colombian ceramic bowl with a twin-headed jaguar design that tells me it was recently smuggled out of Ecuador.

Morse is bent over a computer screen, protected by two bodyguards large enough to park their boss's limo by pushing the other cars out of the way with their hands.

"So this is the elusive Mr. Morse. And I thought you were just a logo," I say to Morse as he straightens up.

"What?" he says. "Oh, is it time to make with the cute one-liners? Then allow me: That pisshole of a building you live in? I just bought it. Effective today, your lease is terminated."

"You let me up here just so you could tell me that?"

"Oh no, there's more, honey. You're out on the street by five p.m., with a court order for your arrest if you don't vacate and if you ever re-enter the premises again. And for a real surprise, look behind you."

My heart sends out a jolt; I jerk my head around, half-expecting to come face-to-face with my own death. I'm not that far off. Hanging on the wall behind me is an original 6' x 9' Wilson McCullough painting in 23 shades of black. One of the late ones.

"Thanks for tipping me off about McCullough's paintings. They're *great* investments. I went right out and bought four of them. That one's already worth $150,000."

"Sacred shit," is all I can say, my voice clenched into a hoarse whisper.

And he laughs at me.

I turn to face him. "Tell me, were you born this way or did you have to study to be an asshole?"

"Sticks and stones, Officer Buscarsela—"

My voice makes a quick recovery. "Don't try to get cute with me. Now that I know what a roach feels like when you gas it, I'll think twice before using that spray can again. But what about you, scumbag? How many more lives are you going to poison?"

The two bouncers stir into motion. I guess the secret word was "scumbag."

"Tell Ziegfried and Roy to leave us alone for a few minutes—or do you want them to think you're afraid of being left alone with a scrawny lung case armed with a bag of mangos?"

The two bouncers chuckle. At least someone here has a sense of humor. Morse looks at them sharply, then dismisses them.

I put my purse down and stand alone in the middle of his office. I'm still holding the bag of mangos. I try to sound conciliatory: "Did we really have to go through all this? Couldn't you just modify your manufacturing processes to produce less of these so-difficult-to-get-rid-of hazardous wastes?"

"You know how many millions of dollars that would cost us?"

"No. And ask me if I give a fuck." So much for being conciliatory. "So you just ship it all off to some crummy underdeveloped countries because it's cheaper, is that it?"

"You're overlooking all the good we're doing—"

"I am, huh? I suppose some of those countries are only too happy to be taking your money. People are funny that way at first, before they wise up. The Ecuadorian Indian tribes welcomed the Spanish *conquistadores* as liberators from the Incas—until the Spanish started raping the women and peeling the gold foil reliefs off the temple walls."

"What are you talking about?"

"I'm talking about environmental and cultural genocide. You should study some South American history. There are a lot of tips for a man like you. For instance, the Incas used to skin the bodies of their murdered enemies and make man-drums out of them, which when beaten forced air out through flutes sewn to their mouths.

You should try it the next time you kill someone. It would sure fit in with the rest of your trophies."

"All right, Buscarsela. Have your laughs now. Because one of these mornings you're going to be found taking a shower with a kitchen knife through your heart. Or maybe you'll be walking down the street and a pay phone is gonna ring and you'll pick it up and a voice'll say, 'Remember me, Buscarsela?' and then a phone on the next block is gonna ring and say, 'That's right, Buscarsela, I'm watching you. Just keep on walking—' "

I recoil in horror from his words. It's a feint to build momentum. He goes for it—he leans forward to give his words more emphasis—and I twirl round and belt him across the face with my home-made sling of a shopping bag and three hard mangos.

"Sit down," I say, panting for breath. "That's *one* I owe you."

Mr. Morse sits down, blood dripping from his nose. He tries to wipe it away with a silk handkerchief, but I stop him.

He's beginning to look a little less cheerful. I go on:

"So, Grendel," I say, showing off my command of ancient literature, "so you have a charm against the weapons of the legal system, but not against my naked anger.—And believe me, you've really got me pissed off." I'm breathing as heavily as if I just ran two miles, and my lungs are burning like hell. I steady myself against his desk. Hot pins are shooting through my chest. I go on: "Because if you ever threaten me again I will toss everything and waste your wife, your children, your cousins, your parakeet—I'll cut off your dog's paws and write nasty messages on the walls in thick streams of blood—and *you*: I will *definitely* come after you. I got in here easily enough." I can barely breathe. The room is spinning. I grab a statue. It's a heavy bronze Bourdelle of Daphne metamorphosing into a tree.

"Keep your hands away from that call button." I manage to croak the words out.

His hand springs back to his side. I start to catch my breath again.

"Fine. Now let me tell you what's going to happen," I say. "Two of your so-called 'low-level' disposal facilities are going to be shut down, now that Federal investigators have discovered that plutonium is leaking into the local ground water."

"Peanuts. We'll make that up in no time."

"Not after you get the subpoena for all your waste-disposal related documents you won't."

"They'll be shredded by this afternoon."

"The E.P.A. has already seized the computer software containing the original data."

"We erased those files," he says with a smirk.

"Yes, but they weren't destroyed. Remember, if the tracks haven't been occupied with new information, then the E.P.A.'s computer specialists should be able to retrieve the original data."

Now Mr. Morse is looking a little grayer. As gray as the face of a $100 bill. I find the resemblance almost amusing.

"But don't worry about yourself, Mr. Morse. You'll get six months to a year at most on some Federal country club. You'll be out in no time. I just want to see a bite taken out of your profits. And that's what's going to happen. But don't worry about yourself. Six months is no sentence. Not for what you've done."

He almost smiles. My hands tighten reflexively around the Bourdelle and the next thing I know it's high in the air, poised to strike. The blood runs out of his face. But that's it. I can't do more. I just wanted *him* to feel it. To feel that *fear*.

Slowly, I lower the statue.

"You ever fuck with me again," I say, "and I will kill you. Do you believe that?"

For once, Mr. Morse is not talking.

"Say yes," I say.

"Yes."

"Now—" I reach into the shopping bag.

Morse's eyes widen and freeze there.

"Don't be ridiculous," I say. "I'm not a superhero. I couldn't slip a hatpin past your security and you know it. But there is something I want you to do."

I pull the soft, ripe mango out of the bag. It's a bit gooey from being squashed by the green ones when I smacked him with the bunch. Perfect. I bite through the skin, tear some of it off and toss the mango in Morse's lap. He jumps as if it were a live hand grenade.

"Eat it," I say.

He doesn't move.

"What's the matter?" I ask. "Don't you like mangos? It's not poisoned.—Well, what I mean is that I certainly haven't injected any poison into it, if that's what you're thinking. But I will tell you one thing: That mango came from Ecuador, one of those countries you send your illegal chemical pesticides to—the pesticides that have been declared unsafe by the U.S. Food and Drug Administration. But they graciously allow you to dump them overseas. Places nobody cares about, right? Well now it's come back to haunt you. Go ahead, eat some. I want you to taste the poison you export to those countries no one cares about." His eyes flit to the door. "—Eat!"

I pick it up and jab the exposed fruit into the space between his bloodied nose and his whitening lip. Hard. He takes the mango and starts eating it. It's a big, overripe, juicy, squashed mango, and there's no way in the world to eat one of those without making a mess. Sweet, orange mango juice is dripping all over his hands. It mixes with the blood running down his face and makes a nice mess on the front of his suit and pants. When he's through, he looks like someone's been working him over with a billy club, even though I only hit him just that once. For the first time, I find that I can smile.

"Next question: Who loaded Tommy Osborne's nail gun with a full shot of powder?"

I never get my answer. The doors fly open and the two bodyguards come rushing in. I thought he ate that mango rather will-ingly. I raise the Bourdelle again. Morse dives out of his chair as I hurl the statue through the computer screen. Glowing shards of green data leak all over the table and die a cold death. The statue is unharmed. That Bourdelle really knew how to cast.

The two boys earn their pay, and before I can breathe, I am pinned between what feels like the Pacific and North American continental plates vying for control of the fault line. Who am I kidding? You can't punch a corporation.

Morse strides up to me and slaps me across the face with an open palm. The sting exhilarates me.

"Come on," I taunt him. "Show a frail, recovering alcoholic being held down by two offensive linemen just how tough you are."

His face flushes like a little boy being teased about the length of his shorts by two cruel teenagers.

To my astonishment, one of the linemen dislodges an arm large enough to raise a barn with and uses it to ease Morse back from this situation.

"You want *us* to work her over, boss?"

That strikes Morse worse than anything I could have said or done. His own men are telling him that he's embarrassing them in front of one undernourished female.

"Or we could call the cops on her for this," says the other lineman, flicking a thumb towards the shattered computer screen.

Morse wipes the muck off his face with his handkerchief. His hand is shaking. "Get her out of here."

"Yes sir, Mr. Morse." The opposing forces release me.

Morse takes a step closer to me, although keeping out of striking range.

"I don't want to see you in my building again, *ever,*" says Morse.

"Fine.—And don't let me catch you in my neighborhood, *ever.* In fact, you'd better just stay the hell out of my hemisphere. I have some *nasty* friends in Ecuador who aren't afraid of your *gringo* lawsuits. Mess with them and we'll send your wife your shrunken head via express mail, you got that?"

Pause. I think he gets it.

"By the way, your boys are right," I confirm. "You can have me arrested for this. I'm not a cop anymore."

He looks at me stunned. I'm wiping my fingerprints off the statue.

"And I could file some interesting counter charges. But you don't want them to put me on the witness stand again, do you? So why don't we just forget any of this ever happened?"

"Get out of here," says Morse.

"Oh, don't worry: I'll be out there all right."

One of the boys yanks me over by the door. The other goes to help Morse mop off his reddened face. Morse twists and shoos him away.

"Can I take this?" I ask, demurely picking up the pre-Colombian bowl. "I know a museum that needs it."

My handler plucks it from my fingers and delicately replaces it on the marble bookshelf.

"Next time," I say.

I give Morse one last parting death stare from the door, and nobody tries to kill me on my way out.

My usher gives me a bit of advice that he may not be aware is a direct paraphrase of a preserved mud-and-reed fragment of third-millennium B.C., Sumerian literature: "Take your staff and don't look back." Only he modernizes it: "Beat it."

I walk outside the building and start breathing again. But not too deeply.

I'm thirsty, but I'm *not* going for a drink. I want to go swimming in the Pacific. I walk a few blocks before becoming sufficiently aware of my surroundings to notice a Korean fruitstand. I feel like buying some of that succulent summer fruit to sooth my thirst, but, somehow, although at first they look so ripe and luscious, when I get closer they no longer look so appealing.

And I walk off down the street that's already beginning to show signs of cooling down for another interminably long, cold winter.

CORE COLLECTION 2010

LaVergne, TN USA
07 April 2010
178380LV00002B/323/A